D0457243

The
Bachelorette
Party

The Bachelorette Party

Karen McCullah Lutz

ST. MARTIN'S PRESS   NEW YORK

www.stmartins.com

Book design by Michelle McMillian

Library of Congress Cataloging-in-Publication Data

Lutz, Karen McCullah.
The bachelorette party : a novel / Karen McCullah Lutz.
p. cm.
ISBN 0-312-32619-X
EAN 978-0312-32619-7
1. Young women—Fiction. 2. Friendship—Fiction. 3. Weddings—Fiction.
4. Parties—Fiction. 5. Cousins—Fiction. I. Title.

PS3612.U895B34 2005
813'.6—dc22   2004056652

First Edition: February 2005

10 9 8 7 6 5 4 3 2 1

The
Bachelorette
Party

one

There was no one in the state of California, on the planet, or in the ozone who wanted to watch *Days of Our Lives* less than Zadie Roberts. But there she was, stuck in the waiting room of a Jiffy Lube on Ventura Boulevard, forced to stare at Jack Cavanaugh as he portrayed "Nate Forrester," bad boy with a heart of gold. She watched him take off his motorcycle helmet and shake out his shaggy black hair, smoldering all the while, before she got up to change the channel, only to be met with severe opposition from a middle-aged black woman who was painting her nails in two different, alternating shades—pink on one finger, red on the next. "Don't you even think about it. That man's the only thing that gets me through the day."

Zadie sighed and sat back down. She had no desire whatsoever to explain to this woman that she was once engaged to Jack Cavanaugh. That she once stood in the foyer of a church in a big white wedding dress waiting for Jack Cavanaugh to show up. That she once had to hear Jack Cavanaugh's pill-popping mother say, "Well, dear. I guess he's not coming."

Zadie fucking hated Jack Cavanaugh.

She'd met Jack before he was a soap star, back when he was a lowly waiter at Chin Chin. A waiter with the kind of eyes that said, "It'll be a mere matter of seconds before I get your panties off and pleasure you like you've only dreamed of." Those eyes got him his job on *Days*. And his job on *Days* got him a big fat ego. And Zadie was no longer being pleasured.

Two years were wasted with Jack. Two years and many thousands of dollars. She paid for the wedding that wasn't. She paid for the acting classes that taught him to smolder. She, who made forty-seven thousand dollars a year in a city where most of the people driving down Sunset in their Escalades and SL500s made that much in a month. At least. So Jack was really the last person she wanted to watch as she waited for her Camry to get lubed. Unless, perhaps, his character was scheduled to die a horrible death.

She sighed and looked at her watch. She still had plenty of time to kill before meeting Grey. He never left the office until seven, because he was in The Industry. And for some odd reason, people in The Industry—the industry being entertainment—worked from ten until seven every day. Although if you called Grey's office at nine, his assistant would answer and pretend he was in a meeting. Entertainment lawyers are always in a meeting or on a call or eating lunch at some overpriced restaurant with their overpaid clients.

For a guy in The Industry, Grey was surprisingly decent. When Jack had pulled his lame-ass disappearance, Grey was the one who sat up with her all night, feeding her tequila shots and Cheez Doodles. Grey was the one who let her vomit on his sea-grass carpet. And now, Grey was the one meeting her for their Thursday night ritual of potato skins and Coors Light at Barney's Beanery on Santa Monica Boulevard. The food was cheap and the jukebox had Rick Springfield songs. What more could a girl want? Aside from a husband and a nice house in the Hills.

Zadie looked down at the stack of essays in her lap, wishing they were written on a more interesting topic than the rhetorical strategies used in the work of Frederick Douglass, but such is the nature of twelfth-grade English at Yale-Eastlake, a private school for very smart and very rich teenagers. When she was engaged to Jack, her students had bought her a La Perla nightgown for the honeymoon. When she came back to work on the Monday after the wedding—unmarried—they felt so bad for her they had her car detailed and bought her a spa day at Burke Williams. Her students loved her. Jack, for some reason, clearly did not.

Before Jack, she'd had the normal number of boyfriends that an attractive thirty-one-year-old woman should have had. She'd done her share of dating. And fornicating. And kissing strangers at the valet stand. But she didn't want to kiss strangers anymore. She didn't want to kiss anyone at the moment. She wanted a fucking beer and a plate of potato skins loaded with bacon bits and melted Swiss.

Right at the moment that Jack (as Nate Forrester) was about to make out with an anorexic redhead sporting severely overplucked eyebrows, the mechanic came in to tell Zadie she needed a new gasket of some sort. Her car always needed something new. As soon as she had paid it off, the exact amount of money that used to make up her car payment was now needed to repair some random defect each month. The car gods hated her.

"Do I have to replace it right this second?"

"No. But you should do it in the next couple weeks." He could care less if her car broke down. She could sense it. He had that steroid-fueled "I wanna get to the gym" look. But she couldn't sit in that waiting room for a second longer, so she left it to fate. She'd rather break down on Mulholland than watch Jack pretend to emote.

She got to Barney's Beanery early and sat down in one of the red Naugahyde booths. The kitschy license-plate and assorted-hanging-crap decor never changed. Neither did the graffiti. For as long as she'd been coming here, the words "I licked Vince Vaughn's testicles" had been inked onto the door of the ladies' room stall.

Grey was going to be at least another half hour. She ordered a pitcher of Coors Light and wandered over to the jukebox. Def Leppard was playing. She stuck a dollar in and dialed up "Summer Nights." Then "Jessie's Girl." When John Travolta's sweet voice came booming out of the speakers, she looked over at the bikers sitting at the bar.

"Sorry, guys, I've had a shit day." They scowled and went back to their beers. Zadie didn't care. She needed solace. She'd been forced to watch Jack, and every memory of her Day of Humiliation came rushing back at her: explaining to her parents that the wedding was off because Jack was "missing." Seeing the pity on her cousins' faces. Watching Jack's parents stammer and look at the ground as they tried to make excuses for him. Realizing that none of Jack's groomsmen had shown up, which meant he'd made the decision early enough to tell them, but not her. Realizing that the man she loved valued her feelings so little that he couldn't be bothered to spare her this agony.

Zadie downed her beer and poured herself another. She didn't care if she was drunk by the time Grey showed up. Grey had seen her in far worse condition—snot flowing down her face, mascara streaked to her chin, and in the midst of the aforementioned puking episode. Grey had seen every ugly, petty, disgusting part of her and that's why he was her best friend. Any guy who can watch you hurl Cheez Doodles is a keeper. And when they drove to Tijuana for a night of mindless drunken fun, he let her play the entire *Grease* soundtrack and even did the "Greased Lightning" moves along with her, through the sunroof. You don't just find friends like that on the street corner.

She'd met Grey at the eighteenth-birthday party of one of her students. It was one of those overblown Hollywood affairs where a Protestant parent felt the need to equal the bat mitzvah of his best friend's daughter, so he hired KC and the Sunshine Band to perform in his Bel Air backyard and invited everyone his daughter knew and everyone he knew and wanted to impress. Grey was his lawyer. And Zadie was the daughter's favorite teacher. Since neither one of them knew anyone else there, they ended up together in the gazebo, doing shots of Jägermeister and making up bios for everyone. The wife was an arms dealer, masquerading as a San Marino debutante. The business partner was a porn star, trying to pretend he had an MBA. None of it was true, but it made them all more interesting.

After the party, they'd ended up at Mel's Diner, devouring cheeseburgers. At two in the morning, they drove up and down Sunset pointing out the hookers. She hadn't had a night that fun in ages. At the time, she'd been engaged to Jack, and Grey had been in a live-in relationship with Angela, an agent at William Morris. Two weeks later, he caught Angela making out with an Asian hip-hop singer at the Viper Room and eight weeks later, Jack left Zadie at the altar.

If they had been really pathetic, they would've ended up sleeping with each other. But since they were only semipathetic, they ended up drinking and eating with each other. A lot. And bitching and moaning. A lot. Pursuits at which they were highly skilled. Besides, Grey had issues. He was a freak about pronunciation. For a surfer, his car was immaculate; if you dared to drop your empty water bottle on the floor, he would pull over. He once broke up with a girl because she drank too much coffee. Issues. She no longer slept with "issues." She was out of the issues business.

When Grey walked in, he looked as if he were ready to kill. As much as, say, Richie Cunningham could look ready to kill. He was far too wholesome looking to convey any actual sense of malice. He plopped down in the booth, dropped his briefcase on the floor, and reached for Zadie's beer, downing it in one gulp and slamming the glass back onto the table.

"Why do I do what I do?" His blue eyes narrowed, as if he'd been pondering this question the entire drive over.

"Because it pays well."

"It doesn't pay well enough for me to have to listen to an actor tell me he should get a million-five when he only got three-fifty on his last project, which bombed and he should've been shot for. I hate actors." He signaled to the waitress for another pitcher. "Yet I am their slave. There is something very wrong with my life."

"If you're looking for an argument from me as to why actors are decent people, you're talking to the wrong girl."

"It's my own fault. I could've been an environmental lawyer. But then I wouldn't have a house. Or a car. I'd have a nice studio apartment and a bus pass. Why does the choice between good and evil have to involve personal comfort? I like my TiVo. I need my pool. Yet to pay for these things, I'm forced to listen to high school dropouts who can't pronounce the word 'sorbet' tell me why they should be making twenty million a movie."

When the pitcher arrived, Zadie asked for a double order of potato skins and filled their glasses. It was obviously going to be a late night. She had enough to bitch about, but if Grey had his own agenda, they'd be there until closing. Which was actually quite a happy thought. It beat going back to her apartment and watching *ER*.

"I fantasized about one of my students today." She liked opening with a shocker.

"What?!"

"He's eighteen. It's legal. He's also an Abercrombie and Fitch model. I've actually masturbated to the thought of him."

Grey just stared at her, then hoisted his beer in her direction. They clinked glasses and he took off his suit jacket and loosened his tie. "I want details."

"His name is Trevor. He's on the cover of the catalog without a shirt and with khakis so low you can see those little V-shaped muscles that frame his crotch. How am I not supposed to look at that?"

Grey seemed highly amused by this. "Do you get all twitchy when you talk to him in class?"

"No, I'm a professional. Today I handed him back his essay and suggested that he read *Dharma Bums* if he liked *On the Road*. Then I watched his ass as he walked away." She took a sip of her beer. Cold Coors Light and salacious gossip. A perfect combo.

"Where did said masturbation take place?"

"Where do you think? In my car. On the way home."

Grey grinned. "I worship you. Have I ever told you that? You are the only woman I know who would admit to masturbating as she drove down Coldwater Canyon."

She rolled her eyes. "Save your praise. I watched *Days of Our Lives* today. By accident."

"And?" He looked worried. Zadie liked it when he looked worried about her. His worry was merely friendly concern, as opposed to her parents' worry, which was a burden that occasionally sapped her will to live.

"I watched Jack kiss another woman with the same cheesy look on his face that he used to have when he kissed me, which means he acted during our entire relationship—not that I didn't know this." Jack had acted even after their relationship. When he finally called two weeks after the aborted wedding, he pretended he'd been in a Mexican jail. Eventually he admitted that he'd got cold feet and stayed in Vegas with his bachelor party buddies. He felt that he deserved recognition for admitting his flaws, but all Zadie thought he deserved was her foot up his ass. She hadn't talked to him since. She and Grey had driven past his condo once and thrown a beer bottle at his door, but she wasn't proud of it. Or of the time she used a Web site that sends dog-doo to people in the mail. Raging anger and profound aching grief tend to make one act out of sorts.

Grey dug into the potato skins as soon as they hit the table. She respected a man who would eat carbs after five o'clock. Very hard to find in L.A.

"At least you never caught him." He was referring to the Viper Room incident, which he still carried like a vial of mental poison.

"You're dating the most perfect girl in the world. Why do you even care that Angela cheated? You're so beyond her." She spooned some ranch dressing onto her potato skins. Everything's better with ranch dressing. Her life was shit, but as long as it was shit with ranch dressing, she could survive.

"The ones that screw you are burned into your brain. Like I have to tell you." Very true. But Zadie didn't like to admit that Jack still had any power over her. In effect, he didn't. Not over her heart. Only over her ego. Which had begun to erode since the day she took off her veil and put on her "I'm okay" face.

"Have you talked to Helen, by the way?" He said it casually, but his face got all tense, like he was either constipated or concerned about telling her something.

"Don't even tell me you two broke up." Helen was her cousin. When Helen's sister Denise got married last fall, Zadie had dragged Grey along with her to the happy occasion. It was a mere month after her own nonwedding. Zadie had needed him around to ease the pain. However, the pain was not eased by the fact that Grey ended up sucking face with Helen on the dance floor during the reception. People were not supposed to be getting married when she couldn't and people were not supposed to be hooking up when she wasn't. But it wasn't just a hookup. Grey and Helen had actually started dating. And fallen in love. And taken a trip to Napa. You don't take a girl to Napa unless you have intentions.

"Although getting dumped at a wine tasting isn't the worst place I can think of," Zadie said. "At least you can drown your sorrows in a nice merlot." She was joking, but then realized this was actually a possibility and felt bad for saying it. Grey was smitten and she wouldn't wish a broken heart on anyone, despite the fact that Helen wasn't exactly her favorite relative. There were several reasons for this distinction, the most prominent one being that Helen had never done a single bad thing and she never let anyone forget it.

"We're engaged." He said it as he shoved a forkful of melted Swiss into his mouth. As if he were announcing that he just traded in his Saab for a Volvo.

Zadie stared at him. "I'm sorry, it sounded like you just said that you and Helen got engaged. But I know that can't be true, because you would've called me the second it happened, not waited four days to tell me while we're listening to 'Hurts So Good' on the fucking jukebox."

"I couldn't call you from Napa, it would've been too weird. She would've heard, and I can't talk to you in front of her. She's always grabbing the phone and looking at me weird whenever she hears me call you 'Loser.'"

"You're engaged. You and Helen. Are getting married."

"Yes."

There was a buzzing noise in Zadie's head. It was most likely all the blood in her body rushing to protect her brain from this news. "And when is this blessed event taking place?"

"Soon. She told me she booked the hotel the day I told her I loved her. She already bought her dress."

"Helen? I'm sure she bought her dress when she was eighteen. She's had a wedding scrapbook waiting to be filled since her twelfth birthday."

Grey frowned. "You sound angry."

"How could I be angry? My best friend is marrying my cousin and my only semblance of a love life is touching myself while lusting after a teenage boy that I'm supposed to be educating. Why would this upset me?" Zadie rubbed her temples.

Grey refilled her glass. "You're overreacting. Besides, I want you to meet my friend Mike. I'm going to ask him to be one of my groomsmen. I think you'll like him."

Now Zadie was really pissed. "If you mention Mike to me one more time . . ."

"What? He's a great guy."

"So you've told me," she said.

"So why won't you meet him?"

"Because I don't want a pity setup. I'm not going to go out with your lame-ass friends just because you don't think I'll ever find anyone on my own."

She motioned to the waitress for another pitcher. The night just went from really long to really short. She might just drink enough to pass out in the booth by ten o'clock. She pictured Grey having to carry her to his car. And then carrying her up the stairs to her apartment in Sherman Oaks. And dropping her because she was too heavy. Then picking her back up and shoving her through the door, placing her face down on her couch with her little wicker trash basket from Bed Bath & Beyond next to her head. You can't puke in wicker. It leaks. She couldn't stand the thought of half-digested potato skins leaking onto her floor while Grey and Helen were nuzzling in front of the fire back at his place. Helen was so fucking judgmental. She could just hear it. "Why does Zadie have to be so self-destructive? Jack left her six months ago.

She should be over it. He's only a soap actor. With a back-burner story line. What's the big deal?"

"I'm not setting you up out of pity. I'm setting you up because I want you to be happy."

"If you want me to be happy, then spare me the blind dates."

"Glory Days" came on the jukebox and she started to tear up. She was no longer young. She was no longer a size six. She was no longer a girl who could bear the thought of dating a man she feared would leave her. And she was no longer a girl who had a best friend to take care of her. Now he'd have a wife to keep him occupied. A perfect wife. A twenty-eight-year-old wife whose hair didn't even need to be highlighted.

"I'm never going to see you again, am I?"

Grey squinted at her. "What the hell are you talking about?"

"You'll be off buying furniture at IKEA and preregistering at nursery schools and ovulating. We're never gonna come here again, are we? This is my last potato skin. This is my last pitcher. This is my last glory day."

"Okay, you're drunk. Which is normally not a bad thing, but considering the mood you're in, I have to question if it's the best choice."

"Fuck you, Grey. I am not drunk." With that, Zadie got up, grabbed her purse, and headed toward the door. Not that she wasn't drunk, she just didn't want to be told she was. At least, not by her best friend who had just betrayed her by getting engaged when she wasn't. She walked past the bikers. "Happy? I'm leaving." They gave her a blank look as she slammed her beer glass down on the bar.

Once she was outside, the valet called her a cab. She'd phone Triple A in the morning, claim gasket problems, and get them to tow it back to Sherman Oaks. Maybe it was a blessing that Jack had been on TV in the Jiffy Lube waiting room, forcing her to flee. And maybe it was a blessing that she was still single. And maybe the girl who'd licked Vince Vaughn's testicles was still in town so she'd have someone to hang out with while everyone else she fucking knew got married.

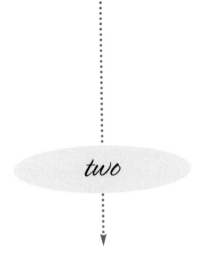

two

When Zadie woke up, she popped two Excedrin, made arrangements to have her car picked up, and started a pot of coffee. The fact that school started so ridiculously early was something she cursed every time she was hungover. Her students weren't exactly bright-eyed at 8 A.M. either. What would be so wrong about having school start at noon?

Her apartment was already hot from the sun streaming in through her sliding glass door. She opened it to let whatever breeze there might be blow in across the seven potted cacti she kept on her balcony next to a faded canvas beach chair and a rusted hibachi that she'd never used. Her mother had insisted that she'd want to grill something someday, but that day had yet to come. Zadie mostly ordered take-out Thai food or bought prepared salads from the grocery store. Why cook when there are trained professionals who have already done it for you?

The neighbor's mange-ridden cat jumped onto her beach chair from the top of the wall that divided their balconies. He then proceeded to run inside her apartment and take a quick tour. Zadie flicked a dish towel at him.

"Shoo. Get out. There's nothing here for you."

Once the cat was satisfied that he'd seen all six hundred square feet, he went back out onto the balcony and climbed back over the wall. Zadie shut the door behind him. It wasn't that she disliked cats, but this particular cat had shat on her beach chair at least twice and she wasn't eager for him to decorate her off-white couch in the same way. She'd bought it with the money she got from pawning her engagement ring. Which meant that every time she sat down on it, she got pissed off all over again. But at least her anger was empowering. Not that it actually empowered her to *do* anything, but it was more energizing than despair.

The fact that her emotional range of late consisted of fury, depression, or numbness was something she wanted to rectify, but she wasn't quite sure how to go about it. People told her it would take time. The *How to Survive a Breakup* book her mother gave her told her to keep a journal and express her feelings on paper. Why the fuck she would want to document what she was currently feeling was beyond her. She wished there was a way to take one of those Native American smudge sticks that her hippie roommate at UCLA used to get rid of negative energy and wave it around inside her head until all her feelings were gone. She didn't want to "work through it" or "let time heal it." She wanted to hit delete.

Before Jack, she'd been optimistic about romance. No matter how many badass poon hounds or neurotic momma's boys she'd dated. She'd always been sure her one big love was out there. Until she found him and he turned into a giant wad of ass. Now the idea of trying to find another big love held little appeal. What would she do with two couches?

Luckily, Jack had never moved in. Her place didn't allow dogs and he had a yellow lab he'd rescued from the pound that he loved more than his mother. And clearly Zadie, in hindsight. Zadie had never moved into his place because it was a shithole. They'd planned on finding an apartment together, but a month after they'd got engaged, Jack got the role on *Days* and bought a condo. Zadie was going to move in after the honeymoon. Good thing she'd kept her lease.

. . .

When Zadie got to school, she parked in the teachers' lot and walked across the quad, passing the Zen garden with its requisite waterfall. Her classroom was in the I. M. Pei–designed main building that had reportedly been feng-shuied by a French guy with a tiny monkey that sat on his shoulder the entire time. They probably paid him more than Zadie made in five years.

The windows in her classroom looked out onto a hummingbird feeder that was attended by the greediest bastards in the ornithology kingdom. Beyond that was a canyon filled with an assortment of nonindigenous trees and the occasional mansion. She took solace in the fact that if her students were bored by her lecture, they at least had a nice view.

When Trevor arrived for sixth period, Zadie tried especially hard to avert her eyes from him, but he was wearing a skintight T-shirt and one of those cute little bucket hats over his shoulder-length surfer-blond hair. She was in hell. How could life get worse than wanting to fuck an eighteen-year-old? It must be hormonal. She had never been attracted to her students in the past. Was there a pill she could take to make it stop?

"*Grapes of Wrath.* What'd you think?" She looked out among the sea of well-groomed teenage faces.

Danielle raised her hand. "It was a little depressing." Danielle was the daughter of the man who ran a television network. The thought of a dust bowl was surely beyond her comprehension.

"What about it depressed you?" She liked Danielle and was secretly hoping she wouldn't say anything that would cause her to repeat it over margaritas with the other teachers.

"They were homeless. They couldn't find work. They didn't have any food. What about it wasn't depressing?"

Thank God she hadn't said, "They didn't have Prada luggage." You never could tell with rich kids. Some of them had parents who made sure they knew how the rest of the world worked, and some of them had parents who kept them in Malibu until they were sixteen and old enough to drive into the 'hood on their own.

After a discussion of poverty and its effect on the human spirit, Zadie let the class go with instructions to read five more chapters over the weekend so she could quiz them on Monday. Jorge approached her as the bell rang.

"My dad's premiere is tonight and we're going skiing in Mammoth all weekend to celebrate. I won't have time to read."

Zadie was used to excuses, some creative, some just plain lame, but Jorge's father was an A-list director who'd left his mother when Jorge was five and moved on to three other wives since. The fact that Jorge was going to the premiere was important. How often does a teenager get to be proud of his parent? And the fact that he was spending a ski weekend with his father was huge. The man was quite frankly a prick who doted on his three younger children with his three younger wives.

"*Grapes of Wrath* can wait," Zadie said. "Go have fun with your dad."

Jorge grinned. "Thanks. I promise I'll read it on Monday." He hurried out behind the rest of the class. All except for Trevor.

As he walked up to Zadie's desk, she ran her hand through her hair, smoothing it down. Teenage boys shouldn't be allowed to be six feet tall.

"Thanks for making us read this. It made me realize that I pretty much don't have anything to complain about," he said.

"Perspective is always helpful," Zadie answered. Wow. That was deep. She tried desperately to think of something else to say, but he was grinning at her and all thoughts left her.

"Is it okay if I change my term paper topic to Steinbeck instead of Kerouac?"

"Absolutely," Zadie said.

"Cool. Thanks." He walked out, allowing Zadie to notice that his T-shirt clung to his lat muscles in a most appealing manner. She forced herself to look away.

After school, Zadie walked to her car and sat inside for ten minutes before she drove away. The thought of masturbating during her drive yesterday shamed her. And the fact that she'd told Grey about it as if it were a prelude to one of their usual nights of fun enraged her. How could he let her go on about her Mrs. Robinson fantasy life when he was holding back the news that he was engaged? Not that she didn't want him to be happy. Not that she didn't know he was in love with Helen. Not that she hoped they would break up. She just hadn't counted on them getting engaged so soon. What did Helen even see in him? He was the worst dancer on the planet. He couldn't change a tire. He had a bed skirt that matched his comforter. Zadie didn't even have a bed skirt. Who the fuck had a bed skirt?

When she got back to her apartment, she called Helen. "Hi! Congratulations!"

Helen was equally effusive. "Isn't it amazing?! He proposed while we were in a hot air balloon, soaring over the vineyards."

Barf. Did he really? So cliché. Jack had proposed to her while they were sixty-nining. She couldn't even see his face—obviously. She just took his dick out of her mouth and said, "Yes." Looking back on it now, it wasn't quite as romantic as she'd previously thought.

"That's so great!" No, it wasn't. It was repulsive. It was incomprehensible. It was so John Tesh. A hot air balloon?

"Obviously, you'll be a bridesmaid." Phew. Zadie was tortured over the thought that she might not get to put on an ugly taffeta dress and stand at the altar next to Helen pretending she was happy. "And don't worry, I promise the dress won't have a bow on the butt." Yeah, right. She wished she had a tape recording of this conversation to play back when she was inevitably standing in a church wearing a lime-green hoop skirt.

"Have you set the date?" Of course she had. She was Helen. Helen had her menstrual cycle charted for the next ten years.

"Memorial Day. It was either that or November twelfth, according to my numerologist, but I have to be tan. Otherwise, how could I wear white?" So Orange County of her. Not that Zadie had anything against the sun, she just didn't plan her wardrobe around it. And not that Helen shouldn't wear white. As far as Zadie knew, Helen had never seen a penis. And she certainly hadn't sucked one. Helen was a virgin. God knows why, but it was clearly something Helen had strong feelings about. Although holding out may not be such a bad tactic after all. How else would you get a guy to propose to you after five months of dating? Poor Grey was probably dying of sperm congestion.

"Wow. Memorial Day. That's soon." In one month, her best friend would be married to her most annoying cousin. What fun! So much to celebrate! "So I guess you're really sure about this."

There was a pause on Helen's end. Then, "Why wouldn't I be?" Helen said it in that really bitchy tone people use when they want to tell you to fuck off, but are too polite.

"Of course you're sure. That's not what I meant at all. It's all just happened so fast, I can't believe it's real. But I do. Believe it's real." Zadie was digging herself into a sizable hole and needed to get out. "I think it's great! I can't wait till the wedding! Whoops—I have another call. I'll talk to you later, okay?" The fake call-waiting ploy. So transparent. So immature. Worked every goddamn time.

After Zadie hung up, she went to the fridge. There was half a Wolfgang Puck Chinese Chicken Salad, but it had been in there since last week and all the dressing was gone. They never put enough dressing in that little cup. And cabbage is not something that can be consumed without proper lubricant. Note to Wolfgang.

She drove down to Ralph's and picked up some supermarket sushi. If she had any money, she'd go get some real sushi. But alas, she had spent her entire last paycheck finishing off her wedding dress payments. Saks doesn't care if you get left at the altar. Saks wants their money.

When she got home with her plastic carton filled with day-old California rolls, she flipped on the TV to watch *The Bachelor,* viable proof that there were still some women left in the country who were more pathetic than she was. Watching these women tremble as they waited to get a rose from some dimwitted yet smug dork who actually used the word "vino" in a sentence—without ironic intent—was the only thing she could think of that could make her feel superior at the moment.

During the commercial, Zadie tried to take stock of everything in her life that was going right. Her job. Things were fine there. She liked her students and at least two-thirds of the books she had to teach. Teaching would never make her rich, but that wasn't something she necessarily aspired to be. Her apartment was clean. There was that. It had taken three months of clutter to finally motivate her to tidy up, and even then it was only because she'd worried that Jack might someday stop by to beg her forgiveness and she didn't want him to see how she'd let things go in the midst of her grief. Not that he ever actually *would* stop by; it was just distracting to have old magazines and pizza boxes in her fantasy that he might. Her hair. She liked her hair. It was long and dark and shiny on most days. And that was pretty much it. Her job, her temporarily clean apartment, and her hair.

This was what she had to live for.

three

Tuesday at school, Zadie ate lunch in the teachers' lounge with Nancy, the biology teacher with giant collagen lips and the misguided opinion that Lycra tops were flattering on her.

"I met this guy at the carwash? While we were waiting? He asks me to dinner and I say yes. Nothing special. Casa Vega. I ordered the fajita taco. But *he* didn't." Nancy said it with a pointed look. As if this were supposed to mean something. Zadie bit.

"So, what's the problem? You can't kiss a guy after he's eaten an enchilada?" Zadie never understood Nancy's dating criteria. She went out with imbeciles and always offered up a play-by-play analysis the next day. Zadie secretly wondered if she went on these dates just to have something to talk about.

"No, he didn't order anything. He just picked off my plate."

"Okay, that's a little weird. I'll give you that," Zadie said.

"Then he asked if he could wipe my face with his napkin."

"Did you have food on it?"

"No."

"A booger?"

Nancy gave her a look that indicated that Zadie was perhaps retarded. "I did not have a booger, my lipstick wasn't smeared, and I wasn't drooling—he was just a sick fuck."

Zadie wrinkled her brow, considering this theory. "Sick fucks generally want you to shit on their chest or some such thing. I don't know if I would qualify face-wiping as being in the sick fuck category."

Nancy gave her the look again. Zadie started to worry. Was she getting so pathetic that she could no longer pick out sick fuck behavior?

"Well, put it this way? He's not getting a second date," Nancy said.

Most of Nancy's dates never made it past the first one. Nancy was close to forty and still believed she was going to find The One. Anything less than The One didn't get a second date. Why would they? She didn't inject her lips full of toxins to attract one-night stands. Those babies were reserved for husband material. Whoever convinced these women that their upper lip was supposed to be bigger than their bottom lip had pulled off the biggest practical joke of all time.

"So did you let him wipe? Was it as good for you as it was for him?" Zadie had no sympathy whatsoever for Nancy's plight.

"Trust me. You won't be making jokes when you get back out there," Nancy said.

Zadie hadn't dated at all since her "wedding" and she wasn't looking forward to the prospect. "Who says I'm going to? You've dated every guy in the city and thrown them all back in. I don't want to fish from your pool of losers."

Right as Nancy worked up "the look" again, Dolores sat down. "Is Nancy trying to set you up again?"

Dolores was what most people would call a spinster. Mid-fifties, dishwater brown hair, no makeup, never married, all of her waistbands elastic. Dolores was what Nancy was trying not to become. And Nancy was what Zadie was trying not to become. In an age when women were supposed to be supportive of one another, it was amazing how many of them just wanted to avoid turning into each other.

What Nancy didn't know was that Dolores had it wired. She was no fool. After a few sour apple martinis at last year's end-of-school party, Dolores confided in Zadie that she often went on those singles cruises and all-inclusive Hedonism weeks and "got some." She wasn't waiting around for The One. She didn't even want The One. She wanted hot, kinky sex with strangers when she was on vacation, and a condo to herself and flannel nighties when she wasn't. Who wants a husband around to make you watch hockey games when *Dirty Dancing* is on TBS? Dolores had a superintendent to fix the toilet when it broke, she had restaurants that delivered, and she had a satellite dish. She was a happy woman indeed. She told Zadie, "When you release your expectations, you can find an amazing peace with yourself." As long as you drive out to Pomona every couple of months for a swingers party and screw a carpet salesman from Bakersfield.

"There's nothing wrong with being set up." Nancy went on at least four blind dates a month. She had a mother who would hang out at the dry cleaners and accost any man dropping off a suit who wasn't wearing a ring.

"Let Zadie find her own guys." Dolores was always one to stick up for you.

"Yeah, but look who she finds." Nancy rolled her eyes, as if Zadie were just the dumbest bitch on the planet for having ever gone out with Jack. She probably was, but still, it was a little rude for people to infer it to her face.

"I love that you've just sat here and told me how you had dinner with a sick fuck, yet it's me who finds the losers." Zadie wasn't putting up with any shit today.

Heading off what was sure to be an argument, Dolores chimed in with, "Have you seen Trevor Larkin in that T-shirt today?"

Zadie and Nancy both turned to stare at her.

Dolores remained unfazed. "How long do you think it would take to lick him from head to toe?"

And with that image in her head, Zadie excused herself.

four

Saturday night arrived amid its usual fanfare—Zadie's clock chimed, her microwave beeped, and her car alarm went off. But this Saturday night was special. She was going to Grey and Helen's engagement party.

She made two stops along the way—one on Hollywood Boulevard to buy an eight-by-ten picture of Steven Seagal from one of the souvenir shops, and one at Aaron Brothers to buy a pewter picture frame to put it in. That was their engagement present. She was sure Helen would take out the picture of Steven as soon as she saw it and probably put in a picture of their hot air balloon, taken postproposal, but that was fine with her. Grey would get the joke. On the first night they met, Zadie and Grey had seen Steven Seagal, by himself, at Mel's Diner. He was eating a plate of waffles and a grilled cheese sandwich. With a milk shake. Grey had secretly paid his tab.

When she got to Newport Beach, she drove around forever trying to find the goddamn restaurant. Normally, she could've made the hour-long drive with Grey. But not when Grey was the groom. No, sir, Grey was down there at ten that morning helping to "prepare." At least she wouldn't have to worry about being flooded with memories of her own engagement party with Jack. They hadn't had one. Never even occurred to them. Isn't the wedding enough? How many times can you expect people to congregate in order to honor your love?

When she finally got there, she was already starting to chafe. Literally. She was wearing a new bra that was supposed to make her look perky in her red sundress, but all it did was dig into her shoulders and let her boobs leak out the bottom. She stopped and stuck a hand in each cup, lifting them back in before she walked inside. The valet gave her a look that straddled between desire and fear.

The restaurant was on the water, overlooking a marina filled with zillion-dollar yachts. A seagull had relieved himself on the potted palm near the door. Never a good sign.

Inside, the normally understated Italian restaurant had been transformed into an explosion of light pink roses. Anyone who knew Helen knew that pink was her favorite color. And roses her favorite flower. And smiley her favorite expression.

"Zadie!" Helen held out her arms and gave Zadie a hug like she'd recently been lost at sea. "My God, you look great!" As if the last time Helen had seen Zadie, she'd looked like fried shit. Which was certainly not out of the realm of possibility, given her post-left-at-the-altar penchant for going out in public in pajama bottoms and a T-shirt.

Helen, of course, looked spectacular. Boob-length blond hair. Brite-Smile teeth. Three-hundred-crunches-a-day belly. Turquoise-blue eyes. Little black dress. Diamond stud earrings. Diamond engagement ring. Holy crap. Grey had spent some bucks. It was huge. At least a couple carats. Zadie's ring from Jack had been amoeba-like.

Zadie hugged her back. "And you're a glowing bride-to-be!" Why was it that wedding-speak was so riddled with clichés? Someone should really break out some new adjectives. Like "fetid" or "moldy."

Grey was across the room, looking dapper in a charcoal suit with a pink rose in the lapel, schmoozing with all of Helen's relatives. Who were actually Zadie's relatives, as well. She could only spot one whom she felt like talking to—Denise. Helen's sister. Zadie had always felt closer to Denise because they were the same age and because Denise was a raging party girl. Which came to a raging stop when she got pregnant. She was now sitting in a booth scarfing down a plate of calamari at an alarming rate. It was at Denise's wedding that Helen and Grey met. No one realized then that Denise was pregnant, but it was pretty hard to disguise at this point. Her stomach was as big as a VW Bug.

Zadie sat down with her and dipped a squid ring into the marinara sauce. "So. Who knocked you up?"

"Funny." Denise looked over at the bar where her husband, Jeff, who possessed a beer belly that rivaled Denise's, was happily imbibing. "He gets to have a Corona and I'm stuck with seltzer. He better be waiting in the delivery room with a pitcher of sangria in his hand when I squirt this thing out."

"Sounds like you two are blissfully happy." Okay, that was a little bitchy, but Zadie was in a mood.

"I'm a bloated seacow. Happiness is not an option at this moment. My only option is food or more food." She moved on to the mozzarella sticks, actually dipping them in sour cream.

"So, what do you think of the pending nuptials?" Zadie looked over at Grey as he slid up behind Helen, wrapping his arms around her waist and smiling at their grandma. "Do you think they'll be happy?"

Denise shrugged and kept eating. "Helen's always happy. And Grey's awesome. Why? Don't you think it'll work out?"

Zadie kept watching them. Smiling. Hugging. Oozing love from every pore. She had to admit that they looked more than happy. Grey was so beatific that most people would've thought he was overmedicated. Helen was levitating. They were perfect together. Helen radiated purity and light and Grey was aglow in her reflection, thrilled to have found a woman who would never do him wrong. Even through her bitter mood and the flying shrapnel from the plate of a ravenous pregnant woman, Zadie couldn't help but be glad that Grey was so happy. She would still be able to hang out with him after he and Helen were married, right? Helen must have someplace to go a couple nights a week. Tupperware parties? Book club? Home for the Criminally Perky?

Grandma Davis spotted her and came wobbling over in a cloud of peach-colored chiffon. "Zadie, you look so pretty." Grandma Davis was legally blind. A compliment from her was always questionable. "Denise, my goodness, you've put on weight." Maybe not so blind.

"I'm six months pregnant, Grandma."

"But you just got married—one, two"—she counted it out on her fingers—"five months ago."

Zadie whisked Grandma over to the buffet before she had time to hear Denise's response. "Grandma, how're you feeling?" Grandma had taken a mighty spill last year and was still in physical therapy. She'd been watching a Ginger Rogers movie and insisted on following along in her living room. Ginger was thirty in the movie. Grandma was eighty. And a little drunk at the time, quite frankly.

"I'm fine. It was no big deal."

"It was a broken hip, Grandma. That's a big deal."

"If Chester had been there, I'd never have fallen."

"Well, I'm sure Grampa Chester would've been there if he wasn't—you know—dead."

Grandma Davis took Zadie's face in her hands. "See what happens to women who're alone, Zadie? This is why you have to find a man."

Right at the moment that Zadie was ready to clock Grandma Davis in the jaw, Grey swooped over, saving the day. "Grandma, look at you!" He gave her a twirl, letting her skirt billow. "Are you sure you're not here to steal me away from Helen?" Grandma Davis squealed with laughter as Grey steered her toward the meat tray, giving Zadie an I'll-be-back-as-soon-as-I-get-some-prosciutto-in-this-woman look.

As Zadie waited, she saw her parents walk in the door. Now the night was complete. She'd been unsuccessfully avoiding them since her "wedding" day. All they wanted to do was smother her with compassion, but their own disappointment seeped through so abundantly that it made Zadie want to cry each time she looked at them. Like she'd let them down somehow by being the girl that Jack didn't want to marry.

Her parents lived in Ventura, where Zadie had grown up. A two-hour drive from this fine restaurant. Dad was a balding CPA who watched NASCAR on the weekends. Mom was an insurance adjuster who did at least fifteen crossword puzzles a day and never missed a manicure. A stable, steady life for a stable, steady couple. Married for thirty-seven years. No concept whatsoever of what it was like for a single girl in L.A. trying to find a man who doesn't want to fuck actresses.

If you took a survey among those in the know, Los Angeles would surely be voted the worst place in the world to be a single woman, Zadie felt. Every prom queen and head cheerleader from every shit town in America comes to L.A. to be discovered. Talented or not. And when they instead discover that every other girl with a fast metabolism and clear skin has moved to said locale for the same reason, they are forced to take jobs making soy lattes or folding sweaters at the Beverly Center while they wait for The Man. The Man can come in many forms—a casting director, a modeling scout, Hugh Hefner, or a short, squat Persian dude with lots of money to blow. The girls without morals are easily corrupted—doing porn in the Valley, spending six months with the Sultan of Brunei as a "hostess," or simply sitting around a West L.A. apartment, waiting for The Man who pays the rent to come have sex with them once a week while his wife is getting her bikini wax. Sometimes dreams of stardom are easily traded in for a steady flow of cash.

The ambitious beauties are harder to nail. Unless you're in The Industry. The men in The Industry are able to entice the young lovelies with promises of connections. "Hey, baby, I can introduce you to my friend Dave. He's directing a movie for New Line next month." Connections are hard to get, so if Balding Bob

knows Director Dave and Pretty Polly wants to be a star, Balding
Bob is gonna get some tail. Broken down into its simplest terms—
men who would kill to fuck you in Topeka are able to fuck the
hottest girls in Los Angeles. So any normal girl at a bar is now
competing with Grade-A snatch to hump a guy who's a "four" at
most.

The single men in Los Angeles are different. Especially the
actors. The male actor ego needs constant encouragement so if
you are a comely lass with encouragement to give, it will fall on
handsome, receptive ears. Jack needed Zadie's kind words when
he was a nobody. Once he became a somebody, he had fans to
give it to him. And an agent. And a manager. And a lawyer. And
a publicist. And a producer. And a costar. And any random bimbo
who happened to recognize him at the Sky Bar. Who needs a wife
when you have all that? Who needs a wife when you are now in
line to get the Grade-A snatch?

Of course there were the men who claimed they were tired of
all the beautiful brainless girls and just wanted a nice, smart,
wholesome teacher to settle down with. These men were full of
shit.

Grey returned to her side right as her parents made their way
over. "Mr. and Mrs. Roberts—thanks for coming!" Zadie stared at
him. Did he just speak with an exclamation point? Was it conta-
gious?

Zadie's parents had met Grey at the Get-Zadie-Out-of-Her-
Apartment intervention Helen had organized last winter. It was
successful. They all went to Jerry's Deli. Woo fucking hoo.

"How are you, kiddo?" Her father looked around the room as
he asked it, hoping she wouldn't answer honestly.

"I'm fine, Dad. How are you?"

"Recovering from tax time." He looked over at the bar, spotting
Grandma Davis swigging down a Bellini. "Mavis, your mother is
drinking."

Mavis Roberts (formerly Mavis Davis) pushed her husband
toward her mother.

"Go stop her, Sam." As if it were his duty as her husband to keep her mother from getting hammered.

"Let me help." Grey led Sam over to the bar, where they proceeded to force-feed Grandma some canapés. Oh, God. Zadie was alone with her mother. Mayday.

"You look sick." Always pleasant to hear. But Zadie knew Mavis wasn't done yet. "Are you not getting enough sun?" To the rest of the world, a tan was a deadly thing. To Californians, it was a badge of health. Unless you lived in Beverly Hills, where you would actually see women with parasols, sheltering the new skin they just bought from a baby seal away from the blistering sun.

"I'm fine, Mom. I've just been working a lot."

"You get off at four. The sun's still out."

"Not on my balcony."

"You can't go to the beach?" Mavis and Sam had met at the beach during a pig roast in the late sixties. Very Gidget. Mavis was convinced that Zadie's destiny was lying in the sand near the Santa Monica pier. All Zadie could find in Santa Monica were homeless men who wanted her change. She recently gave a bum a dollar because he told her she was pretty.

"Mom, stop. I'll get some sun when school ends." Oh, God, it was almost summer. What was she going to do for three months? Maybe she could pick up a summer school class. Or teach a creative writing elective. Maybe Trevor would sign up and come without his shirt on. She downed her glass of wine, trying to block out the thought. Thank God he was graduating.

"There're some handsome men at this party. Have you noticed?" Mavis asked.

Zadie looked over her mother's head, which wasn't hard to do given that Mavis was barely five two, and saw a guy with dark hair and a green shirt standing by the bar. He had the shape Zadie liked. Tall and broad shouldered. Some women preferred the skinny, androgynous rock star type, but Zadie wasn't one of them. If women were expected to uphold the Betty Boop body ideal, then goddammit, men owed them some muscles. She watched as Green Shirt took a sip of his beer and made her Aunt Josephine laugh. Three years ago, Zadie would've had no problem sidling up to him and making clever conversation, but now there seemed to be little point.

She looked back at her mother. "No. I hadn't noticed."

Before Mavis could protest, Zadie's father and Grey came back, having safely sequestered Grandma Davis with Helen and Denise's parents in a booth. "She's only got one real hip left. You'd think the woman would know not to tango in heels." Sam sat down in a chair and hefted his Guinness.

Grey put his arm around Zadie's shoulders and looked at Mavis. "Do you mind if I borrow Zadie for a few minutes?"

"Go right ahead." Mavis thought Zadie was crazy for not looking at Grey as a potential husband. When Mavis and Sam met Grey on Intervention Day, Mavis had pulled Zadie aside and said, "He has a full benefits package and you just *gave* him to Helen?" Zadie wanted to explain to her mother that Grey once sent back a cheeseburger three times, but what was the point?

Grey dragged her outside to the deck overlooking the marina. Zadie willingly followed. She would have driven to Detroit just to get away from her family at the moment.

Grey looked at her, worried. "How are you?" Wow, the question of the night. Couldn't anyone ask her the time? Or what she thought of the Iraqi situation? Or how many times she'd burped after eating the salmon?

"For the ninety-fifth time tonight, I'm fine. How are you, groom-to-be?" She said it with the proper ironic inflection, so as not to be cheesy.

"I'm great. Ready to shit myself, but great."

"You look like you're having fun." She meant it. He did. No need for ironic inflection here.

"I am. I can't imagine why, but I really like your family."

"Well, don't sign up for the fan club. You're the only one."

"I'd introduce you to Mike, but something tells me you're not in the mood."

For a brief moment, Zadie wondered if Mike was the guy in the green shirt, but it didn't matter. She had no interest in meeting him.

"You're a wise man," Zadie said. "Besides, this is *your* night. You're not supposed to be worried about pairing off your friends. You're supposed to be attending to your bride."

"Helen can't stop smiling." He looked proud of this fact.

"Helen has never stopped smiling. She smiled the day I shot her in the knee with a BB gun." That was a good day. Fourth grade. Summer picnic. The savage beauty of childhood.

"Is that what that mark is?" Grey honestly looked concerned.

Zadie rolled her eyes. "Christ, you've actually memorized her skin?"

"That makes me sound pathetic, doesn't it?"

"You are pathetic."

Grey smiled at her. They clinked beer bottles and looked out at the marina. "Helen's dad? Drug dealer. Colombian. Fifty kilos a day."

Zadie smiled at him, picking up the thread. "My Aunt Josephine? Call girl. Runs a few handguns on the side."

"Your Grandma Davis? Man in drag." Zadie spit her beer over the railing of the deck and into the harbor. Grey started laughing. And all was right with the world again.

"I'm happy for you, you know. I really am. Helen will never cheat on you, she'll always stay beautiful and happy and you'll have smiley little babies that will never need braces."

"You think she'll put up with me that long?"

"I guarantee you she'll choose her own bed skirt, but aside from that, I think you'll survive."

He put his arm around her shoulders and gave her a squeeze as they continued to look out at the marina. At the end of the dock, a fisherman pissed onto the side of a yacht. It was a beautiful night.

five

As Zadie sat through homeroom on Monday, she couldn't help but obsess about the fact that Helen had actually asked her if she was afraid she might cry during the ceremony. Meaning cry in a bad way. Zadie hadn't cried during her whole heart-wrenching fiasco. She'd waited until she got home and then she imploded. Grey as witness. The fact that Helen thought her own precious nuptials would set Zadie off incensed her. No, she wouldn't fucking cry. She might puke, but she wouldn't cry.

And wasn't it just like Helen to make Zadie hate her again right when she was trying so hard to like her?

Zadie had never had a problem with Helen—at least not a *severe* problem—until high school. When Helen hit puberty, she sprouted the perkiest of breasts. Not too big, not too small. Phoebe Cates tits circa *Fast Times at Ridgemont High*. And she still had them. Unlike Zadie, who was sporting C cups that were far more susceptible to gravity than she would've preferred. Certain months seemed to feel the pull of the earth more than others. August, for instance. Whenever she put on a bikini, her boobs seemed to hang in a distinctly southern direction. The left one hung a good half inch lower than the right. Which was not something Victoria's Secret cared to address. Had she a need for sexy lingerie, she might've been moved to write a letter. The fact that she was currently spending every weekend hiding out in her apartment allowed her to not give a shit. Except when she saw Helen's tits.

But it wasn't just Helen's physical superiority that angered Zadie, it was her incessant good will. Helen had once given Zadie a kitten. For her sixteenth birthday. Helen had always given her a birthday present. Zadie could barely remember when she was supposed to change her Brita filter, let alone buy her cousins charming birthday gifts. Denise didn't seem to mind. They'd never exchanged gifts. But Helen sent her one every goddamn year, like a plague. Reminding Zadie that she was too disorganized and callous to do the same.

Sometimes Zadie felt that Helen was only well mannered in order to point out to others that they weren't. Not to mention that there was a vengeance in Helen's thoughtfulness. The kitten had peed on every square inch of Zadie's comforter. And the beautiful wall mirror framed by Italian tile that Helen had given her for her thirtieth birthday only served to make Zadie ashamed that she left the house without makeup so often. Why would you give someone a gift that reminded them how inadequate they were? Why didn't Helen just send a framed picture of herself with a card that said, "You suck and I don't"?

By the time homeroom ended, Zadie had a raging headache and was fairly certain that Helen deserved to be tortured by angry bees. Before the engagement, Helen and her spiteful perfection were merely a thorn in Zadie's side. Now they felt like a pine tree jammed right up her ass.

When Trevor arrived for sixth period, his crack was showing. Plumber's butt on the middle-aged was fodder for *SNL*, but a hint of crack on an eighteen-year-old boy whose round globes of ass-cheek were just a scant bit below said crack was something to be worshiped. Zadie had once stood behind him at the Coke machine, imagining what it would be like to put her lips on the back of his neck—so smooth, so tan, so soft. Would he sigh? Would he turn and kiss her on the mouth? Would he get hard? She looked away. The sight of his ass crack sent her into a spiral of shame. No, no, no. Trevor was *not* lickable. He probably didn't even taste good.

As she tried to distract herself with the attendance sheet, he walked up to her desk. "Ms. Roberts, do you think you could hook me up with someone who could get me into Stanford? I got wait-listed."

Zadie glanced up, trying not to look directly at him. "Have you talked to your counselor about it?"

"He doesn't know anyone."

"What makes you think I do?"

"You're cool. You have to know somebody." The fact that her students thought she was cool because she'd been engaged to Jack was something she generally ignored. But now it occurred to her that Trevor might think she was hotter than he'd normally think she was, due to this fact. The tragedy and joy of this discovery danced in her brain, giving her a worse headache than she'd had before.

"I'll try to find someone, but I can't promise you anything."

He smiled at her. "Thanks. You rock." Oh, yes she would. She'd rock his fucking world. He'd go off to Stanford with a whole new understanding of the clitoris. She'd actually be doing him a service. And the women of Stanford. Yet she'd have to live with the fact that she'd defiled a teenager, and that was just too sad to comprehend. As demented as she was, she had a conscience.

Nancy waved her over at lunch from a picnic table outside, but Zadie kept walking and got into her car, on a mission. She drove down Ventura and pulled over in front of the Sportsman's Lodge, parking near the entrance. She'd read in *Soap Opera Digest* that *Days of Our Lives* was having a fan club luncheon there. She wasn't going in. Christ, she wasn't that pathetic. She just wanted to see him walk by. Just to make sure she wasn't upset anymore. She shouldn't even be reading *Soap Opera Digest,* but her subscription was endless. It just kept showing up. She happened to notice the mention of "Eat Quiche with the Men of *Days!*" on the cover. It's not like she was here to stalk him. She just wanted proof that he was a cheesebag who now wore leather pants.

The day that Zadie realized she was in love with Jack, it had been pouring rain. El Niño rain, which somehow seemed wetter than normal rain. Jack was lying on his stomach in the mud, changing her tire on the side of Laurel Canyon. Cars were whizzing by, water was rushing down the hill in a stream that was about ten minutes away from being a flash flood, and Zadie was warm and dry inside the car while Jack spun her lug nuts off. Most guys would've called Triple A. At least, most L.A. guys. Most guys would've yelled at her for hitting the curb and slicing the tire open on the edge of a grate. Jack simply said, "Stay here, I got it," and got out to change the tire. The fact that he'd been capable was a plus. The fact that he'd been willing was a four-star bonus. Zadie was overcome with such a huge rush of love for him in that moment that she rolled the window down and stuck her head out in the rain to tell him. He got up on his knees, kissed her, and told her that he loved her too. They'd been dating for two months at the time.

Zadie checked her watch. She'd been waiting for thirty minutes. If she didn't leave soon, she was going to miss eighth period. Right as she turned on the ignition, she saw a Porsche pull up. Jack got out and sauntered into the restaurant, waving at the screaming housewives who clamored up behind him.

He had sunglasses on.

It was cloudy.

There was no conceivable glare that he needed to shade his eyes from.

Zadie started her car and drove away. She felt nothing. Except overwhelming nausea and a blinding stab of rage.

Once she was back out on Ventura, she saw a drunken homeless man sitting under the awning of a doughnut shop, holding out a cup. She pulled over and stopped, rolling down her window.

"Hey. I've got a job for you."

The homeless man looked up, not sure if he was excited or dismayed at the prospect. "What is it?"

Zadie pulled out a twenty-dollar bill and handed it to him. "See that parking lot over there? There's a silver Porsche Boxster in the last row. I want you to piss on it."

"You want me to piss on a car?"

"Make sure you get the door handle on the driver's side."

"Whose car is it?"

"Osama bin Laden's."

"No shit? We should call somebody."

Damn. A responsible drunk. "It's my ex-fiancé's."

"Was he mean to you?"

"He made me cry for a very, very long time."

The homeless guy frowned, then nodded. "I'm your man." He pocketed the twenty and unzipped his pants as he walked toward the Sportsman's Lodge.

Zadie drove off, trusting him to do his job well.

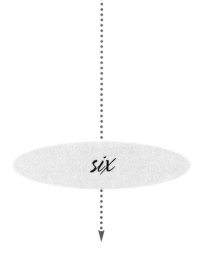

six

When Grey picked her up to go surfing on Saturday, she was in the midst of trying to deodorize her wet suit. She'd left it in the trunk of her car after the last time they'd gone and it had been cooking in there for the past month. It now smelled like something a bulimic would sniff in order to vomit.

"You ready? Waves are at three feet. Glassy and clean."

She was definitely ready. She wanted that feeling. The feeling you got when you stood up easily and got a nice long ride into the beach. There was something magical about standing on the ocean, sun shining down, feeling like you were doing something truly cool. Even if it wasn't cool, she would've done it, though she was admittedly what she thought of as a "tourist" surfer. She didn't particularly like carrying her board, or any of the other exhausting aspects of the sport, like paddling out to the break or fighting the current to stay in position. She heard that in Waikiki you could just walk down onto the beach and rent a board right there, along with a big Hawaiian man to push you into the waves. This was her dream. Someday, she would treat herself.

In the meantime, she was spending twenty minutes strapping her board on top of Grey's car. They were heading south to Bolsa Chica in Huntington Beach. A nice beach break, if you could avoid the stingrays. Shuffling your feet in the sand was supposed to scare them. Zadie usually shuffled so thoroughly it looked like she was doing some type of clog dance. If you stepped on one, someone had to douse your foot in boiling water. Big fun.

When they got there, the waves were only two feet, and not so glassy. So much for the surf report. A two-foot break was easy to paddle out in however, so she couldn't complain about that. Grey had taken her to San Clemente on a five-foot day where she got slammed in the face by waves for forty-five minutes while trying to paddle out, never even making it to the break. Those were the days when she wondered why the hell she liked surfing at all. It was hard. It was frustrating. But here she was again, paddling out in the cold green water, so there must be crack in the ocean. Calling them all out for another fix.

When they got out to the break, they sat and waited. Along with twenty or so other surfers.

"I hear Helen's planning a bachelorette party," Grey said.

Zadie rolled her eyes. "Something tells me it won't be the kind of party where she carries around a blow-up penis." Given Helen's disdain for alcohol, how could her party possibly involve fun of any kind? It would be lame and painful and Zadie was annoyed that she'd be forced to attend.

"Do me a favor and make sure she has a good time. Maybe loosen her up a little."

Zadie raised her eyebrows. "Like make-sure-she-uses-a-condom good time?"

"Funny. Here it comes. Paddle."

Zadie turned around to look at a three-foot wave coming up behind her. She was in perfect position, near the peak. She lay down on her board and paddled hard, waiting for the wave to catch her. When it did, she raised herself into a push-up position and popped up, landing in the middle of her board, perfectly balanced. A miracle. Her first wave a perfect ride. Usually, she pearled for at least three waves, the nose of her board going under water, causing her to get spun. Yet, here she was, standing up, smiling, stomach pulled in, riding the wave. Life was good. As the wave ended, she sank back down onto her board and turned it around to paddle back out.

"Nice one." Grey was still at the break. Waiting for his wave. "You got your foot forward. That's what was holding you back last time."

In the midst of Zadie's postnuptial depression, Grey had insisted that she go surfing with him. She balked, of course. Why would she do something she knew she would suck at? Not that Zadie wasn't athletic. She played softball in high school. She went to the gym. She could kick ass in a beach volleyball game. She played tennis a couple times a year. But surfing required one to go from lying down to standing up in one smooth motion, while balanced on a piece of fiberglass that was shooting across the ocean. Not the most graceful thing one could be doing on a Saturday. But it beat watching reruns of *American Gladiator* on TNN, no matter how hot Nitro was.

Their first surfing excursion was an exercise in torture. Paddling was a fucking drag. Her sunscreen melted in the salt water and ran into her eyes. Her wet suit weighed a million pounds and felt like a full-body girdle. Zadie didn't even like wearing a bra. Why was she doing this? She was convinced that Grey was trying to kill her, when all of a sudden she was up. On a wave. For a good ten seconds. And then everything changed. Now that she'd done it once, she had to do it again. And all of the paddling and all of the salt water in her eyes didn't matter. She had to catch another wave.

"Promise me you'll take charge of the bachelorette party if it gets too pathetic."

Zadie looked over at Grey as she sat up on her board, facing the ocean. Never turn your back on the waves. She'd learned that early on. That, and to keep your mouth closed when you're underwater. The Pacific Ocean is neither tasty nor nutritious.

"Do I sense preplanned guilt in your plea? Like you're having an orgy and want to make sure Helen has a quality pedicure to make up for it?"

"You know what I mean. Helen isn't like you. And I don't think her friends are like you, either."

"Yes, thank you for reminding me that I'm a big alcoholic slut. But sadly, I'm not going to apologize for that."

"I don't want you to. I wish—"

"Wave." Zadie pointed at the incoming peak behind him and Grey started paddling, popping up and showing off until the wave died out. Grey was good. To meet him on the street, you would never imagine he could surf. You might imagine that he would take a Dustbuster to his car after every trip to the beach, and you'd be right. But anal or not, the man could shred. When he paddled back to the break, Zadie was waiting.

"You left off at the point where you were saying that Helen is pure and I'm a big whore."

"How're you a whore? You didn't sleep with anyone but Jack the whole time you were dating him, and you haven't slept with anyone since."

Zadie thought about this. He was right. It was just in her mind that she slept with eighteen-year-olds and tried to dry-hump the maintenance man who installed her trash compactor.

"I just want you to try to get Helen to have fun. Sometimes, she seems—a little uptight," he said.

"Because she won't fuck you?"

"Well, yeah, there's definitely that."

"Don't worry. I'm sure it'll happen once you shower her with rose petals on the honeymoon bed."

Grey rolled his eyes. "Why do you think she's held out this long? It's not like she's religious."

"Some girls need a thing. Virginity is Helen's thing. Otherwise, she'd be just another beautiful Orange County fashion merchandising major."

"Come on—she manages a boutique. That's not embarrassing. She's great at it."

"Of course she's great at it."

Grey sat back on his board, ignoring a perfect wave as it passed him by. "You know, sometimes you sound like you really don't like her." He looked her right in the eyes, making it hard for her to lie.

"Sometimes I don't."

"She's your cousin. She's my fiancée. You *have* to like her." He looked upset. This was obviously important to him. "She's the sweetest person I've ever met. What's not to like?"

"I do like her. Of course I like her. I love her. I have to. She's family. I just don't like the way she makes me feel about myself sometimes."

"Wave." He pointed out a perfect one behind her. She started paddling, glad to escape the conversation. And she pearled. Goddammit. She was too tense to surf now. Grey was making her analyze why she hated Helen. She hated to analyze her feelings. Because then she had to feel them. Denial and repression were her friends.

She paddled back to the break, after wiping the ocean snot from her face. "Can we not talk about Helen right now? She's fucking up my surfing."

"How the hell does Helen make you feel bad about yourself?" Clearly, Grey wasn't listening.

"I didn't say that."

"You implied it."

Zadie sighed. There was no use avoiding a conversation that Grey was determined to have. She'd learned this on their fourth night out when he insisted she explain her repulsion for men who wore open-toed shoes. Not Tevas or flip-flops, just the leather-banded open-toed sandals. There was something so wrong about that.

"Sometimes, I feel like Helen is perfect to remind me that I'm not."

Grey looked at her like she was insane. "You realize that's psychotic."

"How is it that I can tell you how many fingers I stick inside myself without shame, yet when I make a general statement about my cousin, I get a big dose of judgment?"

"Helen can't *make* you feel anything. Only you can make you feel something."

"Thank you, Oprah. Can we just surf?"

Grey looked at her for a moment, then pointed behind her. "Paddle." She lay down on the board and paddled hard. Catching the wave and popping up. Then falling off the board to the left. Balance completely shot. Fucking Helen.

seven

Zadie's Monday started out decently, then quickly deteriorated. Nicole, the daughter of a boozy actress who'd been the second lead on an Aaron Spelling show in the eighties, showed up to class in an outfit that could only have been purchased at the Whore Store. Since it was hard enough to teach Chekhov without the added distraction of Nicole's tits disrupting her class, Zadie gave up halfway through and had them write an essay on dualism.

When she got home, she found that not only had she left her balcony door open, but that the neighbor's cat had leaped across the divide, dug up her cactus pots, then wiped his muddy paws on her couch—giving shabby chic an entirely new meaning. And she was pretty sure the dead sparrow on her coffee table wasn't something she'd picked up at Pier One. Too annoyed to clean it up, she sat down on the ottoman and opened her mail. And now the day was complete. The invitation had arrived. Light blue type on white linen with a lemon-yellow gingham border:

HELEN'S BACHELORETTE PARTY AND BRIDAL SHOWER
An All-Day Fun-Filled Event!!!

9:00 A.M. Breakfast at Barney Greengrass (Yum!!!)

11:00 A.M. Kundalini yoga at Golden Bridge
(I swear it will change your life!!!)

1:00 P.M. Tonics at Elixir (Mind-blowing!!!)

2:00 P.M. Shopping at Fred Segal (Everyone's favorite sport!!!)

4:00 P.M. Tea at the Peninsula (Elegant!!!)

6:30 P.M. Dinner at the Ivy (Grilled vegie salad!!)

Zadie read it with a sinking sense of dread. The kind of dread one gets when faced with attending an event where the most commonly used phrases will be "Cute!", "You'll never believe what Courtney/Zachary did this morning!", and "There're no carbs in that, right?"

The women who would be attending this shindig were generally the types of women that Zadie avoided. Dull women. Women who will have a two-hour conversation about the contents of their children's diapers. Women who only wear designer labels. Women who hire interior decorators. How could you let someone else decorate your house? You should be able to point to things and say, "I got that in a tiny shop in Tuscany," or "some hippie store in Santa Fe," or "at a flea market in Mexico." Not, "Oh, you like it? Thanks. I didn't pick it out and it means nothing to me." Women without souls.

Maybe she was overreacting. Denise would be there. She liked Denise. When they were in tenth grade, they went to see *About Last Night* together for seven weekends in a row, because they were both enamored of Rob Lowe's naked butt. When they were twenty-five, Denise won paragliding lessons from a radio station and took Zadie with her. After a day of instruction, they were both jumping off the side of a cliff with parachutes on their backs. They felt like badass superheros for months afterward. And when Zadie and Jack were still together, they'd gone camping with Denise and Jeff a couple of times and Denise could always be counted on to stay up drinking with Zadie until she passed out, which was the only way Zadie could fall asleep in the woods. Camping was Jack's idea of fun, not hers. Zadie usually lay there staring at the roof of the tent, praying for daylight.

But now Denise was very pregnant and, as Zadie had witnessed at the engagement party, that didn't spell *f-u-n*. Pregnant women tended to talk about things like prenatal vitamins and the size of their nipples.

And Grey's sister, Eloise, would surely be there, which was yet another reason not to attend. Eloise was of the opinion that if Zadie and Grey were best friends, then that automatically meant that Zadie and Eloise were friends. She did not take into account that she was a deeply annoying person. Eloise was a one-upper. If you had a good time, she had a better time. If you had a terrible time, she had a worse time. Her favorite expression was "I can top that." Someone really needed to tell Eloise that she was repellent.

The other women would likely be Helen's coworkers, customers, and sorority sisters. Zadie's head was hurting already.

To head off the tide of cheerful women she was sure to be drowned in, Zadie called Dorian, her best friend from high school and her matron of honor. Well, *proposed* matron of honor. "You will not believe the bachelorette party I have to attend."

"Can't be any worse than yours."

"That was low." Low, but accurate. Zadie and her friends had taken over one of the cabanas at Firefly and ordered a staggering amount of cocktails. Unfortunately, the male stripper Dorian had procured bought his lunch from one of the roach wagons at the construction site where he performed his day job. His burrito turned out to be rancid, and when combined with a tequila shot, it spewed out all over the table full of women. "I should have taken it as a sign."

"Why the hell haven't you returned my last three phone calls?" Dorian was not one for pleasantries.

"I've been busy. It's the end of the school year." Jesus, that was a lame excuse. Especially given that it was over a month away.

"Bullshit. You're avoiding me."

Dorian was right. Zadie had been avoiding her. And her other bridesmaids as well. At first, the groundswell of righteous indignation had been welcome. There was rampant man-bashing. Talk of castration. But after a month or so, it just got old. The fight had gone out of her. And talking to Dorian and the others only served to remind her of that. Zadie didn't like to think of herself that way.

"Let's go to lunch," Zadie said. "I'll drive up on Saturday." There were worse things to do on a Saturday than drive to Santa Barbara and eat a crab cocktail on the pier.

"I can't. Lissy has a recital." Dorian gave birth to twins when she was twenty-six. This was perhaps another reason Zadie didn't hang out with her as often as she should. Small children were so damn needy. "Did you hear that Olivia's boyfriend turned out to be married?"

"Olivia has a boyfriend?" She really needed to return phone calls more often.

"What are you doing tonight?"

"Nothing."

"Then get in your car and drive your ass up here for dinner. I can't talk to you on the phone. You always sound like you're watching TV on mute or something."

"I'm not." Zadie was lying. *Melrose Place* reruns were on E! every single blessed day, how could she not watch?

"We're having lasagna."

Zadie frowned. "Did you make it, or did Dan?" Dorian was not known for her prowess in the kitchen.

"Zadie?"

"Yeah."

"Get in your fucking car."

· · ·

By the time she got to Santa Barbara, it was getting dark. She drove up the hill and parked in Dorian's driveway, behind the minivan. She grabbed the bottle of Chianti she bought along the way and was about to knock on the door when she was accosted by two small creatures wearing clown wigs and tiaras. Dorian's children. They came bolting out of the house and wrapped themselves around Zadie's shins.

"Josh! Lissy! Let Miss Zadie come in the house." Dorian slumped against the door frame in her terry-cloth sweatsuit, looking tired and annoyed. She'd looked that way since the day these two endless sources of energy and mayhem had shot out of her. As soon as they disengaged, Zadie stepped around them and headed toward the kitchen.

"They keep getting bigger."

"Maybe I should stop feeding them." Dorian picked some Play-Doh out of her hair and opened the wine, pouring them two glasses. Zadie sat down at the kitchen table, pushing aside the crayons and headless Barbies. The kids went careening into the playroom, presumably to change costumes.

"So, did I tell you Grey and Helen are getting married?"

Dorian set down her wineglass in mid-sip. "Uh, no . . . Are you okay with that?"

"I'm not sure I have a choice."

"That's so rude of them." Dorian was always good at reframing any event to make it seem like a slight. "How are you supposed to hang out with Grey if they're living in the same house? She'll always be there."

"Yeah, that's occurred to me."

"No wonder you're depressed." Dorian spooned a piece of cork out of her wine and looked at Zadie with concern.

"Am I depressed?" Zadie asked. "I hadn't noticed."

"You didn't return my calls, so you damn well better be depressed." She got up from the table to pull the lasagna out of the oven. "Shit. I burned it. We'll just have to eat around the crusty parts."

Dan walked in, one of the twins attached to his back, the other wrapped around his waist like a belt. "Do I smell dinner?" Dan was one of those guys the word "strapping" was intended to describe. He leaned down to kiss Zadie on the cheek. "How was traffic?"

"Fine." Zadie never understood the male fascination with traffic.

Dorian looked at Dan and motioned with her head toward the kids. "Get them in their seats. The sooner they eat, the sooner we can get them in the bath."

Now that Zadie looked closer, she could see that Lissy was covered in Magic Marker. And Josh had some foreign substance on his face that she didn't have the stomach to identify. Dan peeled the children off his body and got them in their seats as Dorian spooned out the charred lasagna. Josh stared at Zadie. Clearly bothered by something. "What's on your eyes?"

Zadie had no idea. Had a bird shit on her?

Dorian stepped in to explain. "It's makeup, honey." She looked at Zadie and shrugged. "He never sees me with it on." Given the criminal amount of eyeliner Dorian used to wear in high school, Zadie found this amusing.

"So, Zadie. How're things at school? Any rotten kids this year?" Dan was always so polite. He couldn't possibly care about her class, but he always asked.

"Can't say anything too bad about them. They're all pretty well behaved. And they have really good drugs, so that's always a plus." She was kidding, but as soon as it came out of her mouth, she wanted to grab it back.

"Mommy, what's 'drugs'?" Lissy asked.

"It's a grown-up thing, Lissy. Miss Zadie was just making a grown-up joke." Dorian gave her a look like "Zip it on the grown-up jokes." "Why don't you tell Miss Zadie about your dance recital?"

Oh, yes. Please do.

"I'm going to be a ballerina."

"That's great, Lissy. What color is your tutu?" How many times in life do you get to ask someone what color their tutu is? She'd best make use of this opportunity.

"Pink!"

"Will you show me your dance?"

Lissy got up and twirled, despite the fact that she was holding a forkful of lasagna, which was now all over the kitchen.

Dan bent down to wipe it up. "I got it." He was a good dad. And a good husband. Dorian lucked out the day she sat next to him in Econ. People who meet their spouses in college should have to pay dues into a fund for the people who don't.

After dinner, Zadie and Dorian sat in the Adirondack chairs on the back porch, inhaling the night-blooming jasmine and finishing the wine while Dan bathed the kids. Zadie was always amazed that you could actually see the stars up here. At least a few. And the ocean in the distance.

"I think you need to go on a date," Dorian said.

"And what exactly do you think that will accomplish?"

"It'll get you out of that fucking apartment, for one."

"It's actually a non-fucking apartment at the moment. That's part of the problem." Zadie hadn't been laid in seven months. She had wisely made Jack go without for two weeks before the wedding so that their honeymoon would seem special.

"So fuck someone," Dorian said.

"I'll get right on that."

"You're a beautiful girl! All you have to do is walk into a bar and say yes."

"I think you're overestimating my appeal."

Dorian refilled their glasses. "Bullshit. I bet half the boys in your class fantasize about you. That's how Dan lost his virginity, you know. One of his high school teachers gave him detention and then had sex with him in the teachers' lounge."

"Don't tell me things like that." Trevor, Trevor, Trevor. No. Absolutely not.

"I'm not suggesting it, I'm merely pointing out that you're still hot and you could get laid if you wanted to. Maybe you don't really want to."

Zadie shrugged. "Maybe I don't."

"Why the hell not?"

A wet and naked Josh and Lissy came running up to the French doors, smooshing their noses against the glass.

"Hi, Mommy!" They giggled and ran off as Dan chased them with a bath towel.

Zadie lowered her voice. "I can't talk about my need or lack thereof to fornicate when your kids are running around naked. It's unseemly."

Dorian turned to look back into the house. "They can't hear you."

"I just don't know if dysfunctional sex is going to be the cure for my dysfunctional breakup." Christ, she sounded like her therapist.

"Who says it has to be dysfunctional sex?"

"Well, since I'm not going to have sex with anyone that I'm currently acquainted with, it would have to be a stranger. And if it's a stranger, I'll have to go to his place, because I don't want him at mine. And if I'm at his place, I'm going to be wondering if his sheets are clean, and if he was with someone else the night before, or that afternoon, and eventually, any positive benefits I've gotten from the sex will soon be replaced by a shame spiral that will crush me under the weight of knowing that I've just screwed someone I don't even know."

"There's a very simple solution to that. Sleep with someone you know."

"I realize I've been out of touch, but seriously, you're blissfully unaware of the lack of men that populate my world." Aside from Trevor, there wasn't a single guy she could think of who was even remotely appealing. The maintenance-man fantasy was not a possibility. He and his Latina girlfriend lived in the building and she was not a chick whose man you wanted to steal. Her tires had spikes on them.

"Fine. Don't have sex. But at least go out on a date. You need to get back in there. Who was your last date with? Before you met Jack?"

Zadie had to think about this one. She vaguely remembered someone named Bill who'd taken her to a Moroccan restaurant where the belly dancer had practically given him head. He'd then proceeded to flirt with the bespangled dancer while Zadie sat in silence and ate from a plate of food that resembled pita bread and mud. "No one I'd go out with now."

Dorian scrunched up her forehead. "Where'd you meet Jack again?"

"He waited on me. No wonder I liked him. He brought me food. Just think of the pain I could've avoided if I didn't like Chinese."

"Well, I guess lightning could strike twice. Go out to eat and hit on the waiter."

"Definitely not. Every guy who's a waiter is waiting to be something else, and if I'm going to date someone, I'd like him to already *be* what he's waiting to be." Wow, that was profound. She'd never realized what an accurate job title "waiter" was.

"That made absolutely no sense."

Her profundity was wasted. "I'm tired. I should go."

"Okay." Dorian turned around and looked back into the house. "Now that the kids are asleep, it's time for me and Dan to watch porn."

"Are you serious?" Zadie had a newfound respect for marriage.

Dorian laughed. "No, I'm not serious! It's time for me to wash the snot out of my shirt and go to bed. Trust me, you're not missing much."

Zadie sighed. "Aside from love and companionship."

"Well, yeah. There's that."

eight

Zadie woke up the next morning and realized that it had been at least two months since she'd seen her therapist. Of course, this was because she was actively avoiding her. It was ridiculous that she was paying someone to listen to her problems to begin with. Her friends did it for free. It was especially ludicrous given that Zadie didn't *want* to talk about her problems. Didn't that just give them *more* validity? Wouldn't it be better to just ignore them altogether and hope that someday she'd forget about them?

Obviously, seeing a therapist had not been her idea. Her mother had insisted she go and Mavis Roberts could be a giant pain in the ass when she set her mind to it. She made the case that Zadie didn't have the luxury of processing the end of her relationship in a normal fashion. It didn't take the natural route of dating, things souring, and then breaking up. It went from "Here I am, about to walk down the aisle" to complete and utter devastation. She had to instantly start hating Jack right at the moment she was at the peak of her love for him.

In order to shut Mavis up, Zadie went to see Dr. Reed. Seven times. By then she'd had enough of "How did you feel about that?" It wasn't helping.

But on this particular morning, Zadie felt the need to air her agita with a trained professional. Someone who would notice how profound she was because they were being paid to do so. More important, someone who would agree that she did not need to go on a date.

She drove over the hill to Sunset and parked in the underground parking garage. Was it possible to build one that wasn't creepy? The sign stating that the state of California found there to be toxins in the garage that were harmful to unborn fetuses always unnerved her. Where would she park if she ever got pregnant? Every parking structure in the city had that damn sign.

Dr. Reed always had *In Style* magazine in her waiting room, so while you were waiting to purge your soul of the world's injustices, you could find out what kind of shampoo Debra Messing uses. There were also several framed nature prints on the wall, clearly meant to be soothing. Although Zadie had never once been soothed by the sight of a raindrop clinging to a lily pad.

When the good doctor called her in, Zadie took off her shoes and sat on the couch, tucking her legs up underneath her. She always tried to make it seem like they were just two gals shooting the shit over their morning coffee instead of doctor and tragically fucked-up patient.

"I wasn't sure you were going to come back." Dr. Reed gave her a placid smile. She was dressed in her usual perfectly pressed Casual Corner silk separates.

"Why? Do I seem cured?"

"Interesting choice of words."

"Here we go—"Zadie rolled her eyes.

"Cure implies an illness."

"No, I don't think I have an illness." Zadie grabbed a piece of butterscotch from the dish on the coffee table.

"Well, that's good. How *would* you describe what you're feeling?"

"Annoyed." She popped the candy in her mouth.

"Why do you think you feel that way?" Oh, Lord. An exploration of her feelings. The very thing she hated. Why the hell had she come here?

"Because everyone I know wants me to go out on a date. As

if that's going to solve something." Between Grey, Nancy, and Dorian, it was like an irritating song she couldn't turn off. Her friends had all turned into Kylie Minogue.

"And you don't agree?" Dr. Reed asked.

"No, I don't agree. I think it will only make me *more* annoyed. I won't have a good time, and I'll end up wishing I was at home reading a book."

"So, you've already sabotaged any date you'll go on by making up your mind that it will be bad?" Ooh, that was judgmental. Dr. Reed must be feeling feisty this morning. Do therapists argue with their husbands?

"It *will* be bad. There's no question in my mind. Either he won't like me, which will be depressing, or I won't like him and it'll be painful to sit through dinner."

"What if you both like each other and have a delightful time?"

And what if Jack happened to lie down behind her car so she could run him over? Good things like that just don't happen.

Dr. Reed leaned toward her. "Your self-esteem is in a low place right now. Understandably so. And as painful as it may sound, going on a date could help to raise it back up." What?! She was on *their* side?

"Or—going on a date could further lower my self-esteem to a new level of hell."

"There are no guarantees, but there are things you could do to stack the odds in your favor." Dr. Reed crossed her legs and leaned back.

"As in?"

"Pick someone you feel comfortable with. Someone you're not intimidated by."

"You're telling me to go out with an ugly guy?" Zadie asked. She was *paying* for this?

"I didn't say that, but if you're intimidated by good-looking men, then a less attractive date might be a good idea."

"I'm not intimidated by good-looking men. I'm just a little annoyed with their complete lack of humanity," Zadie said, reaching for another butterscotch.

"I think you're projecting your anger at Jack onto other men. Just because one good-looking man turned out to be a poor choice doesn't mean they all will."

"Whoa, whoa, whoa—'a poor choice'? That implies that *I* did something wrong just by going out with him." Zadie put the butterscotch down, too pissed now to eat it.

"Zadie, you didn't do anything wrong. Sometimes we choose people who aren't right for us. Sometimes we choose people who are."

"Uh-uh. You're still putting the blame on me with that scenario. The fact is—I *chose* a perfectly decent guy who turned into a total shit." Jack *had* been a good guy. Otherwise she wouldn't have fallen so in love with him. That's what upset her the most—the fact that *that* version of Jack no longer existed. She missed him.

Dr. Reed nodded. "People can change. That's true."

"So it's not my fault," Zadie said. Damn right it wasn't.

"That he changed? Of course it's not your fault."

"Because you made it sound like I was supposed to take responsibility for it or something."

Dr. Reed took a sip of her tea. "Do you *want* to take responsibility for it?"

"No." Why would she?

"Sometimes people take responsibility for the actions of others so they can feel like they have some control in the situation. A child of divorce for instance. 'Daddy left because I was bad.' That way, they don't feel as helpless. It was their doing. But what starts out as a feeling of control turns into self-imposed guilt for something that was never their fault to begin with."

"And you think I'm doing that?" Zadie asked.

"Are you?"

Was she? She'd always denied that Jack's transformation into the devil was her fault, but did she really believe that? Was it just her way of drowning out the voices in her head that said it *was* her fault? *Had* she driven him away? Or had she just convinced herself that she'd driven him away in order to feel like a participant in the whole meltdown instead of a victim?

Zadie sighed. "I don't know."

"Now we're on to something." Dr. Reed smiled, making a note on her clipboard.

Zadie's head was starting to hurt. And her coffee was cold. Whatever they were on to was not something she cared to address at the moment.

"When Jack didn't show up at the wedding, you must've felt like you had no control over the situation."

"I didn't."

"And that feeling, that lack of control, was mixed in with your grief and your anger and every other negative feeling you were experiencing at the time."

"I guess." There were homicidal tendencies in the mix, but it was probably best not to bring that up now.

"So it would only be natural to try to take that bad feeling— lack of control—and subjugate it by assigning yourself blame, which in essence, is your perception of control. You convince yourself that Jack's rejection was your fault and now you're back in control—*you* caused it. *You're* the one who made it happen."

Zadie leaned her head back against the wall. "This is really depressing. You're telling me that somehow I've blamed myself in order to make myself feel better?"

Dr. Reed leaned forward. "But you don't feel better. You feel worse."

"Agreed." She felt like crap. Pretty much all the time.

"That's why you need to let it go."

"Let what go?" Zadie asked, looking back at the doctor.

"Your false sense of control."

"Okay . . ."

"Stop blaming yourself for what Jack did. You can take control of your life in other ways. More constructive ways."

"Any suggestions?" Zadie asked.

"Go on a date."

And it was back to that.

nine

When Zadie got to school, she stopped in the teachers' lounge to stash her lunch in the fridge. She set it in the only space left, next to a Tupperware container full of ramen noodles that had been there as long as she'd been teaching. There was probably a colony of sea monkeys living in it by now, or some revolutionary cancer-curing mold, but no one was brave enough to open it.

As she made a cup of green tea, Nancy walked in, completely aglow. Coral lipstick on her big fake lips. "You will never believe the date I had last night."

"Let me guess. He took his penis out in the restaurant?"

Nancy rolled her eyes at Zadie, indicating that she was clearly far too wise to date anyone of such ilk. "No . . . he was a perfect gentleman. It was the best second date I've ever had."

"Second date? Congratulations. What's his name?" Zadie was neither impressed nor interested, but Nancy didn't pick up on it.

"Darryl."

Zadie bit her tongue. Did Nancy not realize that in the vast and far-reaching history of the world, there has never been a cool guy named Darryl?

"And he has a brother named Doug who's single, if you're interested."

There were few things that Zadie was *less* interested in than Doug. The particulars of gum surgery, perhaps. How many miles to the gallon her car got. J.Lo's love life.

Nancy put her lunch in the fridge and shut it with a jaunty swish of her hip. Clearly in high spirits. "He's thirty-five and he's a software engineer."

Just as Zadie was about to decline, she had a thought. Doug was a harmless-sounding man whom she could possibly bring herself to have a meal with and, in the process, get Grey, Dorian, and Dr. Reed to shut up about the "you need to go on a date" thing.

"Any visible defects?"

"I haven't seen him, but if he looks anything like Darryl, you're a lucky girl."

Dolores got up from the table where she'd been downing a bowl of Lucky Charms. "Are you really considering this?" She didn't say it in a judgmental way, she merely echoed Zadie's own thoughts. Was she?

"I think I am. Maybe it's time." Fuck, no, it wasn't time, but she could go through the motions and pretend it was time in order to prove it wasn't to those who insisted it was.

Nancy clapped her hands with glee. "This is going to be so much fun! We'll all four go to dinner!"

Zadie thought about objecting, but then realized this could actually be beneficial. As painful as it would be to watch Nancy on a date, at least she wouldn't have to carry the conversation herself. "Yeah. Okay."

"Are you free on Saturday?"

"Unfortunately, yes."

Dolores shook her head in wonder. "I was starting to think this day would never come."

Zadie had been *sure* this day would never come. Now that it had, the universe seemed somewhat askew.

"I'll call Darryl at lunch and we'll work out all the details." Nancy gave Zadie a squeeze, pleased as punch to be a participant in what was clearly, in her mind, a foregone love match.

Zadie entered her classroom with a belly full of dread. She knew nothing about Doug. He could be heinous. He could be gorgeous. He could hate her on sight. She could cringe at the sound of his voice. All this effort just to get her friends to shut up? She was far too giving a person.

The bell rang and her first-period students took their seats. Jessica Martin raised her hand, most likely to show off her manicure. "Okay, I know that William Faulkner is supposed to be a genius and all, but is it just me or are the first three chapters of As I Lay Dying completely incoherent? Who are these people? What the hell are they talking about? And why do they keep repeating themselves?"

Zadie had to think carefully about her answer. She completely agreed with Jessica, but saying that would not be politically sound. "Well, you have to remember, it's a story about people who live in a different time and place."

"Well, why does Faulkner have to write about those people? They're annoying."

"Just think of it as a window into a part of humanity that you would never get to see otherwise," Zadie answered.

"Okay, but can you maybe pick a book that's more interesting next time? I don't care about where these people bury their mother. It's gross."

"I'll do my best."

Zadie could've explained to Jessica that the head of the department was the one who picked the books, but why bother? She'd just spent the morning explaining to Dr. Reed why she didn't need to go on a date and now she was going on one. People don't listen. So why bother to talk? They're just going to hear what they want to hear, or ignore you altogether.

It occurred to her that this was perhaps an unhealthy attitude for a teacher to have.

On Saturday morning, Zadie decided to go to the gym. It had been at least a month and it seemed like a good pre-date thing to do. At least it would distract her from the fact that she would soon be saying things like, "So, what do you do for fun?"

She threw on a ratty T-shirt and shorts and called Grey to meet her there. Their gym had several million cardio machines, all facing a giant window overlooking Ventura Boulevard, as if the sight of traffic would be inspirational. As they rode on neighboring Lifecycles, Grey looked over at her, offering half a Red Bull.

"I'm proud of you."

Zadie drained the Red Bull, hoping that whatever "taurine" was would help make exercise less boring. "What'd I do?"

"You're going out on a date. I think this will be good for you."

"Yes, I'm sure Doug will be just like a shot of wheat grass juice." She upped the resistance on the bike. As long as she was here, she wanted to sweat.

"Are you going to have sex with him?" he teased.

"Of course. In the car on the way over, at the restaurant, and probably in the parking lot after dinner. But only if we can do it up against the Dumpster." She was starting to breathe heavily now. And not from the thought of Doug against a Dumpster.

"I'll take that as a no," Grey said, pedaling faster.

"I'd say there's better odds of you and Helen having sex tonight than me and Doug."

"I'm not even seeing Helen tonight."

"Well, there you go." She lowered the resistance. Her heart was pounding. Enough of this shit. Grey hadn't even broken a sweat yet. "So, what's the deal? Is Helen cheating on you already?"

"She's going over some wedding details with her mom."

"Did they hire the horse-drawn carriage yet?"

Grey looked worried. "Why, is that what she's planning?"

Zadie looked over at him and smiled. "I'm kidding. It's always been her dream to get married on the edge of a lake and arrive in a boat pulled by swans."

"Funny."

"You better show up, you know."

Can you imagine? Helen getting left at the altar? Never in a million years.

"I'm planning on it." Grey was the one guy in the world Zadie would trust to keep his word. There was something so pure about him. He was just a truly decent guy. No surprises. She used to think that she wanted a man who would constantly surprise her. Then she got one.

Zadie got off the bike, pulling her T-shirt out so it wouldn't cling to her now sweaty boobs. "Come spot me on the leg press?"

Grey followed her over to the machine and helped her load the weights onto the rack. "How much?"

"Sixty on each side." Zadie neglected to mention to Grey that if she squeezed her thighs together just right while she did the leg press machine, she would have an orgasm. The more weight, the easier it was. It's not like she felt the need to hide this fact from him. She just didn't want him watching her while she had one. They weren't *that* close.

"You sure?"

"Pile it on." Zadie lay down on the machine and started her set. Listening as Grey chatted on, relacing his shoes, no idea that she was pleasuring herself.

"I'm leaving all the wedding details to Helen. Partly because I don't have time, but mostly because I don't give a shit. Is that inconsiderate?"

"No. That's what you're supposed to do." She was barely listening, but she knew she had to respond to keep up her cover. She wondered if all women knew about the leg press or if it only worked on her.

"Are you sure?"

Jesus, must he go on about this? "Here's a thought. Ask her. I'm sure she'll be more than happy to tell you if she wants your input." First Helen fucks up her surfing, now she's interrupting her orgasm.

"What's the matter?"

"Nothing's the matter." Did he have to talk right now? Why was he looking at her? He was supposed to be watching the weights.

"Your face is all red."

"Probably because I'm repeatedly thrusting a hundred and twenty pounds into the air." And because she just had an immense wave of bliss wash through her loins.

"Why were your eyes rolling back in your head?"

"They always do that when I lift."

Grey frowned. "I don't think you should drink Red Bull before you work out anymore."

He helped her up after she finished and started loading more weight on the machine for his set. "So, I told my buddy Mike about you."

Zadie frowned. "What'd you tell him?"

"That you're a nut job, but that he'd probably want to bang you anyway." He lay down on the machine and started his set.

"Charming."

"I'm kidding. I told him—you're hot—you're funny"—he was talking in between thrusts—"and you're a quality babe." He lowered the weights and stood.

"I love it when you speak in early Keanu." She pulled the weights off the machine until it was back to her level. "But I'm still not going to let you set me up. My date tonight is all the trauma I can take for now."

Grey motioned with his head toward the cardio machines. "There's a guy on the StairMaster checking you out."

Zadie didn't even look. Why bother?

"Red shirt, black sweats. Take a look," Grey said.

Zadie rolled her eyes and turned to appease him. A passably cute guy in a red T-shirt and black sweats was engrossed in a magazine.

"He's not checking me out."

"Not *now*, but he was."

Zadie lay back down on the machine and started lifting again. "Your attempt to build my confidence before my date is transparent, but appreciated."

"He just looked again."

"Stop—"

"What? I'm just reporting the facts."

Zadie closed her eyes. The second leg-press orgasm was never as good. Too fleeting.

"Oh, fuck." Grey was still looking over at the cardio machines, but now he was frowning.

"What?" Zadie asked.

"The guy on the treadmill. I think it's Jack."

Zadie let the weights slam down. "What?!"

The vein on Grey's temple was throbbing, like he was preparing for battle. "Should we leave or should I kick his ass?"

Zadie started to panic. Why did Jack have to show up *here*? She looked like crap. Out of all the millions of times she fantasized about running into him and saying something pithy, and haughty, and Bette Davis–like, she never once imagined that she'd be red faced with a sweaty ponytail and wearing a T-shirt she'd had since college.

"Don't let him see me." She hid behind Grey, grabbing him like a shield. What the hell would she say if he came over? Hi, remember me? The girl who was supposed to be your wife? Can I have my heart back?

"Make sure it's really him before I hit him," Grey said.

"You can't hit him." As much as Zadie would like to see Grey smack Jack upside the head with a dumbbell, she didn't want him to get arrested for assault. Jack made a living with his face. He would surely press charges.

"Here he comes. He's heading for the ab machine."

Zadie steeled herself and peeked around Grey's shoulder. She saw a guy with shaggy black hair and rock-solid delts sit down on the ab crunch machine and bend forward.

It wasn't Jack.

She let herself breathe again and swatted Grey on the shoulder. "Jesus. Don't do that to me."

"It's not him?"

"No, thank God." Grey and Jack had only met twice. When Grey was still with his ex, Angela, they'd all gone to dinner at Koi. Jack instantly hated Angela because she said something degrading about actors before they even got their edamame, so he was sullen for the rest of the night. The second time was post-Angela and Grey had met Zadie and Jack at the Cat & Fiddle, where Jack was supposed to set Grey up with one of his costars, but apparently, she'd met George Clooney at a premiere the night before and was still in his bed. Jack had felt bad and tried to get the bartender interested in Grey, but Grey ended up going home with a makeup artist from *Six Feet Under* who made the dead people look pasty. Neither time had Grey been spectacularly impressed with Jack, Zadie found out later, but he also hadn't foreseen that Jack would pull what he'd pulled. He'd merely thought Jack was a little too concerned with what people thought of him, and a little too handsome for his own good.

"Sorry about that." Grey squeezed Zadie's shoulder. "Didn't mean to scare you."

"Let's go," Zadie said. "You owe me a drink."

Her workout was over.

ten

Some women enjoy trying on several outfits. Some women just pick the first one that looks decent. Zadie opted for the first thing she could find that was clean—jeans and a turquoise peasant blouse. She also opted for a glass of wine while she blow-dried her hair, which left her looking flushed. Maybe flushed was the new sexy.

As she put on her makeup, she tried to keep herself from imagining how the night might turn out. Even though she was only going on a date to shut everyone up—a ploy that clearly hadn't worked with her mother, who'd asked at least sixty-five questions about Doug before Zadie got off the phone—she was still vaguely nauseous at the thought of meeting a prospective suitor.

When she was younger, first dates were always exciting. They held so much hope. The promise of a new and perfect relationship hovered above her every time she met someone for a drink or coffee. On her first date with Jack, they'd gone hiking with his dog in Runyon Canyon. When the dog got too tired to finish, Jack carried him the rest of the way. Zadie knew then that she could have babies with him.

So much for hope and promise.

She met Nancy and the team of Doug and Darryl at Pinot Grill on Ventura, a casual California bistro not too far from home, not too expensive. As she walked in, she saw Nancy waving from a table. Doug and Darryl both turned to look at her and she didn't know whether to be disappointed or relieved. Both were average. Nothing to get lubricated over.

"Hi, I'm Zadie." The two men stood up as she sat down in the empty chair next to Nancy. The guy across from her held out his hand.

"I'm Doug. Great to meet you."

She smiled at him. "Great to meet you, too." Not really, but there was no need to be ill-mannered. She inspected him over the rim of her water glass. Sandy hair. A little too pale. Eyes too small. Narrow shoulders. Not a wimp, but not the type of guy to carry you out of a burning building.

"Nancy tells me you teach English."

"That's right. And you're in computers?"

"I write code."

"Ah." Morse code? Secret code? Dress code?

He grinned at her. "I did horrible in English class."

"Well, I'm sure you've made up for it in other ways." He probably made at least four times what she did. What did he care if he couldn't quite grasp *A Tale of Two Cities?*

Nancy piped up. "Doug is *very* successful."

Doug blushed as he foraged through the bread basket. "I paid her to say that."

He was modest. That was a plus. She hated the "Wanna see my Hummer?" crowd. They were almost as bad as the men who drove piss-yellow Ferraris. Who the hell buys a hundred-and-fifty-thousand-dollar car the color of urine?

They ordered a bottle of red wine and looked over the menu. Zadie opted for the mustard-roasted chicken. The French fries that came with it were so good it wouldn't matter how the date ended up. Although, as of now, it wasn't too painful. Doug seemed pleasant enough.

Nancy leaned over and whispered to Zadie as Doug and Darryl ordered. "Well?"

Zadie knew this was coming. "I just met him. I can't answer that yet."

"But he's kind of cute, right?"

"Kind of." If she passed him on the street she wouldn't even notice him. But she wasn't here for love. She was here to prove a point.

After the guys ordered, Darryl joined the fray. "So, Zadie, is Nancy as strict in her classroom as she is with me?"

Mayday. Was Darryl implying that Nancy was some kind of dominatrix? This was not information Zadie wanted to know. Nancy swatted Darryl and giggled.

"Don't listen to him. He's just mad I wouldn't let him pick the restaurant."

Darryl played along. "There's nothing wrong with Hooters." Nancy swatted him again in that "Oh, you silly!" way. He held up his napkin as a shield.

"So, Darryl, what do you do?" Zadie was being oh-so-polite. She really didn't care.

"I'm a dentist." No wonder Nancy was excited. Darryl was Husband Material. In Nancy's opinion at least. Zadie had always gone for soulful eyes over a steady paycheck. Her mother had literally wailed with pain when she'd told her that Jack was a waiter.

"He has two offices." Nancy beamed with pride, as if they were her own. Zadie made the appropriate "I'm impressed" noise and tried not to notice that her date was staring at her with a weird intensity.

"I can't believe you're still single," Doug said. "You're really cute."

Was she supposed to say thank you? Before she could decide, Nancy answered for her.

"She was engaged, but she broke it off."

Wow. Nancy sugarcoating her situation? This was unprecedented.

"How old are you?" Doug asked.

"Thirty-one." Kind of a rude question, but Zadie let it go.

"Still, engagement or not, that's plenty of time for some guy to snatch you up. Are you sure you didn't go lesbian for a couple years in there somewhere?" He laughed as if this were the wittiest bon mot ever tossed across a dinner table. Zadie took a deep breath, getting ready to retort. Nancy put her hand on Zadie's arm, as if to say "Easy."

"Well, Doug, there've been some nights where I've had more cocktails than I should have, but I'm pretty certain that I didn't 'go lesbian' at any point in time. How about you? Suck any cock that I should know about?" She took a sip of her wine, just as demure as can be.

Doug stiffened and turned tomato red, exactly as she'd intended. "Uh, no, heh heh, I'm only into girls."

Darryl and Nancy exchanged looks across the table. Darryl's look said "Why did you set my brother up with this foulmouthed bitch?" Nancy's look said "Calm down, she'll stop." And she kicked Zadie under the table to ensure that she would.

Zadie smiled at everyone. "Well, glad we cleared that up. Anyone seen any good movies?"

She wasn't leaving until she got her French fries, that's for damn sure.

eleven

"He did not."

"He did." Zadie was on Grey's suede couch, Coors Light in hand, recounting the evening. She'd driven straight to his house in Westwood as soon as dinner was over, bursting to tell him all the gory details. "He wasn't so happy when I asked him if he'd ever had a dick in his mouth, but we managed to finish our meal without spitting anything at each other."

"What a dumbass." Grey got up and went to the fridge, bringing back two more beers. "No wonder he's still single." He handed her one of the beers and sat down in his Eames chair.

Zadie frowned. "That implies that single people have a defect."

"I was talking about *him,* not single people in general."

"*He* thought *I* had a defect. That's how the whole lesbian thing came up."

"You have lots of defects, but they have no bearing at all on why you're still single. You're still single because I'm the only guy you talk to."

Zadie put her feet up on the antique coffee table and thought about this. "Not true. I talk to Mr. Jeffries, the gym teacher."

"Anyone you refer to as 'Mr.' doesn't count. Neither does Abercrombie boy."

"Speaking of him, do you know anyone who went to Stanford?"

Grey thought a moment. "I think Karl Jameson did. I'll ask him on Monday. Why? Does he need a reference?"

"Yeah. I told him I'd ask around."

"His parents don't know anyone?"

"They're hippies. They used to manage the Grateful Dead."

Grey looked concerned. "What'd you do, follow him home and peek in his windows?"

"I'm not *that* disturbed. I met them at a parent-teacher conference."

"There you go—aren't there any single fathers you could go out with?"

"No." Jessica Martin's father was on the edge of being hot, but the opportunity never presented itself. Was she supposed to call? Hello, Mr. Martin, Jessica is having trouble with Faulkner, perhaps we should discuss it in your hot tub? I'll bring the merlot.

Zadie drained her beer and set it on the coffee table. A thought just occurred to her. "Why is it, do you suppose, that Helen was single when you met her?"

Grey threw her bottle in the recycling bin and plopped down next to her on the couch. Zadie had longed suspected that the Eames chair was secretly uncomfortable.

"Because she was destined to meet me. But something tells me you have another theory."

Zadie pulled her hair up on top of her head and tied it into a knot. "I don't. I was just thinking that if Doug was shocked to find out *I* was single, he'd shit himself to hear that Helen is available."

"She's not."

"But she was when you met her."

"Helen had tons of boyfriends before me."

"And I had tons of boyfriends before Jack." That wasn't true. Several maybe, but not tons. "The point is, none of Helen's boyfriends ever proposed. And she *didn't* have one the day she met you."

"Lucky for me. Or else I wouldn't be getting married in nine days."

She should've known it was beyond him to question serendipity. She laid her head on the back of the couch and sighed. "You know what Saturday is, don't you?"

"The bachelorette party?"

"I wish you were coming, so I could have fun," she said.

Grey snorted. "Are you high? I don't want to sit through a day of that girly crap."

"Neither do I. It's not fair. I feel like I'm being punished because I have a vagina." The thought of oohing and ahhing over Helen's wedding details while sipping tea with women she was sure to despise was unbearable. Maybe she'd be lucky and get food poisoning the night before. She would feel too guilty if she lied about being sick, but maybe she could eat some bad fish by "accident." Christ. She was actually wishing intestinal distress upon herself. "Can't I just come to your bachelor party instead? Then I'd have an excuse not to go."

Grey looked at her. "Do you really wanna watch a bunch of lawyers get lap dances?"

She thought about it. "Do men actually ejaculate during a lap dance, or do they just get hard?"

"Speaking from personal experience? There's no emission of fluids."

"Then what's the point? In high school, guys gave us endless hours of grief about blue balls, and now men are actually *paying* for it?"

"I'm the wrong guy to ask. The only lap dance I ever had was at my brother's bachelor party. The stripper looked like she hadn't eaten in a week. Her rib cage was visible. I kept trying to feed her peanuts."

"Sexy." Zadie looked around the room, noticing that something was different. "What happened to your beanbag chair?"

"Helen didn't like it."

"What?! I loved that chair."

"She thought it was tacky."

"That's what made it so cool. It made all your designer stuff seem less pretentious."

Grey shrugged. "What can I do? She hated it."

"What else does she hate? Just so I can prepare myself."

"I'm not getting rid of everything she doesn't like." Grey picked up his Turkish snuffbox and held it protectively. "This isn't going anywhere."

"So is this what your married life is going to be like? Arguing over what gets to stay in your house?"

"No. My married life is going to be endless nights of bliss."

"Seriously. What's a typical night with you two going to be? Watching TV? Cuddling in front of the fire? Nonstop sex? Throwing dishes? Give me a rough estimate." Zadie started to panic. What if he said, "Making babies"? She'd never see him again. People with babies fall out of circulation for at least two years.

"I don't know. What'd you picture you and Jack would be doing?"

"All estimations involved his actual presence, which we now know was too much to ask. Back to you."

"The same thing you and I are doing, I guess," Grey said. "Hanging out. Talking. Drinking beer."

"Helen doesn't drink. And if you can get her to talk about ejaculation, I wanna be on speakerphone."

"Well, obviously not *exactly* like this. But a version of this. With sex at the end, hopefully."

"Ah, sex. I remember it well." Zadie sighed.

Zadie thought about Dorian's advice to have sex with someone she knew and realized that Grey was the only possibility. And that was completely ludicrous. She didn't have sex with him when he was available, so she certainly wasn't going to have sex with him while he was engaged to her cousin. Not that he wasn't attractive. Nice smile. Muscular thighs. Strong arms. Pretty blue eyes with those long lashes that girls never get. But there was no way in hell Zadie could ever sleep with him, Helen aside. He was too important to her as a friend. Why risk screwing that up for ten minutes of penis inside of her? She'd much rather give up sex than Grey.

Grey looked at his crotch. "I'm hoping I remember how. Should I flex first?"

"You'll be fine. Besides, she's a virgin. She won't know if you suck at it."

"An encouraging thought."

She stood up, stretching. "I should go."

"Is Doug waiting back at your place?"

"Funny."

He got up to walk her to the door. "I'll tell Mike he's still in the running."

"I don't know—" Zadie said. "I'm thinking I should try someone who doesn't speak English. It'll be harder to get offended if I can't understand him."

Grey leaned over and gave her a peck goodbye. "Drive safe."

As she drove over the hill back to the Valley, she thought about hanging out in Grey's living room once Helen had moved in. It was not an appealing scenario. Her bad dates would no longer be amusing anecdotes. They would be a source of pity. Helen wouldn't understand the humor in the situation. She would make a frowny face and cluck sympathetically. Grey would cluck as well in a show of solidarity with his wife. She would no longer be his pal Zadie who was fun to hang out with, she would be poor single Zadie who never had the sense to find a decent man. He would see her through Helen's eyes.

And eventually, Zadie would end up in the same place as the beanbag chair.

twelve

On Monday, Zadie successfully avoided Nancy until lunchtime. Dolores was spooning some of her macaroni and cheese onto Zadie's plate as Nancy sat down at their table and squealed, "Well?"

"Well, what?"

"Is there going to be a date number two?"

"No, there's not going to be a date number two." Most of the other teachers ran errands or went to yoga class on their lunch hours. Zadie decided to tag along next time. A forty-five-minute downward dog was better than watching those giant puffy platypus lips ream her out for not liking Doug.

"What's wrong with him?"

"He's offensive." She looked at Dolores for backup, having told her the story before third period. Dolores nodded. Loyal friend and sexual deviant that she was.

Nancy opened her bag of salad greens and dumped them in a bowl. "Okay, I know the lesbian thing was a little off-color, but I'm sure he didn't mean to sound racist when he called the valet 'José.'"

"Considering that the valet was Asian, I'm guessing he did."

"He was nervous. Just give him another chance. He really liked you. Even after you called him an imbecile."

"Hard to get works every time," Dolores said. Although Zadie couldn't figure out what "hard to get" at a swingers' party entailed. Wanna screw? No. Wanna screw now? Okay.

"Nancy, I appreciate your concern that I may become an old maid, but I really don't think Doug is the answer to my affliction. I'm sorry. But I'm going to pass."

Nancy pouted through the rest of lunch.

Before sixth period, Trevor approached Zadie's desk. Wearing faded jeans and a tight T-shirt with an "Abercrombie Athletic Club" decal.

"Do they send you those for free?" Zadie pointed at his shirt. He looked down at it, confused.

"Yeah, how'd you know?"

"Well, I just figured, with the catalog and all."

"You've seen my catalog?" He looked baffled. As if it were beyond his imaginings that one of his teachers would look at the Abercrombie & Fitch catalog.

Now Zadie felt uncomfortable. As if she'd outed herself as a pervert who gazes at his shirtless torso. "It came in the mail. I thought I recognized you, but I wasn't sure."

"Yeah, it was me." He grinned at her, lifting up his shirt. "Recognize me now?"

Oh, dear God. Trevor's bare tanned skin only inches from her. Washboard abs, goddammit. Her favorite kind. She flushed and turned away until he pulled his shirt back down. "Yep, it's you."

"So, did you find anyone who went to Stanford?"

"I may have. I'm working on it."

"That'd be awesome." He gave her that dimpled grin again. Tucking his sun-bleached hair behind his ears. "By the way, if you're not doing anything on Saturday, my band is playing at The Roxy. We kind of suck, but if you catch a buzz, we get better."

Trevor onstage? Singing or playing guitar or whatever sexy thing he did? Out of the question. It would be completely unbearable. "I'll be at a bachelorette party, but maybe I'll try to stop by."

"Bachelorette party? Definitely bring them by! We can always use horny girls in the audience. Even if they're old."

If Zadie had had a penis, it would've become flaccid at that very moment.

After school, she drove to the dry cleaners to pick up her bridesmaid dress from the little old lady who did the alterations. The dress had been too long, but that was the least of its sins. It was pink and shiny and backless. Which meant that Zadie wouldn't be able to wear a bra. Who the hell ordered backless bridesmaid dresses? Designer or not, it was ridiculous. And don't even get her started on the shoes. It had probably taken an entire village in Taiwan a month to make each pair and it would take Zadie a month to pay for them. And because they were fucking pink, she'd never get to wear them again. Helen was evil. Pure evil.

She called Grey from her cell phone. "The fact that I'm going braless to your wedding is a bit distressing."

"You might get lucky. I hear our minister is a real tit man."

"Did you find out if that Karl guy went to Stanford?"

"Hold on."

She pulled up to a stoplight as he put her on hold. A white guy in a Domino's uniform in the Nova next to her was singing along to some rap song and making the accompanying menacing hand gestures. Zadie wondered if he knew how asinine he looked.

Grey came back on the line. "Nope, sorry. San Jose State. I knew it was up north somewhere."

"Crap." Zadie sincerely wanted to help Trevor, but she also wanted an excuse for him to maybe hug her.

"If he doesn't get in, maybe he'll go to USC and you can crash his fraternity parties," Grey said.

"Shut up. I'm wearing pink for you."

"I've gotta go. Helen's on the other line."

"Ask her what I'm supposed to do with my boobs."

"Put 'em in your purse."

He hung up as Zadie pulled up to the next stoplight, the rap enthusiast still next to her, flailing away. Right as she was thinking he couldn't possibly be any more of a loser, he turned and caught her staring, then gave her a big wink and licked his lips.

She was a lucky, lucky girl.

thirteen

The day of the bachelorette party began with the neighbor's cat climbing through the bedroom window and sitting on Zadie's bed, meowing into her face with hot tuna breath that seemed as if it were coming out of someone's ass.

Zadie kicked the cat out, brushed her teeth, and cursed Taco Bell for not causing her to wake up nauseous. Why else would anyone eat refried beans? Certainly not for the aesthetic presentation.

As she made the drive to Beverly Hills, Zadie mentally prepared herself for a day of biting her tongue and flinching with annoyance. She would try to avoid openly cringing if at all possible, but she could promise nothing. If someone started talking about cesareans, colonics, or Dr. Phil, all bets were off.

When she pulled up to the valet at Barneys—not the dive bar Barney's, but the department store Barneys—where the party was kicking off at the restaurant on the roof for a "light breakfast," she saw a large white limo in the parking lot. Since most of the other women were from Orange County, they all came together in chauffeured splendor. Zadie was in her Camry. Three weeks' worth of smog were stuck to it and seven empty water bottles lay on the floor of the front seat, along with an empty bag of Pirate's Booty from Trader Joe's. The valet looked at her with pity.

When she got to the roof, overlooking the unspectacular south-of-Wilshire view of Beverly Hills, the other women were already there in their yoga clothes, bombarding her with cheery hellos. "Zadie! Hi!" Helen gave her a hug. Denise waved a bagel at her.

Eloise squealed, "Oh, my God, I have that same exact purse. Except mine's bigger." The one-upping had begun. Oh, what a fun day it would be. Eloise looked nothing like Grey. And since Grey was handsome, this unfortunately meant that Eloise was not. But she tried to make up for it with a quirky jet-black asymmetrical bob and "edgy" cat-eye glasses in order to make herself look more interesting. It didn't work.

Big Ass Betsy was next in the parade of hellos. Her red ponytail swung from side to side as she moved in for a hug. She was soaked in enough Estée Lauder perfume to make Zadie's eyes water. "I haven't seen you since Helen's twenty-fifth." Big Ass Betsy did not actually *have* a big ass, she *was,* in fact, a big ass. She'd known Helen since high school, where Betsy had been one of those girls who joins every club, runs every event, and chases every boy. To no avail. Thus bringing about years of sexual frustration that had since been finely honed into a severe state of obnoxiousness. "Remember that haircut you had?" Big Ass Betsy rolled her eyes. "I hope you got your money back."

Oh, what a fun, fun day it was going to be.

Helen pulled out a chair for Zadie to sit. "Let me introduce you to everyone. This is Gilda. She was my Alpha Gam roommate and she flew in from Boulder just to be with us." Helen and Gilda had gone to school in Texas, where Helen was the perfect sorority girl and model student. Although how hard could it be to get straight As when your course load was composed of classes like Textiles and Pucci vs. Gucci?

"Hi, Zadie. Nice to meet you." Gilda seemed normal. Pleasant even. She had that well-scrubbed, hair-parted-in-the-middle, baggy-T-shirt Colorado casual look about her. It occurred to Zadie that Gilda was probably the only person there aside from Denise who had ever seen Helen without makeup.

"You remember Marci and Kim from my Junior League fund-raiser?"

Vaguely. They had a suburban-mom look about them—chin-length brown hair and Keds. And they were cutting their fruit into tiny pieces.

"And Jane. From high school."

Ah, yes, Plane Jane. The flight attendant. The girl who didn't realize that sunflower seeds came from sunflowers. A striking Veronica Lake blonde with boobs that rivaled Helen's, but not someone you'd turn to for practical advice. She smiled at Zadie and gave her a lazy wave.

"And this is Cassandra and Phoebe from the shop."

Two surgically enhanced twenty-three-year-old fashionistas in halter tops and yoga hot pants whom Zadie had never seen before. Skinny and Snotty. She hated them and their overstraightened, stripey hair on sight.

"Cassandra's the one who found those amazing bridesmaid dresses for me, so you all have her to thank," Helen said.

Zadie reminded herself to stab Skinny with a fork at some point during the day. In the meantime, she speared a chunk of pineapple and tried to make conversation with the other Orange County gals. "So, you all took a limo up?"

Big Ass Betsy raced to be the first to answer. "Our driver is an idiot. We had to explain to him how to get to Barneys."

Zadie looked around for a mimosa. None to be found. "Well, he probably doesn't shop here."

The other women looked at her as if this had never occurred to them.

Eloise piped up. "So, Grey told me you had the worst date ever the other night."

Why, why, why would Grey share this with Eloise?

"Yeah, it was pretty bad."

"That's nothing. I went out with a felon on Tuesday. Convicted and everything." Eloise buttered her croissant with the pride that only a one-upping felon-dater can muster.

Helen gasped, appropriately horrified at the thought. "What was he arrested for?"

"Insider trading. Spent two years in one of those white-collar prisons. He didn't tell me until dessert."

Zadie was sure that the guy had made it up in order to get out of an after-dinner drink. Eloise probably had dates who would steal a car to get away from her.

Helen was concerned, of course. "Well, I hope you're not going to see him again."

"Absolutely not. Can you imagine his credit after something like that?"

Denise leaned over and grabbed the tub of cream cheese from the center of the table. "Did he tell you if he was someone's bitch while he was in jail?"

Marci and Kim gasped, along with Helen. Prison rape *was* a bit raw of a topic for breakfast. Or maybe they were just horrified that Denise was eating so much dairy.

Eloise wrinkled her nose. "I didn't ask."

Cassandra leaned over and inspected Zadie's purse. "Is that a Balenciaga?"

Zadie glanced at her purse and looked back at Cassandra. "Only if they sell Balenciagas for ten bucks on the Venice boardwalk."

Cassandra didn't even crack a smile. Phoebe was equally stone-faced. Don't fuck with fashion around Skinny and Snotty.

Gilda leaned over and whispered in Zadie's ear. "Do you think we can ditch these two before the end of the day?"

"God, I hope so." Zadie smiled at her, glad to have at least one ally at the table.

Helen put her napkin on the table and stood up. "Who's ready for kundalini yoga?" Big Ass Betsy, Plane Jane, Eloise, Marci and Kim, and Cassandra and Phoebe all leaped up with glee. Denise, Zadie, and Gilda were a little bit slower to rise. "I promise you'll all love it. And kundalini is perfect for pregnant moms, so no one has to worry about Denise," Helen assured them.

Denise didn't look worried about the baby, she just looked nauseous in general as she pushed her plate away. French toast with hollandaise sauce tends to make one a bit woozy.

"Let's go, everyone!" Helen led the way to the elevator, as Denise leaned over and discreetly puked into the bowl of mixed fruit. Zadie stayed behind to make sure she was okay. Denise looked up at her, completely miserable.

"Two more months of this."

Zadie tried to be positive. "But just think. Then you'll have a baby."

Denise didn't look any happier. "Exactly."

fourteen

Golden Bridge Yoga was on 3rd Street, and had no parking lot to speak of, so the limo came in handy. The fellow yogis in the lobby looked out the window, expecting to see Madonna or some such celebrity debark, but alas, it was just a handful of swinging bachelorette party revelers, here to Zen out and discover their kundalini energy.

Zadie had been to a few power yoga classes in the past and had decided that yoga was something she liked having *done,* but in fact, hated the actual process of doing it. Although kundalini was supposed to be a more spiritual yoga practice and some people swore it brought them to heights of ecstasy, so Zadie was hoping it might be like the leg-press experience, which would be a small ray of sunshine in this otherwise dark day.

She plopped down on her mat in the back, next to Gilda.

"Do you think they'll notice if we just fall asleep back here?" Gilda asked.

"Maybe we'll get lucky and it's one of those classes where everyone has their eyes closed."

They watched as Skinny and Snotty pushed their way to the front in order to sit next to Cindy Crawford. Helen sat in the middle, surrounded by Marci, Kim, Plane Jane, Eloise, and Big Ass Betsy. Denise was next to the door in case she needed to hurl again.

When the class started, everyone immediately got to chanting. Zadie chanted along with them, even though she had no idea what she was saying. Hindi wasn't an elective at UCLA. She could be swearing vengeance upon the infidels for all she knew. Along with the chanting came rocking. And breathing. Lots of breathing. Breath of fire. Dog breath. People were actually sticking out their tongues and panting like dogs. Zadie figured when in Rome . . . After a few moments, it actually started to feel soothing. Something to do with releasing emotion through the diaphragm, according to the turbaned instructor.

Most of the class entailed doing the same repetitive motion for six minutes, before switching to another repetitive motion for six minutes. The ecstasy came for Zadie when they were finally allowed to stop. She looked around the room. Some people were actually crying. Others were aglow with their newfound kundalini fire. Helen beamed like she always did. Betsy was digging her yoga pants out of her crack. Eloise was faking spiritual bliss, trying to outdo the person next to her. Skinny and Snotty were checking out Cindy Crawford's butt as she did the plow position, mentally calculating if theirs was any bigger. Marci and Kim were chanting in perfect precision, clearly skilled at it after many episodes of singing along with Barney. Gilda was in child pose, napping. Plane Jane wiped a tear away. Whether it was from boredom or emotional release, Zadie couldn't tell. Denise had long ago left to puke in the bathroom, or maybe just wander the streets.

At the end of the class, they all got to lie on the floor in corpse pose and listen to some more chanting music. This was Zadie's favorite part. But just as she was about to doze off, she was flooded with images of Jack. Damn that dog breath and its emotional release. The images came fast. She and Jack in bed, laughing at how ridiculously horny they were for each other. Jack's infectious excitement after a good audition, and how he'd bring over In-N-Out burgers to celebrate. Jack kissing her in the fog the time they climbed up to the Hollywood sign and the entire valley was covered in a cloud like they were looking down on it from heaven. Jack at her stove, scrambling eggs for breakfast while she watched from the couch, wearing his green Michigan State T-shirt. The day they got drunk at the beach on the one-year anniversary of the day they met, and slept it off in the sand, waking up in the dark, curled up in each other's arms. All of it. All of the moments she hadn't allowed herself to think about in the past seven months. Speeding past her closed eyelids. Her third chakra aching with the release.

And just as quickly as they came, they were gone. Like she'd finally purged him. And as the instructor turned down the music and instructed them to let go of their tension and embrace the peace within themselves and recognize their divinity, Zadie had a brief feeling that her life would be okay. Maybe things weren't so bad. Maybe she would be perfectly fine. She could almost see it.

As they all *namaste*'d and stood up, Eloise looked across the room and said, "Isn't she on *Days of Our Lives*?" Zadie looked to where Eloise was pointing and saw the anorexic redhead with the severely overplucked eyebrows who was kissing Jack the day she was forced to watch in the Jiffy Lube waiting room. She was giggling with her friend as she blotted her face with a towel. Having no idea she'd just stolen someone's bliss.

fifteen

When the limo pulled up at Elixir on Melrose, Zadie was the first one out. She'd just had to endure a running commentary on everyone's reaction to the class, in addition to seeing these women naked in the locker room as they changed into their cute little skirts and sundresses for the remainder of the party. Zadie had brought a pair of jeans and a blue gauzy blouse.

"Did you all love it? Wasn't it great?" Helen was gushing. Everyone agreed, oohing and ahhing about their various states of nirvana.

"For the first time, I honestly understood how the universe works," Eloise said. Zadie looked at her like she was on glue. Eloise didn't know how her ATM card worked, let alone the cosmos.

"Zadie, did you like it?" Helen looked at her expectantly.

"Yeah. It was different." She'd never hallucinated during yoga before, so she wasn't lying.

"Don't you just feel like everything is right with the world now? I always leave kundalini class feeling so centered."

Zadie wasn't sure that she'd *ever* been centered. But that momentary "Maybe things will be okay" feeling she'd had was something she'd welcome back.

Elixir was an Asian-themed herbal tonic bar that sold shaman-approved beverages designed to soothe or stimulate the psyche.

Zadie opted for Virtual Buddha since it was supposed to produce a state of elation, something she hadn't experienced in quite some time. Was this why Helen was so happy all the time? Was life really as simple as yoga and herbal potions?

Helen gave Zadie a squeeze. "I'm so glad you're here." And for a second, Zadie was too. If she came out of this day with a new-found peace, it would be a day well spent.

As they settled into wicker chairs on the wooden deck overlooking a gurgling fountain in the courtyard, Jane handed Helen the Chi Devil tonic which was supposed to make women horny. "We need to get you primed for the honeymoon."

Why Helen would want to be horny while they spent the rest of the day shopping was a puzzle. As she drank it with a blush and a giggle, Big Ass Betsy came roaring up. So much for elation.

"Okay, who's first?" She pulled out a horoscope book she'd bought down the street at the Bohdi Tree while the others were waiting in line at the "bar."

"Me," Eloise said. "I'm a Cancer." Yes, she was, Zadie thought.

As Betsy ran down everyone's horoscope, predicting fortune and travel and love and car trouble, Zadie took a moment to study Helen. Maybe she really was a kind, lovely person. And annoying as her perfection was, perhaps it was not done with evil intent. Her dislike of beanbag chairs wasn't meant to hurt anyone. So she could be a tad judgmental. Who wasn't? Zadie dismissed men on a regular basis simply because of their footwear. And Helen's thoughtful gift-giving wasn't the plague that Zadie had made it out to be. When she'd caught her reflection in the mirror framed with Italian tile before she left the apartment this morning she'd seen a large glob of eyeliner smeared on her left cheek. Much better to catch something like that on your own than to have the valet tell you as you get out of your car. Or not tell you. Helen had done her a favor by sending that mirror. Helen was a caring person.

Zadie looked down at her now empty tonic. What was in this shit? It was like happy juice.

"Zadie, here's yours: 'Don't allow others to color your attitude. You know which way you want the wind to blow. Mercury in retrograde might not allow it, but keep your focus.'" Betsy scrunched her face up. "I hate it when Mercury's in retrograde."

Zadie kept quiet while the others murmured their agreement. She could care less where Mercury was. Her horoscope on her nonwedding day had said, "Joy is the theme today, and those around you will see it in your eyes." It was safe to say she wasn't a believer.

Big Ass Betsy pulled another book out of her bag. "I thought Helen might be able to use this one." She held up *How to Seduce Any Man in the Zodiac*. The other ladies all snickered and mugged as if she'd pulled out a giant dildo. "What sign is Grey?"

"He's a Scorpio," Helen answered.

As Betsy flipped to the appropriate page, Zadie frowned. "I'm pretty sure he's a Virgo." She remembered Grey reading his horoscope aloud one day as they had breakfast at Hugo's, complaining that Virgos never got to have any fun. Then he sent back his waffles because they weren't crisp enough.

"No, he's a Scorpio. I'm positive. That's why he's so mysterious."

Mysterious? Grey? Were they talking about the same guy?

Eloise piped up to settle things. "Actually, Zadie's right. He's a Virgo. He was born in August."

Helen looked stung. "How could I not know that? I could've sworn he told me he was a Scorpio." The rest of the group got quiet, as if this were a bad omen of some sort. Snotty and Skinny shot Zadie a dirty look for bringing said omen to light.

"Does it matter? Are Virgos psychotic or something?" Zadie asked.

An icy pall came over Helen. "No, it doesn't matter. I'm just upset that I didn't know."

Betsy read from the book. "It says Virgo men are into order and perfection."

Zadie gestured to Helen. "See? He likes perfection. You're perfect. It all works out."

The waitress brought out a tray of finger sandwiches for them. Zadie watched as everyone peeled off the bread and ate only what was inside. Helen let hers sit, still miffed.

"I could've sworn we had an entire conversation about him being a Scorpio." She looked at Eloise. "You're *positive* about this?"

Eloise nodded. "I was there the day he was born."

Helen looked down, avoiding Eloise's gaze. "It's just not like me to be so careless." Oh, the shame of not knowing your fiancé's sun sign. Zadie didn't get it.

"You guys have only been dating for six months. It's not like you can know *everything* about each other." Zadie thought she was helping, but the searing glares from the others seemed to insinuate otherwise.

Helen looked to her posse for reassurance. "Do you think six months isn't enough?"

"Six months is plenty," Big Ass Betsy assured Helen.

"Six months is the difference between a pull-up and a potty seat," Marci agreed.

"That's *huge,*" Kim chimed in.

"Six months is longer than I've ever dated anyone," Jane added, clearly not one for settling down.

"Ask any plastic surgeon. It's enough time to completely transform your body. Six months is a *gigantic* amount of time," Skinny said. Zadie took a closer look at her. Could it be possible that six months ago she was short and fat?

"Six months was how long I was pregnant before I had my first hemorrhoid." No one was sure what that had to do with anything, but Denise was exempt from making sense since she'd thrown up three times and it was only one o'clock.

"You could walk across the entire country in six months," Eloise said, always one to make proclamations about things she knew nothing about. Not that Zadie knew how long it would take to walk across the country, but she was pretty sure Eloise had never walked across so much as Burbank.

Gilda leaned over and peeled the bread off Helen's sandwich

for her. "In school you had at least *two* relationships in a six-month period. What's the big deal?"

Helen still wasn't appeased. "I know. I know. I just can't believe Zadie knows more about Grey than I do."

The other women turned to look at Zadie as if she'd just been caught with Grey's dick in her mouth.

"He's my best friend. Sorry." Zadie wasn't quite sure why she was apologizing for this, but it seemed like the thing to do.

Helen patted her hand. "I know. And I'm lucky for that. How else would I find out all of his secrets?" Helen smiled at Zadie and the rest of the women breathed a sigh of relief. Crisis over. But somehow, Zadie knew better.

The day was just beginning.

sixteen

Fred Segal on Melrose was one of those stores that Zadie usually avoided. Not that it wasn't full of trendy items of all types—clothes, jewelry, candles, makeup. It was just that Zadie wasn't willing to pay the ridiculously high prices that scads of other shoppers—lucky for Fred—were willing to pay. A seventy-five-dollar T-shirt? Does it perform cunnilingus? If not, what's wrong with Target?

When the gals disembarked from their fifty-foot car, Snotty and Skinny bolted into the store as if it were giving away money. Eloise was close behind them. Another pair of cat-eye horn-rims surely on her shopping list. Marci and Kim made a beeline for the kids' section, because God forbid their little ones were the only ones at day care not wearing Juicy Couture. Plane Jane hit the lingerie, Denise stopped at the café to replace the food she'd barfed up previously, and Gilda headed toward the apothecary. Leaving Zadie alone with Helen and Big Ass Betsy as they perused the blue jeans. Zadie held up a pair to inspect.

"I know it's been fashionable for a few years now, but does the world really need to see my ass crack? I'm thinking no."

"The lower cut is more flattering," bespoke Helen, whose ass crack was probably lined with gold.

"So, Zadie. What are some more secrets that you know about

Grey that Helen doesn't?" Betsy, cementing her Big Ass status, stood with her hand on her hip next to the Lucky shelf, waiting for Zadie to reveal that Grey had purple warts on his balls or some such thing.

"I'm pretty sure Helen knows all she needs to know."

Helen stiffened. "What does *that* mean?"

"Exactly what I said." Zadie was confused. How could that comment have possibly provoked a reaction?

"So, there are other things that I *don't* need to know?"

Zadie rolled her eyes. "That's not what I meant." She sighed, knowing more questions would follow, so she'd best elaborate. "Grey is an open book. Everything there is to know about him is right there. Trust me, he's not hiding any deep dark secrets."

"That you know of," Betsy said. Helpful as always.

"Well, you know about the thing with the transvestite, right?"

Helen and Betsy both turned such a remarkable shade of white that Zadie had to put them at ease before she was blinded by the glare. "I'm kidding." Once they resumed blood flow, Zadie continued. "She was a transsexual, so technically, that doesn't make him gay."

Helen threw a pair of jeans at her head and laughed, thankfully realizing that Zadie was taunting her. Big Ass Betsy eyed her as if she still weren't sure.

Zadie followed them, for lack of anything better to do, as they wandered into the next mazelike room—note to Fred: knock down some walls—and watched Marci and Kim debate whether or not it was appropriate for a four-year-old to wear a belly tee.

"If it's to the playground, yes. To Sunday school, no," Marci posited.

"But what kind of message does a toddler's belly send? I don't want men looking at Britney Spears's belly and then looking at Madison's belly and thinking it's the same thing and getting aroused," Kim said.

They then questioned whether or not it was appropriate to let Duncan wear pink. Zadie wanted to tell them that it was severely *in*appropriate to spend two hundred dollars on an outfit for a child who was young enough to crap himself, but she refrained in the spirit of Virtual Buddha.

When Eloise and Skinny came clunking down the stairs in their platform flip-flops and stilettos, all heads in the store turned, scandalized by their raised voices. Apparently, there was a Stella McCartney purse that had caught both their fancies and Eloise, being stronger, had wrenched it away from Skinny, who was now in quite a snit about it.

"Clearly, you know nothing about shopper's etiquette."

Eloise, completely ungracious about her victory, snapped back, "I got my credit card out first, and that's the only etiquette that counts."

Helen, distressed at any agita within the corps, stepped in. "Girls, it's just a purse. No need to get upset."

Skinny didn't agree. She stomped off into the apothecary section. Code word for overpriced beauty products. Zadie followed her, hoping to see her cry. Skinny found Snotty by the bath salts and said, "I don't care if she's the sister of the groom. She's a bitch." Snotty agreed with her, and they went off to lick their wounds by sniffing forty-dollar candles.

Gilda looked over at Zadie, holding up some honey-infused shampoo. "This is four dollars cheaper at the beauty supply store."

"This is definitely not the place to come for a bargain."

"Do people actually *wear* those clothes out there?"

"Present company excluded."

"I went to Helen's boutique yesterday and the clothes were just as bad."

"You're preaching to the choir. I watched *Sex in the City* the entire time it ran and still can't figure out how Carrie was supposed to be a fashion icon. In nine out of ten episodes, she dressed like someone who rode the short bus."

Gilda laughed. "Thank God. I thought it was just because I'm from Boulder."

"Is this the first time you've been out to visit Helen?"

Gilda nodded. "I think she's been trying to keep me away from you all. Maybe she's worried I know too much." She winked like she was kidding, but Zadie was intrigued.

If Helen had a dark side, it would make Zadie's entire fucking year.

seventeen

By the time they got everyone into the limo, keeping all warring factions apart, it was time to head to the Peninsula for tea. Yes, tea. Not that any of them were British, but high tea just seemed like a posh, girly thing to do, so it was on the list. Thank you, Betsy.

What the Orange County gals didn't know was that the Peninsula, a fancy-schmancy, extremely pricey hotel in Beverly Hills, was frequented by an assortment of call girls who met their gentleman callers in the dark, discreet wood-paneled bar. Or even in the bright, sunny "living room." The very living room where they'd be having tea. Zadie had learned this by reading Jackie Collins. Just because she taught English, didn't mean she couldn't read the good stuff.

When they were all situated on the tasteful divans, sipping their Earl Grey, pinky fingers in the air, admiring the six-foot floral displays, Betsy decided it was time for "Advice Hour."

"Okay, I think we should all go around in a circle and give our own particular secrets for a happy marriage to Helen. Who's first?"

Clearly, Betsy wasn't taking into account that Zadie, Jane, Eloise, Snotty, and Skinny weren't married, but what the hell. They could listen and learn.

Denise spoke up first. "Don't forget to take your pill."

Helen gave her a playful hug. "Oh, you know you can't wait to be a mommy. And I can't wait to be an aunt." She rubbed Denise's belly.

Denise tried to grin and act excited about her impending motherhood, but the strain of constant nausea was evident. "Good, because you'll be doing plenty of babysitting. I need to go to Mexico and drink Coronas on the beach for a week as soon as this thing comes out of me."

"You say that now, but believe me, you'll change your mind as soon as you see his face," Marci assured her. "All it takes is one smile and you'll never leave his side."

"I don't know if that's good news or bad news at this point," Denise said.

Betsy set down her teacup with emphasis. "This isn't marriage advice. This is baby advice. We're getting ahead of ourselves."

Gilda raised her hand. "Here's my favorite rule—if he ever comments that you're gaining weight, he has to buy you a present before you have sex with him again."

The other women set down their tea to applaud this. Even Betsy approved.

"Well done. Anyone else?"

Marci piped up. "I'm a big fan of date night once a month. You know, where you put on makeup and a bra and actually leave the house."

Kim nodded in agreement. "Especially once you have kids. He needs to think of you as a lover and not just as a mother."

Marci gasped. "Oh, my God, that's *so* important!" She looked at Denise. "Which is why you shouldn't let him watch the birth. Once he sees his child come out of your vagina, oral sex is tainted. I think our mothers had it right when they made our fathers wait in the lobby."

Zadie looked around for the waitress. If she had to hear birth-canal sex references she wanted a drink.

To her credit, Betsy looked equally skeeved out. "Okay, once again, we're getting ahead of things. Does anyone have any marriage advice for Helen that doesn't involve kids?"

Zadie took it as her cue. "Well, make sure you have someone tailing him on the day of the wedding. Just in case." She was kidding. Obviously.

The other women looked at her. Not getting it. Murmuring at what an inappropriate comment that was. Eloise clued them in.

"Zadie's fiancé didn't show up to her wedding."

A collective gasp. All tea sipping stopped.

Snotty spoke up first. "Are you serious? He didn't show at all?"

"Nope. Never made it." Zadie couldn't believe she'd brought this on herself. But at the same time, it felt good to joke about it. Comedy is pain plus time, she'd read somewhere.

The women all leaned closer, eager to hear more. "What happened?" Gilda was sweet. She sounded genuinely concerned.

"I went home, took off my dress, and drank a lot."

"What was his excuse?" Jane asked.

"He was busy. In Vegas. With his buddies. And he decided that he didn't really want to be tied down. Now that he was 'famous' and all."

Snotty perked up. "He's famous?"

"Sort of. He's on a soap. *Days of Our Lives.*"

Snotty immediately hit Skinny on the arm. Skinny almost swallowed her teabag, she was so excited. "Which character is he?"

"He plays Nate Forrester. But his name is Jack. Jack Cavanaugh."

Skinny almost wet herself. "*You* were engaged to Jack Cavanaugh?"

"Uh, yeah."

"Oh, my God! Oh, my God!" Skinny and Snotty were furiously whispering to each other. Zadie was used to it. When she'd been dating Jack, he'd almost been tackled by a group of teenage girls at the grocery store. Every time they went out to eat, there was always at least one woman in the restaurant who recognized him and came up to Zadie while Jack was in the bathroom, asking if it was really him and if Zadie was really his girlfriend. It was exciting the first few times, but then it got old. Possibly because Jack kept a ledger of every time he was recognized.

"What a prick," Gilda said.

"Yeah, he was no prize, that's for sure."

Big Ass Betsy didn't like being shown up. She was saving her marriage advice for last and it was clearly a doozy. "Well, I'm pretty sure Grey will never pull a stunt like that, so I'll offer up what's most important to a successful marriage. Never go to bed angry."

They all just stared at her. Did she not realize this was a fucking bumper sticker? Or refrigerator magnet? Or whatever cheesebag origin it had?

The focus of the conversation immediately turned back to Zadie.

"When was your wedding?" Skinny wanted to know.

"Seven months ago."

"Wow. You seem really strong. Congratulations." Snotty was congratulating her? Why? She didn't need congratulations for surviving Jack, but she'd damn well need a martini if she was to survive this hen party.

"Well, you know, it takes a lot of inner fortitude and soul-searching to get over something like that, but I feel like in the end, I'm a better person for it." Zadie was clearly being sarcastic, not at all willing to share her inner demons with these women. Unfortunately, her sarcasm went unnoticed.

"I completely agree," Betsy said. "Helen told me about your 'wedding' and I felt for you, but I think in the long run, you'll be so much wiser when the next relationship comes along. When I met Barry, I was sure I'd never find anyone as good as Bob, but then Barry turned out to be the one that I could count on, and being able to count on someone is the most important thing."

The last thing Zadie wanted was relationship advice from a woman who'd scared away every man she met until she was twenty-five. As the rest of the women muttered on about how Zadie would become whole again, she shot Denise a "save me" look. Denise complied.

"Forget this marriage advice crap. Let's give Helen some sex advice." Denise held up her teacup in toast. "To the only twenty-eight-year-old virgin in Los Angeles."

They all held up their teacups, for lack of better toasting apparatus, and clinked. Zadie saw Gilda look down and bite her lip, but before she could ask why, Jane spoke up.

"Use your teeth, but not *too* much."

As the other women tittered, Eloise added her expertise. "Kegel exercises. I can't stress that enough. Squeeze him every five seconds and he'll be begging for more."

The thought of Eloise clamping down on some poor man's penis and then advising Helen to do the same to her brother was too much for Zadie. She got up to go to the ladies' room.

Once inside the world's nicest bathroom, Zadie considered stealing some of the plush washcloths, but Jane walked in right as she'd unzipped her purse. She sat down in the upholstered chair in front of the vanity and started brushing her infuriatingly silky hair.

"Do you think we'll actually get anything to drink today? Or are we stuck with tea and herbal tonics?" Jane asked.

Zadie looked at her with newfound respect. "I'm with you. We just have to convince the rest. Grey wants me to make sure Helen has fun, but I don't know if it's possible with this crowd."

"I'm sure Betsy will have something to say about it. She's even more of a butt rash than she was in high school. And Grey's sister— please. Too bad they're not lesbians. They'd make a perfect couple." She snapped her compact open and swiped some powder across her T-zone, even though it wasn't shiny. Jane had poreless skin. All those high-altitude flights must've made them evaporate.

Just then, a call girl walked into the bathroom and began touching up her lipstick. Zadie watched, fascinated. She had no proof that the woman was a call girl, but judging by her beauty, her plunging neckline, their location, and the wad of cash Zadie saw in her purse, it was a leap she was willing to take.

"Hi, Jane."

Jane knew call girls? This was a new wrinkle in the day.

"Hi, Estelle. How are you?" Jane wasn't quite as friendly as the call girl had been, but she was cordial. She looked at Zadie. "Ready?"

As they headed toward the tea room filled with the rest of their crowd, Jane motioned with her head toward the ladies' room. "She flies first class to New York once a week. I think she has a rich boyfriend."

"I think she has a couple," Zadie answered.

Once they were back on the couch, Zadie was horrified to hear that the sex advice was still going on.

"Lick his crack," Snotty said in a knowing tone that implied she'd licked many a crack and had had great success with it. Skinny nodded in agreement. Clearly, they'd compared notes. Crack-licking was high on their agenda.

As the other women "eewwed," Big Ass Betsy scooted to the edge of her seat and lowered her voice to a dramatic whisper. "When he's lying on his stomach, rub your nipples up and down his back."

Betsy's nipples were a horrifying thought. In fact, it sounded like the name of some shitty punk band. Betsy's Nipples. Maybe they could open for Eloise's Dick Squeeze.

"Turn off the lights," was Marci's big suggestion. "It's more romantic." Wow. These girls were on the cutting edge of hot sex.

Skinny kept staring at Zadie. "So, are you still in touch with Jack?"

"Would *you* still be talking to a guy who left you at the altar?"

"Okay, I just wanted to make sure before I told you this." Skinny paused, as if what she had to say was of the greatest importance. "I gave Jack Cavanaugh a blow job three months ago."

All conversations stopped.

"I didn't know you, so you can't get mad at me," Skinny said.

Zadie didn't respond. She didn't have to. Everyone else responded for her.

"Oh, no!" Helen said.

"Where?" Betsy asked.

"Okay, start at the beginning," Eloise said, practically rubbing her hands together in glee at the horror of the situation.

Skinny was cowering at this point. "Please don't be mad at me, I probably shouldn't have said anything, I just felt like I should tell you."

"Why?" Zadie asked.

"It just felt like the right thing to do."

"Again, why?" As far as Zadie could figure, there was absolutely no reason at all that she needed to possess the knowledge that Skinny had sucked Jack's dick. She could've lived a long and happy life without this knowledge. Well, maybe not long and maybe not happy, but it would've been a far better day if this slut had never opened her mouth. Then, and now.

"I met him at a club and I love the show and one thing led to another and we ended up in his car in the parking lot."

"You didn't sleep with him?" Betsy asked.

"No, I had my period. I didn't want him to remember me that way."

"Yeah, you're too classy for that," Denise said. Skinny was oblivious to the sarcasm.

"So, what happened after the blow job?" Eloise asked, not satisfied until she had every humiliating detail.

"I got out of his car and went back into the bar. I never saw him again."

Helen was quiet, horrified that this bit of news had come to light. She reached over and put her hand on Zadie's knee. "Zadie, I'm so sorry."

"I don't get it," Denise said. "You work with Helen every day. You never heard her mention that Jack Cavanaugh left her cousin at the altar?"

Skinny was on the defensive. "I just started two months ago. I didn't know anything about it, I swear."

The other women didn't look convinced, but Snotty held her hand in a show of solidarity. Crack Lickers United.

"You don't understand. I've been watching *Days of Our Lives* since I was in eighth grade!" Skinny whined.

"It's okay," Zadie said. "I don't care. I'm over it."

Everyone looked at her like she was completely full of shit, and truthfully, she was, but she didn't want to have to listen to this dumb bitch in her fuchsia polyester halter top apologize for a second longer.

"I didn't marry the guy, so why should I care who he hooks up with?" She looked at Skinny. "You have my permission to suck off whomever you please." No one seemed to have a response for this. Uncomfortable silence crept across the group. Zadie sighed, hating that pity for *her* was actually able to quiet these women. "Is anyone up for a drink?"

Jane and Gilda raised their hands.

"God, yes," Jane said.

"Do we have to stop at one?" Gilda asked.

Big Ass Betsy wasn't having it. "That isn't part of the plan. Helen doesn't drink. Denise is pregnant. Marci and Kim have toddlers."

"If Zadie wants a drink, I think she should get a drink, what's the big deal?" Helen smiled at her, extra accommodating now that she carried the guilt of having a slut coworker. "Shall we move into the bar?"

"Maybe we should go someplace else," Zadie said. "I'm afraid if we sit in the bar, some guy will think we're his 'date.'" Skinny and Snotty would be picked off in a matter of seconds. Snotty's cleavage alone would have the whoremongers circling the table, wallets out.

"Why would someone think that?" Helen asked, full of innocence.

Zadie hoped she wouldn't have to elaborate any further, and luckily Jane jumped in to the rescue. "Let's go to the Sky Bar. We can sit outside, watch the sunset, have a glass of wine—"

"Sounds great. Let's go." Helen hopped up.

"But . . ." Big Ass Betsy looked to Marci and Kim for support. "That wasn't on the itinerary."

Marci and Kim were in accord. "I thought we were having dinner at the Ivy."

"We can go after the Sky Bar," Gilda said.

"But it's the shower portion of the day," Betsy said. "We're supposed to give Helen her gifts next."

Gifts? Shit. Zadie knew she'd forgotten something. She'd bought Helen a beanbag chair as a joke.

"We can do it afterward," Helen said.

"But . . ." Betsy was completely flummoxed at this change in plans.

"C'mon, Betsy," Denise said. "One drink and then we'll be back on track."

"It's Helen's day," Eloise reminded her.

"Fine," Betsy said, giving in, but making sure everyone knew she wasn't happy about it.

Skinny and Snotty were going to agree to whatever anyone wanted, just to get back in the group's good graces. Once they saw that the majority wanted a drink, they were onboard. "It'll be fun," Snotty said.

"Don't you have to be on a list to get in the Sky Bar?" Skinny asked.

Gilda looked at her and gave her a fake smile. "Maybe you can charm the doorman for us. I bet they have a big parking lot."

Zadie was liking Gilda more and more.

As they left the Peninsula, Zadie caught sight of Estelle sitting with an older man in the bar. Silver hair. Nice suit. Big smile on his face. Estelle was smiling back. And why not? They both knew exactly where they'd stand at the end of the night. No expectations whatsoever, and each fulfilled in their own way.

It occurred to Zadie that Estelle may be the wisest of them all.

eighteen

The valets at the Mondrian Hotel, home to the Sky Bar, were used to limousines pulling up to their doors. Smack in the middle of the Sunset Strip, it was one of those locations that drew the party people. Not that this group could be so classified, but if Zadie had anything to do with it, alcohol would soon be flowing in copious quantities.

As she stepped out of the limo, she heard Eloise and Snotty making lustful noises at some unsuspecting male. When she followed their eyes, she realized it wasn't a male in the flesh, but a giant painted male on the side of a neighboring building—the ever-present Gap ad that provided a focal point for those stuck in the ever-present Sunset Boulevard traffic.

Looking straight into Zadie's eyes was a two-hundred-foot-tall Trevor wearing nothing but a pair of Gap distressed cords. Thumb hooked into a belt loop. Seductive smile. And what appeared to be a very large penis in his pants. What the Abercrombie people had hidden in their baggy jeans, the Gap people sought to highlight. God bless the Gap.

"Can you even imagine? One night. Just one night," Eloise said, all hot and bothered. Which made Zadie want to strike her.

"I know someone who knew him? She said he's amazing," Snotty said. "They dated five years ago, and he used to drive her to the top of Mulholland every night and make love to her under the stars."

"Five years ago, he was in seventh grade. He didn't have a driver's license," Zadie said, interrupting their worship at the church of Trevor. "He's one of my students."

Eloise spun around, tearing her eyes away from his corduroy-covered crotch.

"He's in high school?" Her voice was pained. Fantasy blown.

"Trevor Larkin?" Snotty asked, devastated that her gossip was inaccurate. "Are you sure?"

"I could show you his term paper. I gave him a B."

Helen was at the door of the hotel. "C'mon, girls. We're going to miss the sunset."

Zadie took one last look at Trevor and his bare chest and went inside. Now was not the time to get aroused.

As they walked through the all-white lobby filled with staff wearing cream-colored suits, Jane nodded to a woman at the desk who was waiting for her key with an extremely bored look on her face. The woman nodded back and then turned to snatch her key from the desk clerk's hands, stomping toward the elevator and checking her watch. Jane knew some bitchy chicks.

"I hope we can get in," Skinny said.

"It's early. We'll be fine," Jane said. "No one but Eurotrash and traveling salesmen hang out here anyway."

Sure enough, when they got outside to the poolside area that made up the Sky Bar, the entrance was devoid of the usual large, suited, uppity bouncer, so they breezed through and parked themselves on the giant flowered mattress on the deck. Clearly the Sky Bar believed in doing away with preliminaries and making sure their patrons were in bed together before they even left the premises. Not that Zadie was complaining. Lounging on a bed in the shade of a ficus tree, overlooking hot-pink bougainvillea and a view of the city beat the hell out of a couch in the Peninsula. She looked at Jane. "Good call."

"Drinking outside always seems more festive," Jane said.

"From here on out, we are all about festive," Zadie said. It was time for the fun to begin. She had promised Grey. She looked around at the crowd for potential allies. The blasé crowd of chain-smoking Germans on the next mattress over wouldn't be of any help. Maybe they'd get lucky and some Australians would show up. No one who actually lived in L.A. would be out before dark.

An impossibly beautiful waitress in a sarong and a bikini top came over to take their order. Zadie took the lead. "I'll have a margarita, no salt."

"Gin and tonic," Jane said.

"Pinot grigio, please," Gilda said.

"Pellegrino for me," Denise moped.

"Two Cosmos," Snotty said, motioning to herself and Skinny.

"Dewar's and soda," Eloise said. Proving once again that she had bad taste. Who the hell drinks scotch?

"Diet Coke for me," Betsy said.

"Same here," Marci said.

"Me, too," Kim said.

"Oh, come on, girls. Have a drink. We've got a limo. No one has to drive," Gilda said.

"We won't tell your kids," Zadie said.

"Hangovers are no fun when you have a three-year-old. They don't understand that mommy feels like crap and needs to sleep," Kim said.

Yet another reason not to breed, in Zadie's opinion.

"Can't your husband handle the kids?" Jane asked.

Marci and Kim looked at each other and burst out laughing. Clearly their husbands were either late sleepers or complete imbeciles.

Helen looked at the waitress. "I'll have a glass of chardonnay."

Helen ordering a drink? This was quite a day. Let the sinning begin.

Betsy was beside herself. "But you don't drink."

"It's my bachelorette party. I don't think one glass of wine will kill me."

"I assure you, it will only make things better," Zadie said. "In fact, I'd recommend two."

"Let the party start!" Eloise said.

"This is gonna get interesting," Gilda said, to no one in particular.

Jane kicked off her shoes and muttered, "God, I hope so."

Vintage Prince tunes were playing, the sun was shining, and liquor was on its way. Things were looking up. When the waitress brought their trayful of drinks, Zadie downed her margarita in about four seconds and motioned for a new one. The women rearranged themselves into a large circle and put their drinks in the center.

"Now *this* is a tea party," Eloise said.

"Wait, someone get out a camera," Denise said. "We need to document Helen's first drink."

Marci pulled out a disposable camera from her purse and everyone cheered as Helen took her first sip of wine. "Mmm, delicious!"

Oh, yes, that's all it took. One sip. Welcome to the world of "Did I really say that?" and "Where did I leave my bra?"

Helen took another sip. "Let's play a game. What're some of those games you're supposed to play at parties like this?"

"I'm not sure what kind of party this is anymore, so don't ask me," Betsy said, with what Grandma Davis would call "a big puss on her face."

"Quit being such a prude, Betsy. We're having a drink, we're not fucking sailors," Jane said. Mmm, feisty. Zadie was changing her opinion of Jane more and more as the day went on.

"How about 'I never'?" Denise said. "You know, 'I never had sex in a car'? Whoever's done it has to drink."

"Why would anyone have sex in a car?" Betsy asked.

"Some of us actually got laid in high school," Jane said.

As Snotty and Skinny snickered, Zadie looked from Betsy to Jane. It seemed an all-out war was imminent. Betsy was blushing, more from anger than embarrassment. Jane wasn't sorry though.

She merrily sipped her gin and tonic and looked around the pool area, scoping out guys. A guy with a ponytail and a sunburn gave her a nod.

"That was uncalled for," Betsy said.

Helen set her wine down and grabbed each of them by the hand. "Girls, please. We're old friends. . . ."

"Okay, I'll start," Eloise said. Wanting to take credit for ending the spat. "I never had sex with more than one person in a twenty-four-hour period."

"Well, I'd hope *not!*" Betsy said. Helen blushed and giggled. Gilda furrowed her brow, thinking. Jane drank. So did Snotty. Betsy was appalled. "Jane! What's happened to you? Is it a stewardess thing?"

"Yes, Betsy. We have to screw all the pilots before we board." Jane took another swig of her drink just to piss Betsy off.

Skinny spoke up. "Okay, I never let a guy videotape me."

How did she know? Jack could've had a video camera on his dashboard. Or had a documentary crew following him and getting footage through the back window. Anyone who would keep a journal of each time an old lady recognized him while he was jogging was sure to film every fan blow job he received.

To everyone's horror, Eloise drank.

"It was very tasteful. And I have the only copy."

"Eloise! How can you be sure?" Helen asked.

"Because I watched him take it out of the camera."

"He could have had another one running that you didn't know about," Jane said, trying to stir up some insecurity in the world's most wrongfully secure woman.

"I trust him. He's one of my clients. He knows I can screw him." Eloise was a tax attorney. She specialized in evaders.

"Did you charge him extra for that?" Jane asked.

Damn. Jane was far more savvy than Zadie had remembered. The Jane she recalled from Helen's high school slumber parties hadn't even known that you were supposed to flip pancakes. She let them sit and burn in a bubbling pile of goo before someone clued her in.

"Believe me, I've been screwing him for years with my fee," Eloise said.

The waitress arrived with another round of drinks. "Here we go, ladies."

"We didn't order these," Betsy pouted.

"They're from the gentlemen over there," the waitress said, pointing to a gaggle of guys across the pool who were enjoying their bourbons and cigars. The big ruddy-faced one waved. He had hair that denoted he was perhaps not from Los Angeles. Not quite a mullet, but mullet-adjacent. The girls waved back to him and he gave them a big smile.

"Should we send him one?" Helen asked.

"Sure," Jane said.

Betsy had a cow. "No, we most certainly should not! He could be a psychopath for all we know."

"Some of his friends are cute," Eloise noted, checking out the one with visible chest hair. No waxers in that bunch.

"We're not here to meet men. We're here to celebrate Helen's wedding and bond with each other," Betsy said.

"Is that what it said in the handbook?" Zadie asked. "Why are there so many rules for this gathering? I feel like I'm in Catholic school."

"That's easy for you to say, you didn't spend two solid weeks planning this event." Betsy was a real estate agent. A bad one. In one of the most active, overpriced markets in the country, she only managed to sell one house every six months. She had a lot of time on her hands. Barry, her henpecked husband, paid the bills with his dwindling trust fund. Zadie didn't feel the least bit guilty that Betsy had spent two weeks planning this party and now it was being subverted. How long could it possibly take to decide on breakfast, yoga, tonics, shopping, and tea? It's not like she'd rented out Sea World so they could all swim with the dolphins. Besides, they'd spent the entire day doing Betsy-approved events and if it was time to flirt with some drink-buying, hairy-chested residents of the fly-over states, then so be it. Zadie motioned for the waitress to send the guys a round.

"I never went to the bathroom with the door open," Marci offered. Every other woman drank, including her sidekick Kim. "Are you serious?" Marci squawked. "I could never ever let Tim see me on the toilet."

"Didn't you say he's seen you give birth?" Eloise asked.

"I never had sex with someone who wasn't American," Denise said. "I mean, not that I'm racist or anything, I've just never been laid in a foreign country by a foreign guy."

Gilda drank. "Spring break."

So did Jane. "Perk of the job." She gave Betsy a smug smile.

Helen blushed and put her hands to her face. "We are a racy bunch!" The wine was hitting her. She was getting more animated with each sip, waving her hands when she talked.

"We are indeed," Gilda said, clinking glasses with her. "I never had sex with someone more than ten years older than me."

Skinny and Snotty chugged. Jane took a demure sip.

"Older guys have more money," Snotty said, cementing her status as a gold-digging slut. Not that there was ever a question. The woman wore silver lamé shoes. Manolo Blahnik or not, they were ugly and whory. Zadie never quite understood the hold Manolo had over the actresses and models and tarty shopgirls who wore his shoes. Was there heroin painted onto the instep? Why did women act so fucking giddy when they had them on?

"I never drank so much that I've thrown up," Kim said. Wow. Kim was now the most boring person in the bar. Again, not that there was ever a question. Everyone drank except for Helen. Whose pristine esophagus remained unmarred by regurgitated alcohol.

The waitress appeared again, drink tray full. "Ladies, you have some serious fans." The cigar-and-bourbon crowd waved again and the girls waved back. This was a nice arrangement. Maybe they'd never even have to speak. The women gulped their drinks and accepted the new ones.

Helen giggled. "I'm feeling a little tipsy."

"Two glasses of wine is probably plenty for someone who doesn't drink," Betsy said.

"Three won't kill me, will it? I'm a bachelorette. I'm supposed to get wild." She shook her hair and did a little shimmy. Grey would've been proud, Zadie thought.

"Please tell me we have plenty of film," Denise said, delighted with this turn of events. Marci snapped another picture as Helen gave her a saucy pose.

Jane clinked glasses with Helen. "I think I like this new side of Helen."

"Me, too," Zadie said. She actually did. Tipsy Helen was a hoot. She looked at the others. "I've never seen Helen drunk." They all laughed and drank. Gilda was a little slower on the draw than the others, but she swigged one down.

Betsy had the puss on her face again. "If we're going to play this game, let's find out some real dirt. I've never—slept with Grey."

Everyone stared at her, appalled.

"If you had, I think we'd have to kick your ass," Gilda said.

Betsy stared at Zadie. "I'm just trying to find out if anyone else here has."

Zadie set down her margarita. "Are you kidding me?"

"Well, he's your 'best friend.' Does that include benefits?"

Jane shook her head. "Betsy, you are such an ass. Don't even answer her, Zadie."

"I agree," Denise said, changing the subject. "I never had sex in a bathroom stall."

"Actually—I'd like for Zadie to answer that," Helen said.

They all stared at her. Zadie included, now fully realizing what the word "agog" meant. "You think I've *slept* with Grey?"

"No, actually, I don't, but I figure as long as the question is out there, I should confirm it. Have you?"

"God, no!"

Helen stiffened. "Why? Is he that unappealing to you?"

Zadie couldn't believe she was enduring this conversation. So much for Helen being a hoot. "Let me get this straight. You're *disappointed* that I haven't slept with him?"

"No, I'm just a little offended by the fact that you act like he's so beneath you."

Zadie stared at Helen. Trying to convince herself that it was just the alcohol that had inspired this psychotic break. "Helen, I find Grey perfectly wonderful. He's not beneath me, nor have I ever been beneath him. Does that answer your question?"

"Yes. Thank you." She gulped down the rest of her wine and looked around for the waitress. "Where's the bitch in the bikini top? I need another glass of wine."

nineteen

As Zadie tried to decompress from being accused of screwing Grey, the ruddy-faced bourbon guy walked up to the group.

"Ladies, do you mind if I introduce myself?" His accent was distinctly Southern and his khaki pants could have used an iron. "Or should we keep our romance on a no-names basis?"

Marci and Kim giggled, clearly out of practice at being the recipient of cheesy bar lines. Snotty and Skinny rolled their eyes, clearly not out of practice.

Helen gave him a big smile. "I'm Helen. I'm the bachelorette."

The guy did a double take and put the back of his hand to his forehead like a damsel in distress. "Tell me it's not true!"

"Sorry." Helen giggled.

"Well, let me introduce myself anyway. In case you change your mind." He gave her a wink, finding himself incredibly suave. "I'm Jim James. My buddies and I are here on business from Atlanta. We were hoping that you ladies might want to have a night on the town with us."

Betsy rushed to shoot him down. "We're going to the Ivy for dinner. It's a girls' night only."

"Well, that's a shame. I've got six friends over there just raring to spend some time with you gals." The six friends waved on cue. They weren't hideous, but they weren't exactly appealing. Jimbo was by far the best of the bunch.

"Why don't you guys move over here and join us?" Helen asked, receiving dagger looks from Betsy, Snotty, and Skinny. Clearly Jimbo and his pals weren't up to their high standards.

Zadie smiled at Jimbo. "That's a great idea. You can slide some chairs over here and we'll make a little party out of it." Anything to piss off Betsy and Skinny in one fell swoop. Snotty was just a bonus.

"Well, that's a fine idea. Let me go get those rascals and I'll be right back." He walked over to his friends, relaying the invitation. They tapped out their cigars and picked up their steamer chairs.

The women dive-bombed Helen and Zadie with their protests. "Why did you invite them over? Now we'll have to talk to them!" Betsy whined.

"Oh, relax, Betsy, I'm just having fun," Helen said.

"I wonder what Grey would have to say about that," Eloise said.

Zadie rolled her eyes. "We're sitting in a public place, and everyone is fully clothed. I doubt he'd have a problem with it, Eloise. Why don't you just have another drink and talk to one of these guys and maybe you can end the night with another videotape in your collection."

Before Eloise could retort, Snotty leaned forward to whine. "But they're cheesy! They're not even *from* here."

"Don't be such a goddamn snob," Helen said. All of the women turned to look at her. Had she really just cursed? "We'll have a couple drinks with them and then we'll go to dinner. Quit your bitching. It's *my* party."

Zadie couldn't help it. She laughed. Aside from the whole "have you slept with Grey?" moment, it seemed that alcohol made Helen into someone she could actually hang out with.

Denise's mouth hung open. She stared at Helen. "Who *are* you?"

Helen smiled and held up her glass as the guys carried their chairs over. "I'm the bachelorette."

After introductions and the purchase of another round, conversations were flying. It seemed these gentleman sold vinyl flooring.

A fascinating topic. Thankfully, they were aware of how boring their chosen field was in terms of bar chatter, and they moved on to such subjects as why the South is the best place in the world, how much beef they could consume in one sitting, and the fact that bourbon was the only true drink.

As much as Zadie would've liked to have kept these men around all night in order to piss off the bitch contingent, she found herself completely bored by their company. Her partner in conversation was a man named Billy and he insisted on rubbing her feet as they talked. One of the drawbacks to sitting on a giant mattress.

"So, what's on the agenda for you ladies tonight? Because if you need a stripper, I think I can oblige you." He leered at her as he caressed her instep.

The thought of seeing Billy strip off his button-down shirt and khakis was about as appealing as the offer he'd made earlier to give her feet a tongue bath. She'd laughed it off, but the more he rubbed her feet, the more apparent it became that he was dead serious.

Jane was fending off a charmer named Bobby, who swore he'd flown on one of her flights before and that she'd given him extra peanuts. Gilda was saddled with a full-on redneck who kept asking her to throw ice cubes for him to catch in his mouth. Betsy, Eloise, Snotty, and Skinny were hunkered in the corner talking about how evil Zadie was for encouraging Helen, and Marci and Kim were enthralled by Buddy, who could discuss diaper horror stories with the best of them. Denise was in the bathroom throwing up.

Helen, meanwhile, was officially drunk and talking to Jimbo, who was taking full advantage of her inebriation.

"Something tells me you're not ready to get married yet, Miss Helen." He touched the end of her nose with his finger and she giggled.

"Yes I am. I've always wanted to be a bride." She was about a second away from slurring.

"But are you ready to become a wife?" he asked.

"Of course. I love him."

"But, darlin', I think with a couple more drinks, you could love me more. How do you know it wasn't fate that we met tonight?"

"Because if it was fate, I wouldn't be getting married in two days."

"Maybe you will, maybe you won't." He put his hand on her thigh. She didn't take it away.

Zadie looked over, breaking away from Billy's fascinating story about the time he fell off his horse, and noted with alarm that Helen had not yet removed Jimbo's hand. She seemed mesmerized by his drawl and his big chocolate-brown puppy eyes. Uh-oh. Zadie looked around for backup. Jane was dodging Bobby as he nuzzled her neck. Gilda was holding up her wedding band to fend off her amorous redneck. And Bitches Inc. were still huddled in their corner. Kim and Marci had joined them, growing tired of Buddy's excrement tales.

Billy was coming to the climax of his story. Something about a snake on the trail and the horse bucking. Zadie tried to make the appropriate "Oh, no!" face and nod attentively but when she looked back at Helen, she could've sworn she saw Helen's hand graze Jimbo's crotch. Oh, dear God. Grey had instructed her to get Helen to loosen up. Not to get Helen to give hand jobs to strangers.

"I think we should go." Zadie stood up.

Helen looked up, completely nonchalant. "What's the hurry?"

Gilda was in synch with Zadie. "We should probably go eat."

Jane pushed Bobby away and stood up. "I'm ready."

The bitches and the mommies were more than ready to go. "It's about time," Betsy said. "We're already late for our reservation."

Helen looked up at them. "Screw the Ivy. I want some meat."

twenty

They didn't have a reservation at the Palm, but they decided to try it anyway. It was an unassuming little restaurant on Santa Monica Boulevard in a beige building with green awnings. Inside, the walls were covered in celebrity caricatures and the tables were manned by waiters who had been there for decades. Jimbo told them the Palm had the best steaks in town.

When they walked in, Helen made a beeline for an empty table, without even consulting the maître d'. Once he saw how drunk she was, he decided to let them stay at the table, rather than risk a scene. He retreated in horror when Helen slapped his butt as he walked away.

When the waiter came over, Helen announced, "I think I need a martini."

Betsy immediately became alarmed. "Are you sure? I think you've had enough."

Helen fixed Betsy with an evil stare. "Betsy, if you tell me I've had enough one more time, I'm going to tell everyone you had liposuction."

The table went silent. Betsy blushed so deeply they could almost hear it and looked down at her place setting. "It was only on my upper arms." She pulled her cardigan tighter around her and sulked until Snotty told her she looked toned.

When the drinks came, Gilda held up her glass in toast, trying to keep the peace. "I say we all just relax and have some fun. Now that we've ditched the Atlanta boys, we can get back to girl talk."

Marci pulled a teabag out of her purse and dipped it into a cup of hot water. "Can you believe Buddy has five kids?"

"They probably all have five kids," Eloise said. "It disgusts me when married men try to get laid when they're out of town on business." In truth, Eloise was just angry because none of them had hit on her. Weird haircuts and severe glasses don't fly down South apparently.

"They were definitely looking for some action," Jane agreed.

"I can't believe that Jim guy had his hands all over you, Helen. I was ready to call security," Eloise said, in a way that was highly accusatory. Helen didn't acknowledge it. She was too busy sucking her olive off the little plastic sword in a completely lewd display for the busboy who was watching from the side of the room. He smiled at her and adjusted himself.

Betsy caught sight of it. "Helen! What's gotten into you?"

"Well, we know it's not Grey." She slapped her hands down on the table and looked at them all. "Can you believe we've never fucked?"

Again, silence. Then a barrage of "Oh, my God!", "Where did that potty mouth come from?", and "I've never seen you like this." And the now-familiar refrain "I don't think you should have any more to drink."

But Helen was not to be slowed down. She sipped her martini and continued on her rant. "I bet if the guys in this restaurant knew I was a virgin, they'd be all over me."

Betsy looked concerned. "You're not planning on telling them, are you?"

"I would certainly hope not," Eloise said. "Why would you want to encourage their attention?"

Helen looked at the fifty-something man in a sport coat at the table next to them. He was having dessert with his Botox'd wife. She leaned over and tapped him on the arm. "Ever had a virgin?"

They looked back at her with horror.

Helen proceeded to suck another olive off her plastic sword. "Want one?"

As the women were escorted out of the Palm by the manager, Helen kept shouting, "I was *kidding!* Hello! Do you really think I would screw that guy?" The other women dragged her into the limo. At one point, Betsy's hand was clamped firmly over Helen's mouth.

Zadie stayed behind and apologized profusely to the couple Helen had propositioned. "She's not usually like this. She's getting married in two days. The stress of that alone would make anyone snap. I'm so, so sorry." The couple wasn't buying it. Apparently, having your anniversary dinner interrupted by a slutty virgin was not what they were expecting from their dining experience at the Palm.

When they got back on the road, Helen had the driver stop and get some champagne. She also had him open the top so she could stand up as they drove down Sunset. "Look! Everyone can see me now!" She took a swig of champagne straight from the bottle and then waved to some high school kids in the next lane who were cruising in their daddy's car.

"She's completely lost it," Kim said.

"Can we please go to the Ivy now?" Betsy asked, desperate to get them back on track.

Marci looked worried. "Isn't the Ivy kind of sedate? I don't know if I can handle getting thrown out of two nice restaurants in one night. Maybe we should just go to a drive-thru."

"In-N-Out Burger sounds good to me," Denise said. She tugged on the hem of Helen's miniskirt and shouted up through the moonroof. "Helen, you up for some burgers?"

"I think we should take her back to the hotel and put her in bed," Eloise said.

Zadie was confused. "Hotel?"

"We're staying at the Beverly Hills Hotel for the whole weekend.

We got a discount because the wedding is being held there," Betsy said.

"I think the hotel might be the best idea," Gilda agreed.

Helen pulled herself back through the moonroof and sat down with a look of determination. "You know where we need to go? The Hustler store."

"Why?" Betsy whined. "They sell porn there. And it's owned by Larry Flynt. The man's a deviant."

"Grey's waited six months to sleep with me. I need to give him an amazing wedding night. They have sex toys there, right?"

"Lots of them," Jane answered.

"Then let's go! I need some sex toys!"

Eloise got into the spirit of this suggestion. "I hear they have cock rings. They completely heighten his experience, you know."

Zadie was repulsed. Did Eloise not realize she was talking about her *brother*? Even she felt uncomfortable picturing Grey in a cock ring, but apparently Eloise had no problem with it whatsoever.

"I could use some new lube," Snotty said.

Eloise looked at her. "Dry twat?"

Skinny elbowed Snotty. "That's not where she uses it. . . ."

While Zadie tried to erase the knowledge that Snotty liked to butt-fuck, Helen crawled over them all to bang on the window separating them from the driver.

"We need some cock rings. Turn here."

twenty-one

Zadie had never been in the Hustler store. Not because she was a prude by any means. She liked sex quite a bit, in fact. She just never felt the need to garnish it with vibrators and body paint and butt plugs and whatnot. Call her a purist, but she liked her sex to involve just a man's naked body and her own. And the idea of a rubber penis without a man attached to it held little interest for her. She preferred the whole package.

The driver pulled up and stopped at the curb. The bright neon Hustler sign glared down at them, inviting them in to purchase perversion in all shapes and sizes.

"I think I'll wait here," Kim said.

Denise grabbed her arm and pulled her out. "Come on. Maybe you'll find something to heat up 'date night.' "

Jane took her other arm. "Not everything they have is disgusting. Some of it is fun."

Kim was still unsure, but she let the girls walk her in. Her clone, Marci, was a bit more adventuresome. She headed straight for the lingerie.

Some of the shoppers turned to stare at the sight of Denise's large pregnant belly making its way through the aisles of *Barely Legal* and *Beaver Hunt* magazines, but most were too enthralled with the thousands of porn videos and DVDs on display to be bothered.

Gilda held one up to show Zadie. "*Clownfuckers.* There's a whole series of them! People dressed as clowns having sex!"

Zadie picked up a video and read the title. "*A Load in Every Hole.* Now that's romantic. Do you really think they mean *every* hole? Are ears included? Because I'm thinking that could lead to an infection."

"Oh, my God, wait. This is the best one." Gilda held up a DVD triumphantly. "*Pee, Midget, Pee!*" As they flipped the DVD over to see if there were actual pictures of midgets peeing, they heard a screech from across the store. Zadie was almost afraid to look. Turns out she didn't have to. Helen came running over. Wearing a strap-on.

"Check it out! I have a dick!" She waggled it around at them, not at all put off by the fact that it was bright blue and at least ten inches long.

Zadie swatted at it with a copy of *Granny's Biracial Gang Bang* and Helen ran off to wave it at Snotty and Skinny, who were perusing the nipple rings. "If you'd told me this morning that I'd be watching Helen get drunk and run around with a strap-on, I never would've believed you. She's the girl who used to close her eyes during the love scenes in *Blue Lagoon.*"

Gilda set down a copy of *Honey, I Blew Everybody* and kept her eye on Helen. "Everyone has a wild streak somewhere." They looked over to where Jane was holding up a mesh teddy for inspection. "Jane's a little kinky, I think. Those two idiots from Helen's store are just slutty."

"Oh, come on, who *hasn't* given a blow job to a stranger in a bar parking lot?" As Gilda turned to look at her, Zadie quickly added, "I'm kidding."

"What I want to know is what's Betsy's deep dark secret? She's got to be into something twisted." They looked over to where she was trying on feather boas at the insistence of Denise, who was wearing a faux-fur cowboy hat that said SPANK ME.

"I'm thinking Internet sex. She's probably got a couple boyfriends in prison. She always liked a captive audience."

Helen came running back over, tottering in her heels, out of breath from waving her penis. "You guys, come over to the dressing room. Jane is picking out my honeymoon trousseau."

Five minutes later, the women were all watching as Helen walked out of the dressing room in a black leather teddy that barely covered her nipples, let alone her actual tits. The outfit basically consisted of a giant leather X that crossed her torso and was attached at the hips to a thong.

"What do you think?" Helen asked.

"I think you'll never leave the hotel. Why bother to go to Fiji? Just stay here at a Comfort Inn," Denise said.

Betsy's mouth hung open. "I can see your pubes!"

Marci and Kim covered their eyes. "I can't look," Marci said.

Kim agreed. "It's obscene!"

"I think it's amazing," Skinny said. "Grey will lose his mind."

"Definitely sex-bomb material," Snotty agreed.

"My brother's a lucky man."

"It's pretty hot," Jane said. "But maybe it's too hot. Grey might not be ready for that look on his wedding night. Save it for the end of the week."

Zadie couldn't come up with anything to say. Helen looked like a porn star. A very pretty, well-groomed, virginal porn star. It was the kind of outfit that Zadie would never have the nerve to try on at home, let alone parade around a store in. People were starting to gather. Several men set down their pocket pussy testers and wandered over.

"Maybe you should try on the next outfit," Zadie suggested. She looked around for a security guard in case they needed one.

Helen next came out in a white fur-trimmed silk teddy with matching bridal veil.

"Is this better?"

Jane nodded. "Definitely more appropriate for the wedding night."

Zadie agreed, along with the rest of the women. She'd spent her wedding night in her bathrobe and fuzzy slippers, so she was hardly the expert in this department. Although she had managed to vomit on both slippers, a feat of which she was quite proud.

A short, innocuous-looking man wearing a windbreaker held up a chain-mail halter. "Excuse me, miss? Can you try this on next?"

Betsy turned around and smacked him with the nearest thing she could find—a two-foot, stuffed, red faux-fur penis pillow. "This is not a peep show!" The man skulked off, disappointed. Betsy turned back to the women, still clutching the penis. "Can you believe him? Creepy little perv. People have no appreciation for the idea of girls' night."

"Nice pillow." Denise pointed to the penis and Betsy looked down at what she was holding. Zadie braced herself for a shriek, but Betsy gave the pillow a cuddle.

"This is kind of cute."

Zadie looked at her watch. It was nine-fifteen. She wanted to remember this moment always—the moment when the stick was finally removed from Betsy's ass.

"Oh, my gosh! Look what I found!" Kim had a box in her hand that read BACHELORETTE PARTY KIT. "We should get it. It has games!"

When they left the store, they had with them a bag containing five teddies (including the black leather one), the red stuffed penis pillow, a blow-up doll with a detachable dildo, the blue strap-on, a bag of penis confetti, and the bachelorette party kit. Snotty and Skinny had also picked up some piña colada–flavored lube, and Denise, always thinking about food, bought something called Peter Butter that was supposed to flavor her husband's appendage. Jane had also picked up a bridal veil with devil horns on top for Helen to wear for the rest of the evening, since it only seemed appropriate.

Once they were ensconced in their pimp wagon and stuck in the Sunset Strip traffic, they were left with the dilemma of where to go. The sex toys had reinvigorated the group.

"We can't go back to the hotel now," Jane said. "We have to follow the instructions." She held up the bachelorette party kit and started reading off the items from the scavenger hunt list. " 'Get a guy to wear the bride's bra.' That should be easy. 'Get a guy to lick flavored body gel off bride's neck.' No problem there. 'Get a guy to show his butt and pose for a picture with the bride-to-be.' Now we're talking."

"Are we really going to ask men to do these things?" Kim asked.

"Hey, it was your idea to play games," Denise said, as she threw a handful of the purple penis confetti into the air.

Gilda took a break from pouring her lungs into the blow-up doll. "I think we should get someone to pose with this guy."

"He's better looking than those guys from Atlanta," Snotty said, giving him a poke with her French-manicured nail. Zadie noted that it was the tacky kind of French manicure—the kind where the white started halfway down the nail. There's really no excuse for that.

"What should we name him?" Gilda asked.

"Hans," Eloise said. "He looks like a Hans."

Helen blew up Hans's detachable dildo. "Look, my first blow job!"

As they drove past the Saddle Ranch, the rowdy crowd was already leaking out onto the porch. Through the doors, they could see people riding a mechanical bull. It looked like a giant frat party set in the Wild West. In other words, it was perfect. Helen and her drunken, lewd observations would blend right in, offending no one.

"Stop here," Zadie yelled to the driver, shaking the penis confetti out of her hair.

She turned back to the women. "Ladies, grab your sex toys. We're goin' in."

twenty-two

Inside the barnlike Saddle Ranch, it was crowded and hot and filled with a distinctly nonscenester L.A. crowd. It was more of a mix of college kids, tourists, and white men in sports jerseys who called each other "dawg" mingling among the bales of hay and mannequins dressed as cowgirls.

Within seconds of walking in, Helen had a fraternity vice president from USC wearing her white lace Chantelle bra. Denise dutifully snapped a picture with the disposable camera. When he didn't want to give the bra back, he got an earful from Betsy before she yanked it away from him, causing him to slink back to his friends muttering, "That bitch with the ponytail is psycho."

Moments later, a Swedish tourist who looked like Bono was licking the strawberry body gel off Helen's neck while she smiled prettily for the camera. He spoke very little English and didn't seem to understand that it was a game. He hung around afterward trying to lick Helen again. Skinny shooed him away, saying, "Go away now." Welcome to America.

Jane held up the list. "C'mon, Zadie. Find us a guy who'll show us his butt."

Zadie looked around the immediate vicinity and spotted a wannabe gangster whose pants were so low his butt was pretty much on display already. Too easy.

A hot guy in a blue T-shirt walked by on his way to the bar. He gave Zadie one of those "Hey, you're cute" smiles and she grabbed his arm. "Excuse me. Will you show us your butt and pose for a picture with the bachelorette?" She pointed at Helen, noting that her veil and devil horns were now crooked on her head as she chugged a Bud Light.

The guy looked back at Zadie, confused. "You want me to show you my butt? Like right here?"

"Exactly."

He shrugged. "Okay." Zadie waved Helen over as he unbuckled his pants and slid down his boxers. Denise tossed her the camera.

"Okay, Helen, crouch down right next to his crack and say cheese!" As Helen crouched down, she opted to *bite* his butt as opposed to posing with it.

"Oww!" He yanked his pants back up and turned to Zadie. "You didn't tell me she was gonna bite me."

"Sorry. I didn't know she was hungry."

"Good thing you didn't ask to see my dick." He walked off in a huff.

Helen yelled after him. "Pussy!"

Zadie would've felt guilty but the whole situation was too ridiculous. "Don't let Eloise see you biting strange ass. I think she's planning on giving Grey a full report."

"Eloise can bite *my* ass," Helen slurred. "No wait. Eloise can bite her own ass." She swayed a bit, then flounced off to get another drink. How she was managing to stay upright in her heels was a mystery.

Gilda handed Zadie a beer. "The soccer moms look bored." Zadie looked over to find them ordering Diet Cokes at the bar. Marci was clutching the red penis pillow like a security blanket. Kim was wearing one of the feather boas. Eloise was next to them, trying to pick up a college kid. He looked repulsed. Snotty and Skinny were chatting up two Persian men, probably looking for next month's rent. Betsy was trying to take Helen's drink away, but Helen was stronger. Jane was chatting up a guy with ridiculous sideburns. From what Zadie could hear, it sounded like she was trying to get him to show Helen his balls. Denise was in the bathroom puking.

"Is this what you do on a typical Saturday night in L.A.?" Gilda shouted over the noise.

"I'm usually home with a video and a bottle of wine, avoiding places like this." She looked out at the crowd of men she would never date. "See that guy over there? He keeps wagging his tongue piercing at us."

"I have to admit, it's a relief to be married when I see my options."

"Where'd you meet your husband?"

"In college."

"Fuck you."

"I know. Sorry."

The crowd around the mechanical bull got even rowdier if that was possible, causing Zadie to look over with concern, finding exactly what she feared. Helen was now astride the bull, along with Hans and his inflatable penis. As the bull bucked, Helen and Hans simulated some pretty raunchy sex, much to the amusement of the crowd, who were hooting and hollering their appreciation. Betsy was trying to pull her down, but Helen kept kicking at her until she backed away.

"Oh, Lord," Gilda said, looking concerned.

"Should we try and stop her or just take pictures?" Zadie asked.

"I guess as long as she's not doing that with a real man, we're still in the zone of acceptable behavior. Not respectable, but acceptable," Gilda said, frowning.

Helen was having a hard time holding on to her beer *and* Hans *and* the bull. As she started to slide to the left, a group of guys rushed to set her back on top.

"She has a fan club," Gilda noted.

"She always has," Zadie said. "Did the guys just trail after her in college?"

"There was lots of crying, put it that way. And not from her."

"Grey was blinded the moment he saw her."

Zadie remembered the moment well. They were sitting in the church at Denise's wedding. Fifth row from the front. Helen was the maid of honor, last one down the aisle before the bride. Grey's whole body had stiffened when he caught sight of her. He'd grabbed Zadie's hand and, without dragging his eyes away from Helen, asked, "Who's *that*?" From that moment on, he was smitten. Everything Helen did or said convinced Grey that he'd met the woman of his dreams. And six months later, Zadie was standing in a loud bar watching Helen publicly hump a blow-up doll on the back of a fake bull in celebration of her pending nuptials. Love was grand.

"Oh, my God. Don't turn around." Gilda was gazing over Zadie's shoulder and making a pained face, which of course caused Zadie to turn around. An action she immediately regretted. Eloise was making out with the guy with the weird sideburns. She had her hands on each side of his face, actually making contact with the greasy stripes of hair that went all the way down to his chin. He was probably ten years younger than Eloise, and most certainly blind drunk if he was willing to be seen making out with her in public.

Gilda shook her head. "I don't understand why men would even talk to her, let alone kiss her. Not that he's any prize, but still. If he had any sense, he'd be over here hitting on you."

"Not my type," Zadie said.

"Well, of course he's not. He's probably retarded. I just don't understand why he wouldn't be at least *trying* to hit on you, as opposed to making out with *her*."

"I don't think I give out the hit-on-me vibe anymore. I get the occasional smile, but I can't remember the last time a guy actually tried to make a move on me."

"Well, you're gorgeous, so you must be sending out a pretty strong stay-away vibe if you're not getting hit on." Gorgeous? Hardly. Zadie knew somewhere in the back of her numbed and bitter brain that she was attractive, but "gorgeous" was taking it a bit far. Maybe she'd be considered gorgeous in some Nebraska farm town, population 150, but not in L.A.

"The fact that I cringe and look away when I catch their eye probably does something to damage my chances. But I'm just not all that anxious to talk to men at this point."

"Okay, this is gonna sound really stupid," Gilda said, "but I'm drunk, so forgive me. You know how after 9/11 if you didn't go on vacation and stuff they said you're letting the terrorists win? Well, if you don't start dating again, you're letting Jack win."

Zadie thought about this. It was certainly an alcohol-fueled analogy, which often tend to be the most profound, but regardless, she didn't feel it applied. "It's not really a matter of letting Jack win, it's just making sure I don't lose again."

Gilda sighed. "Okay, I get that. I really do. But there isn't *anyone*? Not even a crush at the gym? Or some guy you saw at the grocery store? You have to have thought about *some* guy in the past seven months."

Of course there was someone. But how could Zadie possibly tell this lovely and normal woman that she wanted to fuck an eighteen-year-old?

Jane appeared with a tray of tequila shots. "Drink up." Zadie and Gilda took their shots and downed them as Jane moved on to Eloise and her hillbilly. "Hey Ya" was blasting out of the speakers, making the bar vibrate. Zadie was starting to feel the pleasant edge of drunkenness.

"Okay, there is a guy. But he doesn't count because it will never happen and it's just a fantasy."

"Who is he?"

"One of my students."

Gilda screeched with delight and grabbed two more shots from Jane's tray as she passed by again. "And I thought Jane was the kinky one."

"He's eighteen, so he's legal. I'm not a pedophile."

"I'm not here to judge." She handed Zadie her shot and they both downed them.

"Remember the Gap ad that Eloise and Snotty were drooling over on the way into the Sky Bar?" Zadie asked. "That's him."

"Oh, honey, I am with you on that." They clinked their empty shot glasses. "He is unbelievable. You get to look at him every day?"

"I keep his Abercrombie catalog on my nightstand. Does that make me a bad person?"

"No, it makes you a normal, healthy, horny woman. Anyone who looks at that kid and *doesn't* want to screw him is either dead or a lesbian."

"His band is playing tonight. He invited me. He invited all of us actually," Zadie said.

"Where?"

"Somewhere on the Strip. The Roxy, I think." She'd seen the band name on the marquee when they passed it earlier, but she was trying to play it cool.

"We should go!" Gilda was practically jumping up and down.

"Really? You don't think it's a terrible, terrible idea?" Zadie couldn't even picture what she would do when she saw Trevor on-stage. She certainly wouldn't dance. She couldn't possibly stand in the front row with the groupies. But maybe she could hide in the back and let his beauty bathe her eyes while retaining her anonymity.

"Well, we can't hang around here and watch Eloise molest ugly men any longer. And Helen's— Oh shit."

They looked up to find Helen now riding the bull along with a very aggressive fraternity boy. Hans was lying on the floor, a few beers spilled on him, slightly deflated by the whole sordid affair. Helen, however, was quite demonstrative in her grinding of the Pi Kappa Phi she was riding with, and he was certainly enjoying her attention. They weren't kissing, but he was in the midst of unbuttoning her blouse.

Zadie looked for whoever was closest to Helen. "Jane!" She pointed at Helen.

Jane turned, dragging her attention away from the cute guy

whose ass Helen had bitten to see her on the bull. She looked back at Zadie, calling out, "I'm on it."

Jane marched over to the bull and dragged the Pi Kap off, causing him to fall on Hans and deflate him even more. Then Jane gently pulled Helen off and maneuvered her over toward the bar, just as Zadie and Gilda reached them.

"What? I was just riding the bull."

"Where the hell was Betsy when that was going on?" Zadie asked. Gilda pointed her out, sitting in a chair against the wall with her arms and legs crossed, scowling at them all. When she saw Zadie waving her over, she got up and stomped toward them.

"Well, I'm glad someone finally took notice of the bachelorette besides me. I tried to stop her from engaging in a public sex show, but she kicked me."

"I didn't kick you."

"You did, too!"

Marci and Kim wandered up. Yawning. "Are we leaving?"

"I certainly hope so," Betsy said.

Denise walked out of the bathroom, spotting them. "What's going on?"

"Your sister has lost her mind and is trying to have sex with strange men. This is not what was supposed to happen today," Betsy said.

"Betsy, if I were *trying* to have sex with someone, I think I'd accomplish my goal," Helen said, with all the superiority that someone as drunk as she was is wont to convey.

Snotty and Skinny appeared. "What's wrong?"

"Nothing's wrong," Helen answered.

"Good, because that guy just asked me if he could take me shopping. I love Persian men!" Skinny said.

"Well, give him your number, because we're leaving," Gilda said.

"Where're we going?" Eloise asked, as she made her way over, oblivious. Leaving Sideburns to pine for her at the bar.

Gilda smiled at Zadie. "The Roxy."

twenty-three

Back in the limo, the whine-fest began.

Betsy, of course, was first. "I don't *want* to go see a band. We were supposed to have dinner and now it's ten-thirty! We never even played the 'Fun Facts About Grey and Helen' game. I called their moms and found out all their favorite toys when they were kids and everything!"

"Barbie's Dream House," Helen said.

"And Grey's was his G.I. Joe," Eloise said.

Denise patted Betsy on the arm. "See? We just played it."

Betsy was not appeased. She crossed her arms and put on her "in a huff" face. "Isn't anyone else here worried about the fact that Helen is drunk and acting obscene?"

"There are many different levels of obscene," Jane said. "I think we're still in virgin territory."

"I'm not drunk," Helen said, as she held the now empty bottle of champagne upside down over her mouth.

"It's about time Helen loosened up and had fun," Zadie said. "Besides, it's what Grey wanted." Well, maybe not the grinding-with-college-boys part, but as long as everyone's clothes stayed on, she could condone it.

Helen looked at her. "What does *that* mean?"

Oh, Christ. Not again. "Exactly what I said. Grey wants you to have fun."

"So he doesn't think I'm fun normally?"

"He thinks you're perfect, Helen. He's madly in love with you. That's why he's marrying you in two days."

"But he told you he wanted me to 'loosen up'?"

Zadie looked from Helen to Eloise, who was now looking at her accusingly. "No. He just said that he wanted me to make sure you had fun."

"Because I'm not capable of that on my own? Because I need *help* having fun?"

"Helen, you're being ridiculous. That's not what he said at all."

"Liar. He thinks I'm uptight." Helen was right. Grey *had* told her to try and get Helen to loosen up. But she certainly couldn't admit that now.

Eloise threw her two cents in. "I think Grey likes Helen just fine the way she is. He *did* propose to her, if you recall."

"That's exactly what I'm saying!" Zadie said. "He loves her and he wants her to have fun." Enough already. Every time she opened her mouth and said anything about Grey she got grilled and skewered. From now on, she was only opening her mouth to drink.

"Well, if Grey wants me to loosen up, then loose I will be. Thank you, Zadie."

Oh, shit.

The limo driver pulled to a stop and turned around. "This is the Roxy." They looked out at a three-story black building with a neon sign and a marquee. Hordes of music fans were lining up on the sidewalk. Some of them were a little skanky looking. Whether it was faux poser skank or actual skank was yet to be determined.

Skinny made a face. "Why are we going *here?*"

Snotty agreed. "I don't care about some lame band."

Marci beamed. "Kim and I went to see Rick Springfield in concert last summer in Anaheim. It was *amazing*. He still looks exactly the same as he did when he was on *General Hospital*."

"When he sang 'Jessie's Girl'? I almost cried, I was so happy," Kim said.

"We were so close to the stage, I got to touch his ankle," Marci gushed. Clearly, Kim and Marci needed to leave the house more often, but Zadie was at least happy to know that she had some common ground with them. She had every Rick Springfield album ever recorded.

Eloise looked up at the marquee. "There're six bands here and none of them are Rick Springfield."

"We're only here to see one," Gilda told her.

"Surf Monkeys," Zadie said.

"And why am I supposed to care about Surf Monkeys?" Eloise snipped.

"Trevor Larkin is in it," Zadie answered.

Eloise and Snotty almost hurt themselves, they got out of the limo so fast. The other women followed them out, confused.

"Who's Trevor Larkin?" Kim asked.

"The guy in the Gap ad!" Eloise informed her. "The one with the big—"

"Oh, my," Marci said. "I've noticed that, too. I felt bad for looking, but it's hard not to see it."

Skinny was still unclear. "You're telling me Trevor Larkin is in this band?"

Gilda glared at her. "Hands off. You are *not* blowing him."

"Can I?" Jane asked.

"He's Zadie's," Gilda answered.

"He's one of my students. That's what she means." Zadie wished she'd kept her big tequila hole shut. She did *not* want these women to know she lusted after Trevor.

"Of course that's what she means." Jane smiled at her and winked.

Helen led the way through the door. "Do you think they'll let me sing?"

Once they were inside, it was impossible to talk, the music was so loud. The room was black and cavernous and the sound of screeching guitars filled the entire space. Zadie checked with the bouncer and found out that Trevor's band hadn't gone on yet. He thought they might be next, but he had a giant tattoo on the top of his shaved skull that said BRAIN LEAK, so his reliability could hardly be counted on.

Jane gave a group of young guys fifty bucks to leave their table so they could all sit down. Flight attendants must make more than Zadie thought. The band onstage finished, leaving the women a window of conversation time.

"It smells like old beer and armpits in here," Betsy said, wrinkling her nose.

Helen held up her newly procured martini. "To loosening up." She took a big swig, then looked at Zadie. "Do you think Grey would like seeing me this way?"

Zadie looked at her. She was still wearing her bridal veil with devil horns and carrying Hans's blow-up penis. She had the strap-on on backward, so that the blue dildo was poking out of the back of her chair.

"I think Grey would love seeing you this way. I think he'd love seeing you *any* way." Humor the drunk girl. Always the best policy.

"He'll never see me puke, like he saw you do that time."

Why would Grey tell Helen that she'd puked? That was hardly information that she needed to know. Not that Zadie was ashamed. Most women left at the altar probably vomit on someone shortly thereafter. But she was pissed that he'd told Helen about it. Was nothing sacred? Were all of her secrets fodder for Grey and Helen's pillow talk?

"Well, that's probably a good thing. It wouldn't be very romantic," Zadie said, still humoring her, even though she felt betrayed.

"You know what's romantic?" Eloise said. As if she had the remotest idea. "Sitting in complete and total darkness and touching each other."

Zadie tried to tune her out. Any sex tip that Eloise gave was immediately nauseating by virtue of the fact that it was she who had given it. Zadie was worried that by the end of the night, Eloise might ruin all possible sex acts for her.

Betsy looked at the stage, still in a snit. "Is that the big-penis model?"

Zadie followed her gaze to see several young guys, not as young as Trevor, but young, tuning up their equipment and plugging things in. Just as she was about to answer no, Trevor walked out onstage. His green Abercrombie T-shirt was skintight, and his Gap cargo pants were just tight enough to cup his butt, but loose enough to camouflage his package. His blond surfer hair was fetchingly tucked behind his ears and freshly washed. Clean hair was so important in a man. The men who loaded their heads with greasy gel were doing themselves and all those who had to look at them a great disservice, Zadie thought. Someone should really write an article about it.

"Oh, my God, he's so hot." Snotty groaned as if she were being tortured.

Eloise looked at Zadie. "You're positive he's eighteen? He looks at least twenty-three."

"Not unless he was left back five times." She was pretty sure he wasn't, judging by his essays. She was delighted to discover that he was actually quite bright when he turned in his first paper. Which, of course, was just sad. Not that he was bright, but that she was delighted to discover it. She wouldn't have had the same reaction had he been ugly.

As she watched him tune up, she told herself she was just here to support Trevor's musical endeavors. Teachers were *supposed* to be supportive of their students' creativity. She was merely doing her job. There was nothing at all unseemly about the fact that she was here. Nothing at all.

Gilda leaned in and whispered to Zadie, "We're not leaving here until you kiss him."

Zadie rolled her eyes. "Then we'll be here for several years."

"How old are you?"

"Thirty-one."

Gilda calculated the difference. Not an easy feat after several tequila shots. "That's only thirteen years! Demi and Ashton are sixteen years apart!"

Emulating the behavior of people on the cover of *US Weekly* was not something Zadie aspired to.

Gilda wouldn't give up. "He invited you here, right? He probably didn't invite any of the other teachers. So that has to mean something."

Zadie did a quick scan of the dark room, making sure that Nancy and Dolores weren't in attendance. No sign of them. Phew. She didn't see the math teacher or the foreign language slut, either. She turned back to Gilda. "I'm helping him get into Stanford. He was just sucking up."

Betsy leaned forward, superiority bursting out of her. "Do you realize we haven't even given Helen her shower presents yet? They're still in the trunk of the limo. We were supposed to do it at dinner."

"We can do it later. Let's just watch the band," Denise said, throwing Zadie an "I know you need this" look.

Did she need this? Did she really need to watch Trevor onstage and feel guilty for enjoying it? He was adjusting the microphone stand. Oh, Lord. Did that mean he was going to sing? Now that she thought about it, he looked like a younger, more wholesome, blonder version of Jim Morrison. Did Jim Morrison surf? Was Trevor the new Lizard King? Fuck. She was drunk.

When the Surf Monkeys kicked into their first song, Zadie was transfixed. As was every other woman in the room. There was no denying that he was sex on a stick. He had the perfect blend of cocky playfulness and that soulful sad boy wailing that always made Zadie's heart quicken when she listened to the radio. He was a god. The rest of the band was crap, but it didn't matter. Trevor was singing. He was playing guitar. Zadie wouldn't be able to repeat a single lyric or hum any of their tunes if asked later, but that wasn't the point.

She leaned over to yell in Gilda's ear, "Is he surrounded by an angelic haze or am I just really drunk?"

Gilda grabbed her arm. "Listen to me. You are going to have sex with him and give me every single detail afterward. Vicarious fucking is all I'm allowed."

They continued to watch as Trevor got close to the first row of the mosh pit and bent down to sing to various girl groupies.

"Let's go up front!" Snotty said. She grabbed Helen and they raced down there, Skinny close on their heels. Zadie felt the warm glow in her belly turn cold. Why had she shared Trevor with them? Now he was going to fall in love with Helen. Or have sex with Snotty and Skinny in his dressing room. Goddammit!

When they got up close to the stage, they had to fight through a group of teenage girls who had "Under 21" wristbands on. The girls were not at all pleased to have a drunken bride-to-be carrying a blow-up dildo and wearing a backward strap-on in their midst. Not to mention two slutty bitches in designer whore-wear and four-inch stilettos. Helen was forced to start beating some of the girls with her blow-up penis just to retain her personal space. Zadie noticed that a couple of them were in her third-period class and ducked down in her seat.

Trevor looked down from the stage as Helen got particularly nasty with two teenagers in belly tees and bell-bottom cords. Her veil was crooked and her eye makeup was smeared as she bashed the girls over the head with Hans's genitals. Trevor made a face and then gestured to his bass player, who started laughing. As they finished the song, Trevor looked down at Helen and leaned toward the microphone, mocking her. "*Someone's* hammered."

Zadie's glow returned. Trevor was not blinded by Helen's beauty. He was now even more of a god than he was before. This was tragic. She didn't need excuses to like Trevor more. She needed reasons to flee. Dignity. Propriety. These were reasons. Maybe she should move over next to Betsy and Marci and Kim. They would talk her out of her lust. They would set her straight.

The band lit into another song and Helen made her way back to the table. "This band sucks. Let's go."

Betsy stared at the stage with glassy eyes. "One more song."

Marci and Kim were equally entranced. "We can't go until he's done," Marci said.

"Fuck Rick Springfield," Kim agreed.

Zadie felt vindicated. Trevor was irresistible. The most prudish women in California were in accord with her. When the band finished, Snotty and Skinny came rushing back to the table, looking at Zadie. "Do you think you can get us backstage?"

Zadie wasn't about to let these two near Trevor's sweet innocence. "No."

"It doesn't matter," Snotty said. "Let's just wait out here. I'm sure he'll be at the bar in a few minutes."

Which meant Zadie only had a small window of time to talk to him without these bitches horning in. She got up. "I'm going to the bathroom."

Gilda winked at her. Jane gave her a "fuck his brains out" look. Denise merely nodded. Snotty and Skinny were too busy checking their lip gloss in their compacts to notice. Helen was stealing drinks from the waitress's tray as Betsy was putting them back.

Once she was backstage, Zadie felt like an idiot. What the hell was she going to say? Hi, Trevor. Loved the show. Wanna make out? Teachers should never be drunk around their students, but it was too late. She'd been drunk when they walked in. So there was really no point in feeling bad about it now.

She saw a group of swooning teenage girls and figured she was close. They were hovering around the doorway marked GREEN ROOM. Luckily, it wasn't too far away from the bathroom, so Zadie could always pretend she'd gotten lost if Trevor or any of her other students spotted her. She thought about zipping in to pee, but was afraid she'd miss him, only to come back out to the bar and find Skinny kneeling at his crotch.

As she walked past the door she heard, "Holy Shit. Ms. Roberts." She stopped, not sure what she should do. He'd obviously spotted her, so she couldn't just keep walking. She opted for turning back and peeking in the door, but before she could, Trevor was out in the hall, beer in his hand. "I can't believe you came."

twenty-four

Zadie leaned against the wall, trying to look casual and hide the fact that she was drunk. She put a hand against the door frame to steady herself. "Hello." It was all she could come up with.

He grinned at her. "What'd you think of the band?"

"I thought you were great."

"It's okay, you can be honest. We know we kinda suck. But we're better than we used to be." He was so self-aware for an eighteen-year-old. Zadie tried not to swoon, but the black light in the hallway made his skin look so tan and his teeth look so white.

"I think you've got a lot of talent."

"Yeah? Guitar or singing?"

"Both."

"I messed up the third song."

"I couldn't tell."

He turned back to the guys in his band, sitting on ratty couches in the Green Room drinking Heinekens. "Dude, my teacher couldn't even tell I fucked up the bridge." They all laughed. Zadie felt stupid. Was it obvious that he fucked up the bridge? What the hell was the bridge? Why did he have to announce that she was his teacher? He looked back at Zadie. "Sorry. The drummer gave me so much shit about that. I had to bust him on it."

Zadie relaxed. Her stupidity was prized.

"So, weren't you going to a bachelorette party or something?"

"Actually, I brought them with me. I think you saw the bride. She was up front."

He started laughing. "No way. That chick with the veil and the strap-on is with *you?*"

The fact that her normally uptight cousin Helen was a source of wonderment for her lewd behavior was inconsequential at the moment. She was too caught up in his green eyes. God, she liked this feeling. It reminded her of how she felt when she was a girl who went to bars and talked to cute guys instead of a woman who stayed home and hid from them.

"You guys must've had a few drinks before you got here," he said.

"Yeah, we've been to a few bars along the way."

"Where you off to next?"

Was he asking because he wanted to know or asking to be polite? Zadie couldn't tell. "I'm not sure."

"Where'd she get the strap-on?"

"The Hustler store."

He smiled at her. In what might be construed as a lascivious grin. "Did *you* get anything there?"

"Nope. Didn't find anything I needed." Jesus. Could she have been any more boring? She should've told him she bought edible panties or some such thing. No! No! She was his teacher! She had no business talking to him about panties. Shame washed over her. It didn't matter if everyone agreed with her that he was hot. It was entirely inappropriate for her to be talking to him in a bar. She should go. She should walk out right now.

He leaned in close to her. "Don't get mad at me if I say this, okay?"

Her entire body froze. Completely aware that he was an inch away from her face. "Okay."

"I was kind of glad that you didn't get married."

Zadie had no idea how to respond. Was he hitting on her? It

kind of seemed like he might be. Why else would he be happy she wasn't married? Was he just a sadistic bastard?

"Why?"

He smiled at her. "I probably shouldn't answer that. You might fail me."

Okay . . . what the hell did that mean? What did it even matter? She was leaving. She was leaving right now.

She stayed rooted to her spot.

"Your final grade is based on your term paper, not on what you tell me in a bar." *Why* was she encouraging this?

He held her eye contact for a moment, like he was considering whether or not to elaborate on his comment. Zadie felt feverish. Right at the moment that he started to speak—his drummer walked out.

"Dude, let's hit the bar. The cooler is dry."

Zadie couldn't tell if she was relieved or pissed beyond reason.

Trevor shrugged and looked at Zadie. "Wanna head back out there?"

"Sure."

They started down the hall. He was in front of her and she could watch his ass as he walked. But it was no longer just a guilty pleasure. It was pure guilt. She'd come close to allowing herself to think it was okay to lust for him. It was not okay. It was bad. Very, very bad.

As soon as they reached the main room, he was swarmed by his teenage groupies. "Trevor! I love you!" He stopped to sign some autographs. Zadie spotted Amy, Brittany, and Felicia, three of her students, hanging at the back of the swarm. She ducked her head and edged around Trevor, fleeing back to her table before they could see her.

"Let's go," she said.

"Where?" Jane asked.

"I don't care. Let's just go."

"But Trevor will be out here soon," Snotty whined.

Helen stood up on her seat. "Let's go someplace we can dance!"

Zadie looked at her. "Only if you take off the strap-on."

"Deal."

Gilda pulled Zadie aside. "What happened?"

"Nothing."

"Nothing bad or nothing good?"

"Nothing we have to leave before I do nothing good," Zadie said.

Gilda scrunched up her face. "That made no sense."

"Exactly. We have to leave."

Jane joined their huddle. "He hit on you, didn't he?"

"No."

"Something got you all riled up."

"Maybe it was all the tequila shots." Zadie opened her purse and threw some money down on the table. "I'm gonna wait in the limo while you guys pay the check, okay?" She had to get out of there before Trevor spotted her and possibly came over. She could not be responsible for what she might do.

Inside the limo, Zadie was pleased to find five new bottles of Moët. The bushy-eyebrowed limo driver smiled at her. "The bride asked me to restock you guys when you were walking in. She's a handful, that one." Yeah, no shit.

Zadie opened one of the bottles and poured herself a hefty glass. She'd narrowly escaped a horribly embarrassing situation. This was occasion for a toast. She downed a glass as she congratulated herself. Restraint. Willpower. High moral standards. These were good things to possess.

Betsy slid into the limo next, scooting over against the far door. "Thank God you got Helen to agree to take off that blue dildo. I was afraid I wouldn't be able to take any pictures for the rest of the night."

Buoyed by the champagne and her newfound sense of self-righteousness, Zadie leaned over and took Betsy's hand. "Betsy, I'm sorry the night didn't end up the way you thought it would. I know you're disappointed, but I think we all need to remember that it's Helen's night and we're here to make her happy."

Betsy nodded gravely. "You're right. I just don't know what to think about this totally new Helen. Did you see her on that bull? She was perverted!"

Marci and Kim got into the car. "Are we talking about Helen?" Marci said.

Zadie nodded. "I think it's just the alcohol. And the occasion. And twenty-eight years of being perfect. She had to blow sometime." Zadie handed Betsy a glass of champagne. "Drink this. I think it will make the rest of the night easier for you."

Betsy took it and drank it down in one gulp, then looked up at them. "Have you ever noticed that the first sip of champagne tastes a little bit like garbage? I think I need a second one to counteract it." She held her glass out and Zadie poured her another one as the other women began to slide into the car.

Snotty and Skinny were pissed. "We didn't even get to talk to him."

Eloise was next. "I'm sure he's in the back room with Pamela Anderson or someone like that."

Helen and Denise slid in behind her—Helen still in high party mode. "Let's go to Deep! I read about it in some magazine."

"If you read about it, it's already over," Skinny said.

Zadie looked at her like she was an idiot. Which she was. "None of the places we've been tonight are 'hot spots.' If they were, we wouldn't have gotten in."

"Speak for yourself," Skinny retorted.

Just as Zadie was wishing she had honed her projectile vomiting skills, Gilda and Jane slid in the car. "Look what we found," Jane said.

She pulled Trevor into the car.

"Hey." He climbed over Gilda and plopped down next to Zadie. "Where we going?"

twenty-five

Oh, holy God.

Trevor was sitting next to her. In the limo. "Can I have some of that?" He pointed at the champagne.

Zadie shook her head. "I can't be responsible for contributing to the delinquency of a minor."

"I can." Gilda poured him a glass. Winking at Zadie. Oh, that evil, evil Gilda.

"So, your friends said we're going dancing." He motioned toward Jane and Gilda with his head.

"We're going to Deep," Helen said.

Trevor smiled. "Cool. I like that place."

"How do you get into bars?" Zadie asked, completely baffled that Trevor had more of a nightlife than she did.

"Fake ID. I've got a really good one. My dad made it for me."

"Your father wants you to go to bars?"

"He's pretty cool about stuff like that. He's a hippie. He's not really into the whole 'follow the rules' thing." Good, Zadie thought, then he wouldn't report her for having sex with his son.

Skinny and Snotty had just been staring at him, mouths open, until this point, but unfortunately, Snotty found her powers of speech.

"Trevor, hi. I'm Phoebe. I think you used to go out with someone

I know. Josie Altman?" Clearly, Snotty was completely discounting what Zadie had told her earlier, even though it was obvious that Zadie knew him and therefore knew of what she spoke. Snotty was an idiot of the highest order.

"Never heard of her. Does she go to Yale-Eastlake?"

Snotty frowned. "No. She's a waitress in Newport."

"Never been there, sorry."

Skinny leaned forward and put her hand on his knee. "I loved your band. You guys are really awesome."

"Thanks. You must be really drunk."

Gilda leaned back and eyed Zadie behind Trevor's head, giving her a "So?" look. Zadie gave her a "I can't fucking believe you did this to me" look in return.

Trevor bent down and picked up the deflated Hans off of the limo floor. "Who's this poor guy?"

"Helen's boyfriend," Denise answered.

"He died," Helen said, pretending to be sad.

Trevor scooped up the red stuffed penis pillow from its resting place next to Hans. "This has to be yours." He looked at Zadie.

"Nope. It's Betsy's."

Betsy, now on her third glass of champagne, grabbed it from Trevor. "I like it because it's furry."

Trevor raised his eyebrows and looked at Zadie. She smiled back at him, shrugging.

And then Skinny grabbed his knee again. "Trevor, are you guys going to cut an album?"

He looked at her and laughed. "Cut an album? We can barely play our instruments. We only got that gig because of my modeling."

"Oh, you're a model?" Eloise asked. Zadie looked at her. No, she did not just pretend not to know he was a model. Was this her idea of playing the coquette?

"I did a couple ads. It's no big deal. Just travel money so I can go to Europe this summer and not have to sleep in some hostel in a puddle of piss."

Betsy was confused. "Do you wet the bed?"

Trevor laughed. "You ladies are wasted."

Zadie giggled as if Trevor were just the most apt commentator on female behavior she'd ever had the pleasure of listening to. But the fact that he'd referred to them as "ladies" was less than sexy. She wanted to be a chick in his eyes. A hot chick.

Helen chugged from her glass of champagne, getting her steam back. "So, Trevor, are you a virgin?"

"Helen!" A collective protest was heard from each woman in the car.

Trevor took it well. He looked at Zadie and rolled his eyes, then looked back at Helen. "Why, are you offering to relieve me?"

Helen batted her eyes. "You should be so lucky."

Eloise gave Helen a sideways look then looked back at Trevor. "I'm sure Trevor has a girlfriend."

"Nope. I'm free and clear at the moment. The last girl I went out with was too possessive, so I swore off the whole girlfriend thing for a while." He rested his hand on Zadie's leg. She looked down at it. Did he mean to put it there? Maybe he just needed a place to rest his hand. He'd been playing guitar all night. Perhaps his wrist was tired.

Jane noticed it and gave Zadie a "oh, yes, it's going to happen" look. She poured more champagne into Trevor's glass. Zadie closed her eyes in shame. Her new friends were getting a teenage boy drunk in order to up her chances with him.

"This stuff kind of tastes like—bad. I think I'll hold out for a beer when we get to the club." He handed the champagne glass to Zadie. "You want it?"

Zadie took it and drank it down in one gulp. His hand was still on her leg. Snotty noticed it and glared at Zadie.

"Trevor, is it true that Zadie is your English teacher?" She gave Zadie a smug look, as if to say, "I will de-sex you in his eyes in a matter of seconds."

"Yeah, she's the only teacher I like."

"Why's that?" Denise asked, angling her pregnant belly to block out most of his view of Snotty.

"Because she's cool."

Zadie blushed. She *was* cool, goddammit. And being validated by a sex god only made her more so.

"And she doesn't give me a lot of shit, like the other teachers do."

"Who gives you shit?" Zadie asked.

"Ms. Johnson."

Nancy. Of course.

"What does she do?"

"She's always trying to get me to do extra-credit stuff."

Zadie was enraged. Extra credit meant staying after school and spending extra time with the instructor. Nancy was hitting on him! Or at the very least, hogging him for herself. How was he supposed to take Zadie's creative writing elective if Nancy was keeping him around to peer at petri dishes?

"It doesn't matter. In four months, I'll be in college and out of that place." He looked at Zadie. "Did you find me anyone who went to Stanford?"

"I went to Stanford," Betsy said. Skinny and Snotty glared at her, beside themselves with jealousy. If only they'd managed to get past community college, they, too, could help Trevor Larkin.

"Really?" Trevor was excited. "Can you give me a recommendation?"

Betsy poured herself another glass of champagne, now the life of the party. "Sure."

"That would be awesome." He looked at Zadie. "I knew you'd hook me up." He squeezed her knee.

"I'm sure the dean remembers me," Betsy said. "I reorganized the entire student government." Betsy probably reorganized the curriculum and the housing plan as well, but now that she was getting Zadie into Trevor's good graces, Zadie was in no position to judge.

Eloise kept staring at Trevor. "I just can't believe you're only eighteen."

"I'm not," he said. "I'm nineteen. When my parents were touring with the Dead, they forgot to register me for school, so I started a year late."

He was nineteen? Zadie couldn't have been happier if someone had just given her a small country. She wasn't quite sure why one year made such a huge difference, but it did.

The limo stopped and the driver turned around. "We're at Deep."

Betsy turned to him. "You know, we don't even know your name."

"It's Jerry."

"Thank you, Jerry. We appreciate your services." Betsy was on a roll. Full of good will for everyone.

As they slid out of the car onto Hollywood Boulevard, they were greeted with a giant line to get into the club, which appeared to be nothing more than a green boxy building on the corner with no sign. Denise looked back at Helen. "Maybe we should go someplace else."

The bouncer at the door looked over the sea of heads in front of him and spotted Trevor getting out of the limo.

"Yo, bro, come on in." He motioned for Trevor to come to the front of the line.

Trevor gestured at Zadie and her group. "They're with me."

"No prob, man." The bouncer opened the door and ushered them through, much to the consternation of the other people in line. Especially when they spotted Kim and Marci in their Lady Dockers and Keds.

A girl in a black minidress turned to another girl in a black minidress and said, "Okay, either I just got fat while we were standing in line, or those two chicks fucked someone to get in here."

twenty-six

Once they were inside, Trevor put his hand on the small of Zadie's back as he guided her through the hipster crowd. He was so smooth, so full of confidence. He had loads more than Zadie had. He'd just sat in a limo full of grown women and managed to shut down Helen, Snotty, Skinny, and Eloise with no effort at all. Granted, they were hammered, but still.

Deep's hook was that they had scantily clad women dancing inside three Plexiglas cubes in the wall. There was also a small dance floor for the patrons, surrounded by walls of two-way mirrors. But Helen was not content to dance with the masses. She immediately became fixated on the idea of entering a cube. The women who were currently manning the cubes looked bored out of their minds, but Helen thought it looked like great fun.

While she went off to find the secret cube entrance, the rest of the party went to the bar. Trevor ordered a Red Stripe and Zadie ordered a margarita. Tequila had gotten her this far, so why stop?

Snotty and Skinny were immediately asked to dance and they went out to grind with their new marks. Marci and Kim plopped down on some bar stools, while Betsy, Eloise, Gilda, and Jane ordered shooters. Denise went off to puke in the bathroom.

Zadie stood at the bar, every fiber in her body aware that Trevor was standing next to her. He threw some money on the bar when the bartender brought their drinks, then handed her her margarita and clinked his beer against her glass. "To new experiences."

Zadie took a sip, wondering what new experiences he was toasting. Europe? Stanford? Fucking her? He turned to face her, leaning against the bar.

"You're not gonna get pissed at me, are you?"

"Why would I get pissed at you?"

He smiled at her. Not answering. Zadie noticed a few women around them recognizing him. He either didn't notice or pretended not to notice as he took another sip of his beer, then set it down. "Let's dance."

Every last working brain cell Zadie possessed told her this was a bad idea, but she let him lead her out onto the dance floor. She tried to view the situation as if she were floating above it. There she was. Dancing with Trevor. His arms were around her waist. Her hips were against his. He was smiling at her.

"I always hoped you'd be like this, but I was never sure," he said.

"Be like what?"

"You know."

"I don't think I do."

Before she could question him further, she was distracted by the sight of Helen, now inside a cube, performing a strip show.

"Oh, shit."

"What?"

"My cousin is taking off her clothes."

He turned to look—he was still nineteen after all—and sure enough, Helen had her top off and was struggling to unhook her bra. Once she got it off, she threw it in a ceremonious gesture, but it just hit the Plexiglas window and fell to the ground.

Zadie scanned the bar. "How do I get in there to stop her?"

Trevor shrugged.

She looked around to find Betsy and the others and saw them merrily knocking back shots at the bar, completely unaware that

Helen was showing her mammaries to a room full of strangers.

Guys at the bar started to whoop and holler, encouraging Helen to slide out of her skirt. Luckily, it also encouraged a large black bouncer to yank Helen out of the cube from behind.

"Stay here." Zadie removed Trevor's hands from her waist—reluctantly—and went to find the entrance to the cubes. It wasn't hard to spot, because the bouncer came out of it pushing Helen in front of him. Thankfully, she had her clothes on. The bouncer marched her toward the front door.

Zadie grabbed him. "Wait!"

He turned to look at her and Helen said, "That's my cousin. She'll tell you. I'm a nice girl! I'm a bride!"

The bouncer looked at Zadie. "I don't care what she is. Our liquor license doesn't cover topless dancing."

"She'll keep her clothes on. I promise."

Eloise appeared at their side. "I'm her lawyer. Is there a problem?"

The bouncer looked at Eloise and rolled his eyes, bored with them already. "Tell your client to keep her goddamn clothes on or she's out of here." He went back to man his post in the corner of the room. Helen looked at Zadie.

"He was *totally* into me."

"I'm sure he was."

Eloise was a bit miffed. "Why in God's name are you *stripping* in front of all these people? I was having a shot at the bar and I looked over to see your nipples smiling out at everyone."

"I'm just 'loosening up.'" She grinned at Zadie as if to say "It's all your fault" and then wandered toward the bar.

Eloise turned to glare at Zadie. "Are you proud of yourself? You've turned her into an exhibitionist. I really don't think Grey would've been too pleased if he'd seen that."

"*I* didn't pull her clothes off, she did. Don't you dare blame this on me."

"You encouraged her to drink."

"So did you!"

"Well, you were the one who told her that Grey thought she was too uptight."

Okay, that was true. Sort of. Zadie looked around. Helen was nowhere to be found. "Where'd she go?"

Eloise turned around to look. "Now you've lost her. Great."

Zadie looked over at the bar and saw a flash of blond hair leaping upward. Sure enough, it was Helen, flying into the arms of Jimbo, the floor salesman from Atlanta. Zadie marched over, Eloise right behind her. Helen waved at them.

"Look! It's Jim!" Jim gave Helen a twirl and set her down.

"Darlin', I saw that little show you put on and I'm here to tell you—you are the woman of my dreams," Jim said. His face seemed even ruddier than it was before.

Zadie gave him a tolerant smile. "That's swell, Jimbo, but Helen is getting married in two days. As you're aware. So let's keep our hands outside of her moving vehicle, okay?"

Jim tweaked Zadie on the nose. "You're a snappy one. I like you."

"I'm so glad."

Helen started pulling on Jim's arm. "Let's dance!"

Eloise frowned. "I think you've had enough dancing tonight."

"Eloise, I'm a bachelorette! I'm supposed to be having fun. Dancing is fun. Tell her, Zadie. I saw you out there." She gave Zadie a look that said plenty, then dragged Jimbo out on the dance floor and proceeded to do obscene things, but since they weren't too far from the obscene things the other people were doing on the dance floor, Zadie allowed it.

Eloise set herself up as chaperone on the edge of the dance floor, arms folded, frown in place. She turned to Zadie, still keeping her eyes on Helen. "If he makes a move, he's gonna lose an appendage."

Zadie decided that Helen was safe on Eloise's watch and did a quick lap around the club to find Trevor, not believing that she'd actually left him *alone* in a bar full of easy women. She spotted him at the bar, where Skinny and Snotty were on him like fleas.

She came up behind them so that she could eavesdrop and so Trevor could spot her.

Skinny was in mid-pickup line. "So, if you, like, ever need someone to buy you beer or something, you can call me. I'll come right over." She stuck out her implants and licked her lips. She was subtle and minxy, that one.

Trevor shrugged. "I have fake ID. I buy my own beer."

Snotty gave it a shot. "When you do those catalog shoots, do they let people watch? I'd love to see you work." She cocked her head and tried to look as if she were an appreciative patron of the fine art of modeling.

He looked over Snotty's shoulder and spotted Zadie.

"There you are." He held out his hand and pulled her into the circle. "Did you find your cousin?" Snotty and Skinny were none too pleased. There was much eye-rolling and some disgruntled sighing.

"She's over there. Clothes on." Zadie motioned toward the dance floor, where Helen continued to shake her wares at Jimbo.

Skinny wrinkled her nose. "Eww, is she with that guy from Atlanta? I thought we ditched them."

"I don't like him any better than you do at this point," Zadie said.

Snotty curled her lip. "He's wearing pleated pants."

While Snotty and Skinny performed their sartorial evisceration of Jimbo, Trevor smiled at Zadie. "I was worried you left."

He was worried? Why? Because he needed a ride or because he wanted to continue grinding against her? Trying to decipher Trevor's intentions was becoming an all-consuming task. She couldn't simply allow herself to believe he was attracted to her. Life just wasn't that kind.

Trevor leaned over and whispered into her ear. "I would've rather watched *you* take your clothes off."

twenty-seven

When certain things happen, such as a male you're quite in lust with telling you that he would enjoy seeing you naked, certain other things are supposed to happen in a sure and speedy manner. Zadie could've taken his hand and led him to the limo for some quick backseat action, making Jerry put up the tinted divider window so as not to hear their sin. She could've hailed a cab and brought him back to her place for a night of carnal savagery heretofore unknown in the state of California. She could've taken him into the ladies' room and let him back her up against the wall of a stall and fuck the living hell out of her.

Zadie did none of these things.

Instead, she blushed, she giggled uncomfortably, she looked down at the floor, and she said, "I think we should get another drink." She was torn between wanting to be sober enough to remember it if something did happen, but knowing that she'd have to be plastered to go through with it.

He smiled at her, acknowledging her discomfort without commenting on it. He leaned in close again. "Only if we can get away from these two. They're annoying." He motioned at Snotty and Skinny with his head.

He pulled her by the hand down to the end of the bar where Jimbo's Atlanta crew had descended on the rest of the bachelorette party. Jane and Gilda were knocking back shots with two of them, while Kim and Marci and Betsy were trying to explain to the rest of them why they didn't want to dance to a song by a misogynist who "sings" about killing his wife and mother. Denise was downing every maraschino cherry in the bar prep station, much to the consternation of the bartender.

When Jane and Gilda saw Zadie with Trevor they started making lewd gestures. Jane repeatedly shoved her tongue into her cheek, making the universally known blow-job face. Thankfully the music was too loud for Trevor to hear Gilda shout, "Have you made out with him yet?" Zadie shook her head, gave Gilda a stern look, and moved down the bar a couple of feet just to make sure their actions would go unnoticed.

Trevor handed her another margarita. She couldn't even remember what she'd done with her last one. Did she drink it? Did she leave it sitting on the bar? Was she wearing it?

"So, if we have sex and you don't like it, you won't fail me, will you?"

If this had been a movie, it would've been one of those ridiculously overdone moments where the music stops and everyone in the bar would've heard him. And perhaps Zadie would've done a spit take with her drink. Fortunately, there were no cameras and no bad directors present. Unfortunately, Zadie had no idea what to say. She just stared at him, trying not to allow herself to process what he'd just said.

In reality, it wasn't that hard to fathom that he wanted to have sex with her. He was nineteen. Nineteen-year-olds want to have sex with everyone, don't they? He probably masturbated five times a day. He probably got hard when he touched himself to pee. She probably shouldn't be quite so honored to hear that he was considering her as a sexual option. But fuck it, she was. He was hot. And he'd shunned the halter-top twins in favor of her. He'd rather see her naked than Helen. He thought she was cool. These were all things that would get her through the night for many months to come.

Of course, having sex with him would also give her plenty of material to run through her head on the many long, lonely evenings ahead of her.

"If you mention your grade one more time, I'm leaving." She said it merely because being reminded that she was his teacher was severely unsexy, but it had the unplanned effect of making her sound hard to get.

"Deal." He clinked his beer against her glass. "So, can you tell that I stare at your boobs in class?"

"Okay, let's just avoid school as a topic altogether."

He nodded. "No problem." He took a swig of his beer. She watched the way his face moved as he sucked on the bottle. His cheeks caved in, highlighting his already prominent cheekbones. His jawline was exquisite. How many times in your life can you look at someone and say that their jawline is exquisite?

"Are you drunk?" she asked.

"Not really. Are you?"

"A lot."

"Good." He grinned, tucking an unruly sun-bleached lock behind his ear. "So, have you ever thought about me?"

"I can't answer that." She could—but she wouldn't.

He smiled at her. "I watched you getting into your car once and you pulled your skirt up thigh-high so it wouldn't get shut in the door and I thought about you for the rest of the day."

Zadie tried to imagine the scene. Her pulling up her skirt that she'd probably ordered from the Boston Proper catalog as she got into her Camry. Trevor watching from across the parking lot as he did tricks on his skateboard. Her starting her car, then stalling it, then starting it again as she drove home while masturbating at the thought of him.

He leaned in and whispered into her ear as he nuzzled her neck. "Don't you wanna know what I thought about?"

Yes, she did. But she couldn't bring herself to say the words. She was too busy trying not to melt into a pile of goo at the feel of his lips on her skin. Then she remembered something.

"You called me old."

He stopped nuzzling her neck and frowned. "When?"

"You said that you could always use a bunch of horny women at your show even if they were old."

"You're not old," he said. Playing with a piece of her hair.

"You thought I was old when you said that."

"Well, you're older than the teenyboppers we get at our shows. But I don't like those girls."

"Why not?"

"Did you see them?"

"They were screaming your name."

"Exactly."

He gave her the grin again. "I wanna scream *your* name." Oh, he was smooth. He took her hand. "Let's dance." And he was smart. She realized that *he* realized that the more they talked, the more freaked out she got. Best to keep it to grinding and eye contact.

Once they were back on the dance floor and his hands were on her hips she allowed herself to think it could actually happen. She could actually take him home and strip his clothes off and do nasty, nasty things to him.

"I've slept with four girls, if that's what you're worried about. I know what I'm doing."

Uh, no, it never concerned her at all whether or not he knew what he was doing. Just the joy of his presence and naked flesh would be enough for her.

The song lapsed into something that was pure bass, offering them plenty of opportunity to mash their hips together in a preliminary fuck. She was going to do it. She was going to have sex with him tonight. As Zadie shut her eyes and pretended that he was at least twenty-five, she was rudely interrupted by Gilda.

"We may have a problem."

Zadie opened her eyes and looked up at Gilda's frown. She pointed to Helen and Jim, who were now in the throes of something untoward. Helen had her legs wrapped around Jim's waist and he was backing her up against the wall, nibbling on her ear.

Eloise was trying to pull Jim off her, but Helen wasn't helping in any way. In fact, she seemed to be enjoying herself.

"Oh, God."

"I think we should leave," Gilda said. "We have to get her in bed."

As the other women joined Eloise in the effort to remove Jimbo from Helen, Zadie realized Gilda was right. It was time to get Helen into bed before she performed a live sex show. Grey would never forgive her if Helen hooked up with Jim. The wedding would be off and Zadie would feel guilty until the day she died.

She looked at Trevor. "I'm sorry, but I've got to get her out of here."

"I'll come with you."

"You know what? I think we should just call it a night."

He actually looked pained. "But . . ."

Betsy and Eloise now had Helen in an armlock and were dragging her toward the door. Jimbo trailing after them.

"I *really* need to get her out of here before something happens."

Zadie started toward the door. Not believing that she was leaving the hottest guy alive standing alone on a dance floor with half a hard-on.

twenty-eight

The limo ride back to the hotel was full of contention. Eloise was apoplectic at Helen's behavior. Not to mention the fact that Jimbo had banged on the back window as they drove away. Once they'd gotten Helen outside on the sidewalk, Jimbo took it as an invitation to join them and Zadie had had to knee him in the groin to keep him from getting into their car. He kept screaming, "But I love her!"

"How do you think Grey would feel if I told him you were carrying on with some redneck in a bar?" Eloise asked. "He'd be crushed. You're getting *married*, Helen. You can't do things like that. You're making a *commitment*. I thought you were the type of girl who understood that, but now I realize that I don't know you at all and I'm worried that Grey doesn't either."

Helen stared at her. Her best ice queen look. "So, are you saying that you're going to tell Grey what's happened tonight? Because I thought the whole point of a bachelorette party was for the bachelorette to have fun. If you don't agree with that, I'm wondering what you're even doing here."

Zadie had to hand it to her. Even drunk, Helen's self-righteousness was strong enough to make anyone question the fact that they had criticized her.

"Why are *any* of you here if you don't want me to have fun?" Helen demanded.

"We do want you to have fun," Gilda said. "We just don't want anything to happen." She gave her a meaningful look to which Helen replied with a shrug.

Zadie decided to step in. "I think what Eloise is trying to say is that your idea of fun used to be yoga and tea, not dry-humping traveling salesmen."

Helen gave Zadie her practiced look of superiority. "Should I be dry-humping teenagers? Would that make me a better person? Because God forbid, I'm not as good as Zadie."

Okay . . .

Zadie wondered what she was supposed to say to refute this. "Fuck you, bitch" was the only thing that came to mind.

Luckily, Jane jumped in before she got it out. "No one's judging you, Helen. We're just trying to make sure no one takes advantage of you in your state."

"What 'state'?"

"You're a little hammered," Denise informed her. "Not that that's a bad thing."

"You know what? I'm drunk, too," Betsy said. "And I kind of like it. I should really do this more often." She poured herself more champagne. "Who's up for next weekend?"

Before Zadie could feel proud for welcoming new converts into the world of a pleasant buzz, Skinny and Snotty brought up Trevor.

"Why didn't you bring Trevor with us?" Snotty whined. "You hogged him all night and then just left him there."

"That was really rude," Skinny added.

"Maybe she had sex with him in the men's room and she's done with him," Gilda said, trying to boost her in the eyes of the two most vile women in the world.

"Oh, my God, did you?" Eloise asked.

"No, I did not have sex with him," Zadie said. She'd chosen Grey's happiness over her own. She didn't trust any of these women to make sure Helen got to bed alone. Even Eloise. Helen was a cagey drunk. There was no telling what she'd do next.

"Why the hell not?" Jane asked.

"Timing," she said, motioning with her head toward Helen.

Helen caught it. "Don't blame me because you're too chicken to have sex again."

"I'm not *afraid* to have sex."

"*Have* you had sex since Jack?" Betsy asked.

"No. But that has nothing to do with anything. I just haven't wanted to."

"I never want to," Marci said. "It's too much trouble."

"Marci!" Kim was appalled.

"Admit it, you're in your flannel jammies, the kids are asleep, you're nice and cozy in bed watching TV, the last thing you want is a big wet wad of semen dripping out of you for the rest of the night."

Kim shrugged, admitting Marci had a point.

Denise looked at Zadie. "You looked like you wanted to when you were on the dance floor. Maybe it's time, and you're just too nervous to go through with it."

"I completely agree," Jane said.

Zadie looked at all the expectant faces staring at her, waiting for her to have a big sharing moment where she explained the contents of her psyche. This was the exact reason she'd avoided all of her female friends and hung out with no one but Grey for the past seven months. Men never wanted you to explain your feelings. Most of them openly discouraged it.

"Have I disappointed you all by not fucking Trevor? Tell Jerry to turn the car around. I'll go back and do him on the bar so you can all watch."

Gilda reached out and squeezed her hand. "That would be the nicest thing anyone's done for me in a long time."

"You can't have sex with one of your *students*," Kim said.

"Excellent point, Kim. And whoops, here we are at the hotel."

Jerry pulled up into the half-circle driveway of the Beverly Hills Hotel, the biggest pink building in Los Angeles. It sat on Sunset Boulevard in the midst of a residential area, making it seem even more incongruous a place for a limo full of drunken, sexually charged women to be disembarking.

"Can someone tell me why we're at the hotel?" Helen asked.

"Because you're going to bed," Eloise said.

"My ass."

Jane took over. "Why don't we just go to the bar and have a drink?" She skillfully guided Helen out of the limo and up the walkway into the hotel. The valets and uniformed doormen all gave her a winking nod. As if they saw drunken brides being escorted in every night of the week.

Once they were all inside the door, they headed for the dark green, horse-themed Polo Lounge. Large leather booths and piano music were awaiting them. As well as an elderly European gentleman at the bar who seemed to know Jane.

"Jane, my love, I wasn't expecting you tonight. I thought Cyndi was coming."

Jane gave him a stiff smile. "Paolo. Hello. These are my friends. We're having a bachelorette party."

"Well, of course you are. Congratulations to the bride."

"That's me," Helen said, prompting Paolo to kiss her hand.

Betsy stared him down. "How do you know Jane?"

"He flies to Dallas once a week," Jane said.

"That's right," Paolo said, looking like he couldn't come up with a reason to go to Texas if someone held a gun to his head.

Zadie frowned. An awful lot of people in hotels seemed to know Jane and fly on her airline. She squinted at Paolo. "What do you do in Texas?"

Paolo seemed to look to Jane for an answer, but then came up with one on his own. "Oil."

Jane steered the group away from him into a large booth. She looked at the bartender. "Dani? Can we get some champagne?"

True, the bridal party was staying at this hotel, but did Jane really have the time to get to know the bartender on a first-name basis? This was the first night of festivities. Something didn't gel.

As they sat down at the table, Zadie looked over at the bar, where two beautiful twentyish women had just arrived with two paunchy middle-aged men trying to look younger by wearing acid-washed jeans. One of the girls was blond and looked like a slutty version of Cameron Diaz. The other one was black and had the best body Zadie had ever seen. They appeared to be having quite the lovefest with their ugly boyfriends. Kissing and cooing and hands on asses. The glaring realization that these women wouldn't normally touch these men unless they were being paid hit Zadie full force as one of them looked over at Jane and gave her a nod.

Zadie turned to look at Jane. Jane nodded back.

Eloise took her glass from Dani's tray. "I'm just going to pretend that nothing I saw tonight happened. I think in the light of day, we'll all be back to normal and none of this will matter."

"Speak for yourself," Betsy said as she swilled more champagne. "I'm going to feel like hell tomorrow, but I don't care. Do you realize I never once got drunk in college? What the hell was I thinking?"

"Helen's never been drunk before *tonight*," Denise reminded her.

"I've probably been drunk, like three hundred times," Skinny said.

"Is that why you blow actors in parking lots?" Betsy asked, without a hint of malice.

"You know, I thought the champagne was helping you, but it's not. You're still a bitch," Skinny retorted.

"Ladies, we're all on the same page, no need to bicker," Denise said, even though she was the only sober one. Even Marci and Kim were sipping champagne at this point. Which caused Marci to be more confessional than necessary.

"The last time I had sex was on our anniversary. It lasted about three minutes. Is this what I have to look forward to for the rest of my life?"

Jane shrugged. "Not if you don't want to. I could teach you some tricks."

As Jane was offering her expertise, Zadie noticed that Paolo's "date" Cyndi had just shown up. The same bitchy girl they saw at the Mondrian earlier. The one waiting for her key.

Zadie kicked Gilda under the table. Gilda looked up at her and Zadie announced that she had to go to the bathroom. Gilda followed.

Once they were in the beige marble-floored bathroom, Zadie told Gilda what she was thinking. "Jane's a call girl."

"What?!"

"I don't have any proof, but I have a pretty strong hunch."

"I thought she said she was a flight attendant."

"Well, she's gotta tell people *something,* right?"

Gilda was baffled. "Why in the world do you think she's a hooker?"

"She's known someone in every hotel we've been to and Paolo acted like she'd shown up as his 'date' by mistake."

Gilda couldn't quite comprehend this. She was from Boulder, after all. Not a high call-girl-traffic area. Granted, Zadie was drunk and she'd read every trashy novel ever written, but she was pretty sure she had a good case. Right as she was about to point out that Cyndi was clearly a pro, the Cameron Diaz look-alike walked in to reapply her makeup.

Zadie took the opportunity to investigate. "Hi. How are you?"

Cameron's clone turned around. "Fine, thanks."

"You and your boyfriend are so cute. Where'd you meet?" Zadie asked.

The woman frowned, not sure where Zadie was going with this. "We met at a party. Last weekend."

"Really? You're so lucky. I bet it's hard to meet a guy like him."

The woman snapped her purse shut and blotted her lipstick. "Thanks. I'll tell him you approve." She gave Zadie a "fuck you" look and walked out.

Zadie looked at Gilda. "See?"

"See, what? You just pissed off some chick in the bathroom."

"She's a hooker."

"She's not a hooker, she's beautiful!"

"You think guys pay to have sex with ugly women?"

Gilda thought this over. "That still doesn't mean Jane's a call girl."

"Then how does she know Cyndi?"

"Who's Cyndi?"

"The call girl that showed up for Paolo."

"Paulo's like—sixty."

"Who exactly do you think it *is* that hires call girls? Trevor?"

Helen burst through the door. On a mission. "Hurry up, you two. The gay busboy just told us about a male strip club."

twenty-nine

They were back in the limo.

Zadie was beyond pissed.

She'd left Trevor to make sure Helen was safely tucked in bed, and now they were going out to see strippers? What the fuck? Her sacrifice was wasted.

"Why are we letting Helen out in public again?" Zadie demanded.

"I agree," Gilda said. "I'm not sure this is a good idea."

"It's a room full of gay men. How much trouble can she get in?" Denise said.

Zadie looked at Helen, who was now trying to revive Hans by blowing into his foot, which did not contain an outlet.

"Helen wants to see naked boy penis," Helen said, now charmingly referring to herself in the third person.

"I *really* don't think it's a good idea," Gilda said.

"As long as it's gay penis, I don't mind. She should probably see at least one before she sees Grey's," Eloise said. Much to Zadie's repulsion. Was it the fact that Zadie was an only child that kept her from thinking it was okay to discuss your sibling's genitals, or was it the fact that Eloise was a fucking freak?

Zadie looked at her watch and then at Marci and Kim, who had opened another bottle of champagne. "I thought you two had to get home to your kids."

"Screw our kids," Marci said. "It's about time our husbands did something useful."

"Paying the mortgage doesn't count," Kim said. "I'm so sick of that argument. I gave birth, I raise the little shits, yet I'm treated like another goddamn bill to pay. Fuck him. If I want a juicer, I deserve a goddamn juicer."

"Tim doesn't flush. Have I mentioned that?" Marci asked. "He thinks he's conserving water, but he's not, because I follow him around and flush every time he leaves his piss sitting in the toilet bowl. Like I don't have anything better to do."

"Roger acts like I'm an idiot because I don't check the price of gas before I fill up the Jeep," Kim countered. "Why the hell would I check? I have to buy it anyway. Does it matter?"

Denise smiled at Helen. "See what you have to look forward to?"

"It's physically impossible for a woman to live with a man and not find something to complain about," Betsy said. "Barry leaves his mail everywhere. I find it in the laundry room. It's like he reads a piece and sets it down, then reads another piece and sets it down somewhere else. If it hadn't taken me so long to find him, I'd make him live in the garage."

As the limo swung onto Santa Monica Boulevard, the women glued their faces to the windows. A fabulous array of handsome and buff gay men were promenading down the street. The kind of men they'd all followed around in college to no avail. Gaydar comes with age.

Betsy pointed to an immaculately groomed gay gentleman. "Look at him. I guarantee you he's never left an envelope any-where but the walnut table in his foyer."

Jerry pulled up to a nondescript building that displayed only a neon address. "This is it. Have fun, ladies."

Betsy turned to him. "Jerry, I hope you're not judging us."

"Not at all. I'd let my own wife come here. It's not like she's gonna get lucky." He laughed in that "you're surrounded by ho-mos" kind of way.

The women got out of the limo and filed in through the door, letting Jane pay the ridiculous cover charge.

Zadie brought up the rear. "Thanks, Jane. I'll pay you back."

Jane shrugged. "Don't bother. I had a good month."

A good month? How does a flight attendant have a "good month"?

As they walked down the dark hallway toward the room filled with loud disco music, Zadie noticed that Jane was carrying a crocodile Hermès bag. She'd heard Nancy going on about the very same bag at lunch one day and had somehow noted the needless fact that it cost five thousand dollars. If Zadie had been solving a crime, that purse would've been her proof.

Jane turned around and looked at her. "You coming?"

"Right behind you."

thirty

Zadie had been to Chippendale's before when her friend Dorian had gotten married, back in the dark ages of men with coiffed hair. But the Chippendale's boys had in no way prepared her for the spectacle of the West Hollywood boys. The crowd was all male, and by the time the girls got seated, there was no pretense of stripping, the men were already down to their G-strings. Tiny, tiny, G-strings. And they weren't shy about letting their parts leak out the side and caress the patrons. In fact, Jane was slapped in the face with an impressively sized penis the moment they sat down.

She pointed to Helen and instructed her accoster to direct his member toward her. "She's the bachelorette. Give her a tickle."

Zadie considered the fact that Grey would not be happy about a penis being stuck in Helen's ear, regardless of the fact that it was a gay penis. She could hear him saying, "A cock is a cock." But Eloise didn't seem to mind, so how could Zadie object? If she did, Helen would probably stick the offending appendage in her mouth just to spite her.

Gilda leaned over to Zadie. "We shouldn't be here. We should've locked her in her room. It was one thing when she was pretending to have sex with a blow-up doll, but with all these naked men, I'm afraid something's gonna happen. Gay or not. There's just too many stray dicks in this room."

Would Helen actually give her virginity to a gay stripper two nights before her wedding? The way the night was going, it was just Zadie's luck. But these guys couldn't seriously pose a threat. Could they? It was Jimbo who was a danger and he was nowhere near West Hollywood.

The other ladies were busy being dazzled by the eye candy. Betsy was tipping a large black man quite heavily for the ass-shaking spectacle he was performing and Kim and Marci were encouraging a Hispanic fellow to flex. Eloise was licking the waiter.

Helen leaped up and joined the current stripper, a hunky Italian named "Mr. Lovepants," onstage for a grope. He humored her and dipped her backward for a chaste kiss. The crowd booed. She grabbed his dick in order to elicit their favor. The men now cheered, happy to see something unsavory going on, despite the fact that it was a girl onstage with their favorite boy.

"See?" Gilda said, worried. "This is where it starts."

Zadie looked at Eloise who shrugged. "He's gay. It doesn't count."

Zadie's head was starting to hurt. She rose. "I'm going to the ladies' room. If there is one."

When she was in the middle of what seemed like a ten-minute stream of piss, she heard the outer door bang open. "Zadie?"

Zadie pushed open the door to her stall to find Gilda looking distraught.

"What's wrong?"

"Okay, I know I should've told you this before, but Helen swore me to secrecy."

Helen had a secret? This was news to Zadie. Helen's pristine past was something she'd spent many years resenting.

"This isn't the first time Helen's been drunk."

Zadie frowned. Baffled. Helen? Drunk? Before? This was too much for her tequila-addled brain to comprehend.

"When we were in college, we went to Cancún for spring break."

"I remember," Zadie said. "She came back with all sorts of stories about Mayan ruins."

"Yeah, well, we didn't see any of those."

Zadie felt that something bad was coming. "What *did* you see?"

"I saw Helen have sex with three guys, break a man's neck, steal a diamond necklace, and karaoke to Lionel Richie."

thirty-one

Zadie's anger at having to leave Trevor, her agitation at Helen and Grey's entire relationship, and her ire at the fact that there was zero toilet paper in the stall all converged into one clear and shining moment of benign confusion followed by indignant rage.

"You're telling me that Helen isn't a virgin?"

"Not even close," Gilda said.

"Helen has had *sex*?"

"It was just that one night. She swore she'd never drink again. And she didn't. At least until graduation. I can't vouch for what happened when she moved back here, but from what she's told me, she's been a saint. I think that night in Mexican jail really scared her."

"Helen has been in *jail*?"

Not only had Helen been lying to Zadie all these years, pretending to be perfect and sin-free, which in turn made Zadie feel *im*perfect and sin-saturated, but she'd lied to Grey, who thought he was marrying the most innocent girl in the world. Not that he set out to marry a virgin by any means, but he certainly didn't set out to marry a liar. Why hadn't she just come clean? Why develop your entire persona around a big fat, incredibly annoying, pious fabrication?

Zadie could understand if Helen had just let Grandma Davis

believe she was a virginal prig who shat marshmallows, but why lie to Denise? Why lie to Zadie? Zadie and Denise had spent many a drunken evening discussing Helen's apparent malfunction and how she could have possibly ended up so pure when they were so very, very fond of drink and dick. And all this time, it had been a lie. Zadie felt betrayed.

Gilda looked guilty. "I promised her I wouldn't say anything, but I'm worried about where she'll end up tonight. I don't have enough cash on me for bail."

Bailing Helen out of jail was something Zadie had been fairly certain she'd never have to do. "She really broke a man's neck?"

"It was self-defense."

"And the necklace?"

"That's why she went to jail, but it was all a misunderstanding. She's just not allowed back in Mexico."

Helen had been banished from an entire country?

"Who were the three guys?"

"The first one was a senior at the University of Texas, the second guy was on his honeymoon, and the third guy was a waiter at our hotel." A guy on his *honeymoon?* Jesus. Helen was a slut *and* a bitch.

"Where did all this take place?"

"His room, our room, and the hotel kitchen." Where food is prepared? Zadie shivered, thinking she would never eat guacamole again.

"And the neck-breaking?"

"That was on the street. Some guy tried to shanghai her and she closed a car door on his head."

Zadie didn't even know what to say at this point. She just stared at Gilda, mouth agape. "So you're telling me that my cousin is a violent, thieving whore."

Gilda bit her lip. "Well, I wouldn't go that far, but it was a pretty wild night. She felt really bad about it when we got back to school. The waiter got fired. She sent him money for a couple weeks, but then I think she got over it."

Zadie couldn't even bring herself to comment on the fact that the *waiter* was the thing Helen felt guilty about.

"At what point did she decide she was going to lie about it?"

"The plane ride home. She said she wanted to start over. I promised her I would never tell anyone, but I'm worried she's going to ruin her future with Grey if she has a repeat performance tonight."

"Uh, yeah . . . I can't see that Grey would be too happy if she fucked a bunch of guys tonight."

"So we need to get her out of here. Like, right now."

Zadie agreed. "Let's go."

As they walked back into the bar, they couldn't help but notice that Helen was onstage removing the flaming Mr. Lovepants's G-string with her teeth. The room was going crazy, cheering and clapping and making lewd suggestions.

Eloise watched it all with a naïve innocence, thinking that Helen couldn't possibly get into trouble in such a situation. Betsy even cheered her on, thinking this was all merry fun. Kim and Marci were still giggling over the Hispanic hunk. Skinny and Snotty were bored, since they'd realized that no one in the room wanted to have sex with them. Jane and Denise were getting lap dances. Watching a gay stripper give a pregnant woman a lap dance was something Zadie hoped to never see again, but she didn't have time to worry about her brain's ability to repress. She had a job to do.

Zadie marched toward the stage and yanked Helen off by the hair. "We're leaving. Now."

"Oww! You're hurting me."

"I don't care. We're leaving."

The crowd booed. Someone pelted Zadie with an olive. It was of no concern to her. She was saving her best friend's marriage and such things take precedence over public scorn.

"Why are you being so mean?" Helen whined.

"I know about Cancún. So just shut up and walk out of here like a good girl or I'll tell the others."

Helen immediately quit her whining. "Fine."

When they walked past their table, the others looked at Zadie as if she were the queen bitch of all party poopers.

"What's going on?" Eloise asked.

"We're leaving. Get in the car."

Betsy was baffled. "Why?"

Gilda had Zadie's back. "Because Helen needs to go to bed. Now."

Jane hurriedly tipped her lap dancer and followed them out. "The guy was gay, what could happen?"

"I don't want to chance it," Zadie answered.

As the other women paid for their drinks and bid their naked gay men adieu, Zadie manhandled Helen into the limo. Gilda was close behind. Helen glared at her.

"You told her! I knew I shouldn't have invited you."

"I did it to save your ass, so maybe you should be thankful."

Before Zadie could point out to Gilda that drunken women being disciplined are rarely *thankful*, Helen turned to her and fixed her with the eyes of Satan. "If you tell Grey, I'll deny everything and he'll end up hating you for trying to break us up."

Zadie stared at her. If she had been more in command of her mental faculties, she was sure she could have come up with some scathing retort that involved the words "lying whore," but since she was hammered and flabbergasted and completely thrown by Gilda's revelation, she just looked at Helen and shook her head. "I have *no* idea who you are."

The rest of the women got into the car before Helen could enlighten her.

"Thank God we got out of there," Skinny said. "It was gross."

"*So* gross," Snotty agreed.

Betsy slid in after them. "Bullshit, if they were straight, you'd be naked on top of the hood of some car right now."

"Okay, you are *not* someone who needs to speak to me for the rest of the night. I have no interest at all in even being civil to you at this point," Skinny answered.

"Of course, you don't. I don't have a penis," Betsy said.

Zadie looked at her, an entirely new respect for Betsy being born in this moment.

Jane got in. "I think Marci and Kim have found their happy place. I don't know if we'll ever get them out of there."

Denise stuck her head in. "How hysterical would it have been if I'd gone into labor during my lap dance?" She climbed across them all to sit near the window, in case a future bout of nausea overcame her. "Can't you just see me telling Jeff that my water broke while some guy was rubbing his man-berries against me?"

Marci and Kim burst into the limo in a happy giggle fit. "Did you *see* Javier? He was beautiful!" Kim said.

"He was like a big hairless caramel with muscles," Marci said.

"He gave me his number," Kim said. "I'm going to hire him to babysit. Why shouldn't *I* get a hot nanny to ogle? Roger looks like he's going to pee himself every time he drives the damn cheerleader home. And the bitch eats all my yogurt."

Eloise was the last one in. And she was in a complete state of agita. "I hope we're leaving for a good reason, because I'm pretty sure I could've converted our waiter."

The fact that the least attractive woman in the car was the most certain that she could turn a gay man straight was the final capper. If they didn't leave within seconds, Zadie's head would surely explode.

She turned to the limo driver. "Jerry, we're going back to the hotel."

"Why?" Helen whined.

Zadie turned and gave her a withering look of condescension.

"Because you're getting married."

thirty-two

When they arrived back at the Beverly Hills Hotel, Helen let Zadie and Gilda escort her to her room, even though she was clearly unhappy about it. It was only one-thirty. There was another half hour of public drinking to be done, in her mind.

Zadie had a firm grip on her elbow as they got in the elevator. "I actually let you make me feel guilty for sleeping with Jack on our third date. How could you have sat there and acted so high-and-mighty when you'd banged three guys in one night?"

"It didn't count. I was drunk."

"So was I!"

Helen shrugged and looked away. Clearly unconcerned by her hypocrisy. Or maybe not. In a tiny voice, she asked, "You're going to tell him, aren't you?"

"Grey? No, I'm not going to tell him! Christ, do you really think *I* want to be the one to break the news to him that you're a giant fake? You get that job."

"It was seven years ago. Why is that any of his business?"

"It wouldn't be, if you hadn't made such a big deal about your high moral standards. You're full of shit, Helen. And Grey is not the type of guy who tolerates people who are—shitful."

The elevator door opened and they stepped out onto the fifth floor. Heading toward the bridal suite.

"So you're saying he'll break up with me if he finds out?"

"I'm not saying anything."

Helen looked confused. "But why do I have to say anything if you're not going to say anything? Can't we just keep letting him think what he thinks?"

Zadie was in no mood for logic. "Just go in your room and go to bed. And try not to kill anybody or steal anything."

Helen looked at Gilda. "You told her *everything*?"

Gilda shrugged. "I was trying to save you."

Helen looked at Zadie and then back to Gilda. "Does she know about—"

Zadie cut her off, hands over her ears. "If the next words out of your mouth aren't 'Lionel Richie,' I don't wanna hear it."

Helen looked contrite and kept quiet. Keeping God-only-knows-what horrific secret.

Zadie looked in Helen's purse. "Where's your key?"

"I don't know."

Zadie groaned, annoyed. She was going to get Helen into this fucking hotel room if she had to break the door down.

After they called the front desk and got Helen inside the bridal suite, she refused to put on her nightgown and insisted upon sleeping in her veil with the horns and the strap-on over her yoga clothes. Zadie was in no mood to argue over the petty things, so she let it go. She set three opened bottles of Evian from the mini-bar on the nightstand and put the stainless-steel trash can next to the bed in case Helen puked. Which, given the amount Helen had had to drink, was a highly likely scenario.

Zadie looked at Gilda. "Did she throw up in Mexico?"

"Like you've never seen."

Zadie wet a washcloth and put in on the nightstand next to the water. Having no idea why she was being so accommodating, but feeling extra guilty on Grey's behalf for letting Helen get so drunk. "If you get sick, aim in here, and wipe your mouth with this."

Helen groaned, already half passed out now that she'd hit the bed.

Once Zadie and Gilda were out in the hall, Zadie let herself relax. She slid down the wall and sat on the floor.

"We did it. She's in for the night."

Gilda shook her hand. "Congratulations. That was an impressive display of control in there."

"Anytime you need a bitch, I'm your gal."

"Grey would be grateful, I'm sure."

Zadie sighed. "If she'd had sex with some guy tonight, it would've killed him. It would seriously have killed him."

"I'm not saying she *would* have, I just didn't think we should chance it," Gilda said.

"*Three* guys in one night?" Zadie still couldn't get over this.

"Did I mention she got crabs?"

Zadie smiled. From this moment on, she would never feel inferior to Helen again.

thirty-three

When Zadie and Gilda walked back into the Polo Lounge, the other women were paying the tab. It was well past last call and they were the only people left in the room, aside from the bartender.

"Is she asleep?" Betsy asked.

"She was out cold and snoring when we left," Zadie answered.

"I still can't believe the way you pulled her off that stage," Eloise said. "She could sue you for physical battery."

"I did it for Grey, so I'm pretty sure he'll drop any charges."

Zadie looked around, noticing that their numbers had grown smaller. Skinny was missing. "Where's Cassandra?"

"Finding her new calling," Jane said.

"What does *that* mean?" Snotty said, wrinkling her little face up into a pug. "God, she's just talking to some guy. I don't know why you're making such a big deal about it. You've been giggling ever since she went out there."

Jane smiled. Mysterious as ever.

Betsy filled in Zadie and Gilda. "She's out in Paolo's limo—'getting to know him,' which I'm pretty sure will involve an orifice of some type."

"I'm taking twenty percent for setting it up," Jane said, winking at Zadie. "He's one of my regulars, so I thought I'd throw him a bone."

"I knew it!" Zadie said.

"Twenty percent of what?" Kim asked.

"Yeah, I'm confused. Regular what?" Marci agreed.

Zadie felt triumphant. She watched in pure glee as Jane broke the news to the others.

"Ladies, I'm a call girl."

They all stared at her. Not comprehending in the least.

"No you're not. You're a flight attendant," Betsy said.

"I used to be. Until I discovered the world's easiest way to make money. C'mon—how do you think I dress like this?" She gestured at her apparently expensive outfit and her reportedly expensive purse.

"Wait a minute," Snotty said. "You set Cassandra up to *screw* that guy?"

"Hello, he's loaded. She would've screwed him either way. I did her a favor."

Snotty snorted as if this weren't true, even though she knew it was.

This was beautiful. Skinny was in a limo with an old man who was going to hand her cash. Zadie wished she could've been there to see her face.

"Whoa, whoa, whoa—back up," Eloise said. "How did you get into this?"

Leave it to Eloise to want the logistics of the situation in case she, too, decided this was a viable career option. Although Zadie couldn't imagine what kind of degenerates would actually fork over cash to pork Eloise. Maybe one of those people who only screw stuffed animals on an off night.

Gilda looked at Zadie. "I can't believe you were right."

Betsy couldn't stand that someone knew before her. "You *knew*?"

"I suspected," Zadie said.

Jane shrugged. "I'm not ashamed of it. I just wasn't sure you all were ready to hear it." She looked at Zadie. "What gave me away?"

"Paolo, Cyndi, and your purse."

Jane raised her glass to Zadie in a salute.

Marci and Kim were just staring at Jane, still completely baffled. "So, wait, you're a prostitute?" Kim asked, alarmed.

"I don't walk the streets. I have a small list of clientele that I rotate."

"How much do you get?" Marci asked.

"Five hundred an hour."

The other women all whistled or gasped or made some exclamation of shock. Impressed shock.

"That's more than I make and I have a CPA with a law degree," Eloise said.

Jane shrugged. "Supply and demand. It's three thousand if they want me to spend the night."

More oohs and ahhs.

Now Snotty was all ears. "Wait a minute. Cassandra's getting five hundred dollars to have sex with that guy?"

"Cassandra's getting three hundred. I gave him a discount because she's new."

"So, you're a madam, too?" Betsy asked.

"As of tonight. I never thought about it before, but that girl's a natural."

Snotty gave an indignant snort.

Eloise looked like she'd never been so envious of anyone in her life. "You still haven't told us how you got into this."

"Same way Cassandra did. I was out with some friends one night, some friends who had way more money than they should have had for being secretaries, and next thing I knew, I had ten regulars."

"What do you have to *do*?" Kim asked, still completely distressed.

"Same thing you do. Except I get paid."

"You have to listen to them take a crap with the door open afterward?" Marci asked.

Jane frowned. "I'd charge double for that."

"Does Helen know?" Betsy asked.

Jane shook her head. Zadie thanked God for small favors. If Helen had found out tonight, she'd have been pulling Skinny out of the limo and taking on Paolo herself. And she would've found the perfect way to justify it. After all, three hundred dollars was one more plate at the reception.

Gilda clinked glasses with Jane. "To my first call girl friend."

"Well, I think it's gross," Snotty said.

Betsy gave her a look. "You're just pissed because she didn't send *you* out to Paolo's limo."

"Just because I'm pretty, does *not* mean I'm slutty," Snotty asserted.

Eloise mumbled into her drink. "You're not that pretty."

Just then, Skinny breezed back in. Calm as can be. No sign of a recent moral struggle of any kind. She sat down in the booth with them.

"Did I miss last call?"

They all stared at her.

"What?"

Jane spoke up first. "Did you like Paolo?"

"Yeah, he was nice."

The other women waited for her to elaborate. She started to look nervous.

"We just drove around in his limo for a while. He's way too old to be my boyfriend, but I told him I'd go out with him again sometime."

"I'm sure you did," Jane said.

"Let's see the cash," Betsy said.

Skinny deepened in color by two shades. "What?"

"We all know he paid you three hundred dollars to have sex with him," Gilda said, "so you don't have to fake it."

Skinny's hand shook as she drained Snotty's martini. "I don't know what you're talking about."

Jane's pager vibrated. She looked down at it and smiled, reading the text message. "Paolo said you were fantastic and he looks forward to seeing you next week."

Skinny almost smiled with pride, before she realized she was now officially busted. She grabbed Snotty's hand and yanked her up. "We're going home." She turned to the others. "If you bitches aren't in the limo in five minutes, we're leaving without you." They stomped off in what they surely thought was an impressive display of huffiness.

"I'll be in touch," Jane called after her. "I've got a guy on house arrest in Encino who would love you."

Gilda looked at the others. "Aren't we all staying here? For the rehearsal dinner tomorrow?"

Marci and Kim reluctantly stood. "Not us," Kim said. "We've got babies and husbands to nurse. We'll see you all tomorrow night."

Kim looked at Marci. "I can't believe we have to spend an hour in the car with those two. I'd get kicked out of Mommy and Me if they knew I was consorting with hookers." She looked at Jane. "No offense."

"None taken," Jane said. Ever the diplomat.

As they all rose to leave, Denise walked out of the ladies' room. "What'd I miss?"

thirty-four

Zadie felt a palpable sense of relief as she walked through the lobby. The night was over. Her taxi was waiting. She'd survived. On top of that, she'd actually made some new friends, found out the truth about her Marcia Brady of a cousin, and managed to prevent said cousin from ripping Grey's heart out, which surely would have been the case had Helen strayed into the arms of a redneck vinyl flooring salesman or a gay stripper. All in all, the night was a success.

Right as she got to the door, she heard a familiar voice behind her.

"Hey."

She turned around slowly, fully aware of who the voice belonged to. He stood there grinning at her, in all his Gap ad glory.

"I remembered your friend saying you all were staying here, so I thought I'd take a shot."

"Trevor."

That was all Zadie could manage to say at this point. Her buzz was slightly worn off, but not enough so that she still didn't find him unbearably desirable.

He walked closer. "You going home?"

Yes. Yes, she was. She couldn't possibly bring Trevor with her.

Was this not against every semblance of propriety she still half possessed?

Fortunately, Jane and Gilda walked out of the ladies' room and through the lobby right at that moment. Greeting Trevor as if he were a long-lost best friend.

"Trevor! We were hoping you'd come back." Jane winked at Zadie as she said it.

Gilda gave him a hug, then looked at Zadie. "Are you guys going back to your place?"

Zadie felt her tongue grow thick with an explanation she didn't quite have. "I don't—"

Jane held out her room key. "Because I'm going to hang out with Gilda in her room for a while, so I really don't need mine for a couple hours. Why don't you guys take it?"

And there she was. Faced with Trevor, a hotel room, and a call girl encouraging her to make use of both these things. What was a girl to do?

The elevator ride up to the fifth floor was excruciating. She leaned against one wall and he leaned against the other. Smiling at her.

"Are you pissed I showed up here?"

"Why would I be pissed?"

"Because you ditched me before, which is usually a sign that a girl doesn't wanna hook up."

The only word Zadie heard in that sentence was "girl" and it made her happy.

"Believe me, you wouldn't have wanted to be at the place we went next."

"What was it—some male strip club?"

"How'd you know?"

"Bachelorette party? C'mon. You're *supposed* to go to a strip club. I just hope you're not sick of naked men."

The realization that she was about to see Trevor naked washed over her. She had no pithy retort. She just looked at him and grinned. Anticipating all the joy that was about to be thrust upon her.

"Can I kiss you now?" he asked.

Zadie nodded. Why the hell not? Jane fucked guys for money. Eloise let clients videotape her in bed. Marci had to listen to her husband shit. She was clearly no kinkier than the rest of them.

He took a step toward her and put one hand on the back of her head, gathering up her hair as he kissed her. It was unbelievable. She was kissing Trevor. In an elevator. On the way to a hotel room. He tasted like beer. His tongue was warm. She felt his dick get hard against her. For the first time in seven months, she felt human again.

The elevator dinged and they got out. Zadie looked at the number on the sleeve on the room key and found Jane's room. Three down from Helen's. She shoved the key in the door and waited for the green light. It happened on the first try. An excellent sign. Trevor had his hands on her ass at this point. Then he moved them up to circle her waist.

"I can't believe I'm with you," he said. "I've been fantasizing about this for so long."

Zadie took a moment to savor the sweet irony before she pushed the door open. She was Trevor's fantasy. If only she could tape-record this to play back later.

The room was a suite, done in tasteful earth tones with maroon velvet drapes. Jane had obviously had a few overnighters lately to afford it. Either that or she got the call girl discount. Zadie kicked off her sandals and sat down on the cream-colored silk couch, nervous now that they were in the room. Trevor took the cue and went over to the minibar.

"Sweet. They have Corona." He popped one open and looked at her. "You want something?"

Zadie spied a small bottle of José Cuervo and figured she'd best indulge the señor in order to perform what her libido required of her but her brain still half-forbade. "I'll take the tequila."

"You want it over ice?" he asked.

"Just give me the bottle." She took a swig and set it down. Realizing she had neither lemon nor salt. He sat down next to her on the couch. "You realize you can never, *never* tell anyone about this," she said.

He pulled his T-shirt over his head. "I swear." He leaned over to kiss her again. Both hands in her hair this time. Why was that so damn sexy? Zadie didn't know, but she wasn't going to stop and analyze it now.

He unbuttoned her shirt and put his hands on her tits. First just touching them, then cupping them. As if he couldn't believe how big they were. Thankfully, she'd worn a good bra. It certainly wouldn't do for Trevor to see her ratty, discolored Target bras. She was wearing her one Victoria's Secret satin demicup, which pushed her bigger breast up a good half inch higher than her smaller one. The way Trevor was squeezing them as if they were made of Play-Doh ensured that he would never notice. When he buried his face in her cleavage, Zadie leaned her head back on the arm of the couch and sighed. Hell, fucking, yeah.

"What's this?" He pulled a piece of purple penis confetti out of her cleavage.

"Oh, God," Zadie said, silently cursing Denise. "Don't ask."

Trevor looked at it and laughed, flicking it aside as he resumed his worship of her boobs. He looked up at her. "These are awesome."

She couldn't bring herself to unzip his pants. It felt too molesty. She waited until he took her hand and put it on his crotch, as nineteen-year-olds are wont to do—that much she remembered from her youth—before she let herself feel the goods that everyone on Sunset Boulevard had been ogling. Oh. Dear. God.

She drew her hand back, startled.

"What's wrong?" he asked. In between kissing her tits. Her bra now off.

"Nothing." She tried to play it cool. It certainly wouldn't do for her to let him know he had the biggest dick she'd ever held in her hand. Jack had been ample, but Trevor was just obscenely large.

No wonder he liked older women. A sixteen-year-old girl would look at this thing and run. Zadie had always assumed that male models stuffed in those billboards. Not so.

"You okay?" he asked.

"I'm—fine. I'm good."

He kicked his cargo pants off and she resumed her fondling as he unzipped her jeans and pulled them off. She had a moment of panic, trying to remember which pair of underwear she had on, then relaxed when she looked down and saw that it was a pair of silky bikinis from Frederick's, left over from her "trousseau." It was as if everything pointed to the fact that the universe wanted her to have sex with Trevor. Her guilt was gone. Clearly, this was ordained by a higher power. She was meant to do this. Why else would she have worn good underwear?

thirty-five

After they were done, Zadie rolled off him and sank back against the pillows on the couch. Three times. Never in her life had she been fucked three times in a row. In the midst of the second round, he'd told her he loved her. She didn't take it to heart, she merely appreciated the sentiment in the spirit in which it was intended.

Trevor laid his head back on the arm of the couch, trying to catch his breath. "Holy shit."

Indeed. Any doubts Zadie had had about her desirability had been erased in one fell screw. Months of therapy had brought her nowhere. Thirty minutes with Trevor had delivered her to new levels of self-esteem, previously unknown. She was a hot piece of ass.

"Remember that time at the Coke machine?"

Zadie came out of her afterglow to pay attention to what he was saying. Was he talking about the day she'd been fantasizing about putting her lips on the back of his neck?

"I turned around and you were *right* behind me," he said. "I almost kissed you then. But I chickened out."

Trevor had almost kissed her? In school?

"It probably would've freaked you out, huh? I'm glad I waited until tonight."

"I'm glad you did, too," she answered. Zadie tried to imagine Trevor kissing her at the Coke machine and having Nancy breeze around the corner catching them. Only bad things would have followed such a scenario. Jealousy. Accusations. Unemployment. "We can never, ever do anything at school. You know that, right? I'd get fired if anyone found out about this."

"I know. It's cool." He looked over at her and smiled, then rolled on top of her to kiss her again. Was it possible he was going for round four? Zadie wasn't sure she had it in her. Or rather, that she was up for having it in her *again*.

She kissed him back, then scooted toward the back of the couch, so that they were side by side again, facing each other. "I think you wore me out."

He grinned. Proud. "So, did you like it?"

In truth, she liked it more in theory than in practice. The actual fucking was fine. Good in fact, although rapid. But his foreplay skills were a bit lacking. She hadn't had an orgasm. Not that she'd expected one, thinking back to her first nineteen-year-old lover in college, who'd let an entire three-second time span elapse in between the moment he kissed her and stuck his penis in her. But Zadie wasn't here for the technicalities of the sport. It was the contact that she'd wanted. Trevor's naked skin on hers. The thought of it had been one of the only things that had gotten her through the last few months and the reality of it didn't disappoint.

Although the cozy aftertalk was a bit awkward. She'd never fantasized about *this* part of the evening. In her head, he'd always vanished immediately afterward, leaving her ample time to watch *The Daily Show.*

She ran her hand over his perfectly sculpted, paddled-many-waves shoulder. "Yes, I liked it." A shoulder like this should be bronzed, she thought. Or carved in marble. When she'd gone to Italy for a semester abroad during senior year, she'd been struck by all the statues in the Vatican of Antonius, Emperor Hadrian's beautiful boyfriend. Apparently, Hadrian had had him declared a god and hired artists to make several Antonius statues, capturing his extreme hotness, and placed them all over the empire. Zadie wished she could have a similar statue made of Trevor so she could put it in her living room to remind her of this night. As well as a copy to place in Jack's front yard with a snippy note.

"I thought you did. You seemed pretty into it." He tucked a piece of her hair behind her ear, looking relieved. "You made a lot more noise than the other girls I've been with."

Zadie blushed. She'd probably woken half the hotel.

He looked at his watch. "I should probably get out of here. My parents get pissed if I'm out past three."

The mention of Trevor's parents immediately quashed any further libidinous urges Zadie had. She took one last pass at his pecs with her index finger and watched as he sat up and pulled on his pants. Once safely buttoned and zipped, he looked back at her, leaning over to kiss her again.

"I seriously think this is the best night I ever had." He gazed into her eyes with such warmth that it almost brought her to tears. She couldn't even answer. She just kissed him and ran her hands up and down his lats. He was a gift from above. Sent here to cure her. Dr. Reed would be so proud. And Dorian—Dorian would crap herself when she told her.

He stood up and pulled his T-shirt on. "So, can I, like, call you or something?"

"Sure." Zadie got tense even thinking about it. It was out of the question.

He grinned. "So, are you gonna give me your number?"

"We'll talk on Tuesday. But not in school. I'll figure something out."

She pulled her jeans back on and buttoned the top few buttons of her blouse. He watched her.

"I wish I could tell Jared how hot you are naked, but don't worry. I won't."

Now Zadie was completely panicked. Jared Blair was the son of one of the school board members. If Trevor and Jared got stoned and Trevor happened to let it slip out that he'd happened to let his penis slip into her, she would be out of a job. And not too bloody likely to get any recommendations. *"Zadie Roberts? Oh, yes. The senior-fucker."*

"Trevor, I can't emphasize enough how important it is that you don't tell anyone. I'll be homeless. You can't call me if I'm living in a refrigerator box under the freeway."

"I get it. Don't freak out."

She slipped her sandals back on and grabbed her purse as they both walked toward the door. He cupped her chin with his hand and kissed her one last time before they opened the door. The sweetest kiss imaginable.

"Sorry," he said, "I just had to do that one last time."

If Zadie hadn't been so preoccupied with thoughts of losing her job, she would've swooned. Instead, she cupped his ass with her hands while he hugged her. If she was going down, she was going down fulfilled.

thirty-six

When Trevor got in the elevator, Zadie gestured down the hallway.

"I should check on my cousin. Make sure she's not choking on vomit or anything like that."

"Okay. See you at school." He gave her a grin that said he'd be picturing her naked all through class.

As the doors shut, Zadie turned and headed toward Helen's room. Frowning as she got closer. Why was there noise?

She put her head to the door and heard the unmistakable moans of two people having sex. A woman's voice saying, "Oh, God! Oh, God!" and then a man's voice saying, "*Goddamn*! You are the perfect woman." The accent was Southern. The man was Jimbo. She was sure of it. Her fears were confirmed when he said, "We sure don't find 'em like you down in Atlanta."

Motherfucker!

Somewhere in the thirty or forty minutes she'd spent with Trevor, Jimbo had found his way to Helen's room and commenced screwing her. Helen must've given him her room key at Deep. Fuck! What was she supposed to do? It wasn't like she could bang on the door and save the day. They were already knee-deep in fornication. The deed was done.

Fuck!

Grey was going to kill her. It was all her fault. She should've stayed in Helen's room and kept guard. She *knew* Helen was drunk. She *knew* Helen was a secret slut. And yet she'd just left her alone, albeit passed out in a locked hotel room, to welcome gentlemen callers at her whim.

Fuck!

She stood there for a couple more seconds, trying to figure out what to do. When Jimbo said, "Let's flip you over and try it from the other side," she had to walk away.

She'd failed. Grey had asked her to make sure Helen had fun, and oh, yes, it appeared that Helen was having fun, but certainly not in the way Grey had envisioned. Poor Grey was home picturing Helen maybe having a mimosa with a piece of decadent cheesecake. Not redneck cock up her ass.

She had the valet call a cab and paced the driveway of the hotel until it got there. She hadn't even given Jane her room key back. She knew if she saw anyone else from the bachelorette party that she'd tell them, and she figured the fewer people that knew the better. She still hadn't figured out what she was going to tell Grey. She'd been balking about telling him about Cancún. Which seemed like a trip to the nunnery compared to this.

When her cab pulled up, she got in and gave the Armenian driver directions. He turned around and looked at her. "You okay?"

She used the opportunity of his concern and his ability to speak English to fish for an answer to her dilemma. "If your best friend was getting married in two days and you just caught his fiancée having sex with someone else, would you tell him?"

"Of course I would tell him," the driver said. "You can't let him marry some slut."

"What if the slut was your cousin?"

The driver sucked in some air and let it back out in a sigh. "That's a tough one. Who's your loyalty to?"

"My best friend."

"The groom, right?"

"Yes."

"Then you should tell him."

"But won't he hate me for being the bearer of bad news? And won't he hate me for letting her get drunk and give some guy her room key?"

The driver turned around and looked at her. "You are a bad friend."

Zadie sighed. Yes, she was.

Fuck.

thirty-seven

When Zadie woke up, she had a headache that rivaled the pain of childbirth. Or so she imagined. Her body was so dehydrated she felt as if her throat were made out of singed parchment paper. There was no possible way she could ever get out of bed again. She was here for life. She would have to teach school by speakerphone.

Thankfully, it was Sunday, and she wouldn't have to move. And then she remembered.

Tonight was the rehearsal dinner. She was supposed to meet Grey at noon to help him pick up the groomsmen's gifts. Grey. At noon. Shit.

She tried to roll over and sit up, but her body wasn't cooperating. Not only was she hungover, but there was an ache in her nether regions that she could only attribute to vigorous boning by an oversized penis. Where were the feminine hygiene products for *that* particular affliction?

When she made it to the bathroom, she looked in the mirror, only to be confronted by a creature with a clammy, pale, guilty reflection. After being chastised by the cab driver for the fifteen-minute ride home, she'd paced her living room for an hour, trying to figure out what to tell Grey. It was an accident. It's just a misunderstanding. A fluke, if you will. Oh, Helen never told you about Cancún? Funny story.

By the time she'd passed out in her bed, she still hadn't come up with an explanation that would spare Grey's feelings while letting him know the truth. There's no easy way to tell someone that the girl they're about to marry just had sex with another guy. She thought back to her own particular moment of searing pain when she realized that Jack wasn't showing up at their wedding. No one sugarcoated it for her. How could they? They simply told her, "He's not here." Maybe that's what she should do for Grey. But the thought of Grey going through the agony that she'd gone through was too much for her to bear. She wouldn't wish that on anyone. There was simply no way she could tell him.

But what if Helen made a habit of this? What if she didn't repent and go back to being Little Miss Sweetness and Light? The Helen that Grey knew could be gone. By telling him, Zadie could be saving him from a fate far worse than a few months of heartache.

What shamed her the most was that she was having sex with Trevor when Helen let Jimbo in. Figuratively. Zadie should have been standing watch instead of giving in to her carnal perversions. Grey could be getting happily married this weekend. Sure, there was the Cancún lie, but that paled in comparison to the Jimbo "let me flip you over" scandal.

After she showered and threw on a T-shirt and jeans, she dumped six Emergen-C packets into a glass of water and chugged it. She even took the liberty of cutting a lemon in half and rubbing each half in an armpit, because she'd read in *Cosmo* that it would help get rid of a hangover. Whether it worked or not, it could only help kill the smell of tequila that was wafting out of her. She tried to calculate the number of margaritas she'd had and lost count somewhere around twelve. And then there was the champagne.

By the time she'd cabbed to her car at Barneys and got to Grey's house, it was twelve-thirty. Grey hated tardiness. She knew she was in for an earful.

"Where've you been?" He looked tense. "We've got a shitload

of stuff to do today." He slid his wallet into the pocket of his cargo pants and grabbed his car keys.

"Let's go," she said, happy to have the diversion of chores to keep her from having to explain her condition. Not that he noticed. Thankfully, people getting married tend to be a bit self-absorbed.

"I need to pick up the groomsmen's gifts first, then we need to get some film and some sunscreen," he said. The sunscreen was for Turtle Island in Fiji. Helen fell in love with it during *Blue Lagoon*. She'd been dreaming about it ever since. Grey had made Zadie look at the Web site close to a hundred times and Zadie had to admit— it looked pretty damn good. Private beaches where you could be alone all day—naked, sipping champagne, eating lobster, making love. It was the type of place she could never have convinced Jack to go to because it didn't have a casino. God forbid he vacation anywhere he couldn't lose a thousand dollars in five minutes.

Once they were in the car, Zadie felt a wave of nausea. Being in the passenger seat always did that to her, even more so when she was hungover.

"So how was the bachelorette party? Helen said it was great."

"She did?"

"Yeah, she said you guys went all over town. Shopping, yoga, tea."

"Exactly. That's exactly what we did."

"She also said you guys went to the Hustler store and got me some surprises for the honeymoon."

Zadie sincerely hoped that Helen wasn't referring to the blue strap-on.

Grey looked at her and grinned. "I would've loved to have heard the conversation where you convinced her to do *that*. It must've been after the champagne."

"She told you about the champagne?" Zadie frowned. How much did he know? Clearly not *all* there was to know, but Zadie wasn't sure how to respond—did he know about the bar-hopping? Had he talked to Eloise?

"Two glasses and she was hammered. I hope she drinks some on the honeymoon. I'd love to see her with a buzz."

Zadie rolled her eyes, hoping the good people of Turtle Island were ready for the drunken terror known as Helen. She'd heard the Fijians were a large people, so perhaps they'd be able to restrain her.

"I tried not to drink *too* much last night," Grey said. "I figured she'd kill me if I was hungover at the rehearsal dinner."

That's right. Grey had had his bachelor party last night. Maybe he fucked a stripper! Please, God, let him have fucked a stripper!

"How was it?"

Grey shrugged. "Steaks and cigars at Mastro's, then a little trip to Crazy Girls for some lap dances and shitty drinks."

"Did you get one?"

"I tried to get out of it, but it's a little hard when you're the groom. I think I had about five."

Excellent. Five naked women rubbing against his crotch equaled anything that Helen did up until Jimbo's appearance in her hotel room.

"Did you enjoy it?"

"Not really. I told you. I always worry about the girl doing it. There's gotta be some sad story behind it all. It's not like these girls graduate from Wellesley and decide to become strippers for fun."

"Come on—biology has to take over at some point."

He shrugged. "Okay, the third girl was hot. I would've done her if I was a total scumbag."

"But you didn't?"

He looked at her, incredulous. "No, I didn't do her! I'm getting married, remember?" Why, yes, she did remember. Pity the bride didn't.

"By the way, I arranged it so you're walking up the aisle with Mike. Before you complain, he lives in San Diego. Close enough for a relationship, but far enough away to ditch if you don't like him."

On a normal day, Zadie would change the subject. But on a day where she felt like complete and utter shit for letting him down, she opted to humor him.

"This is the Mike from USC who kept his gum in his mouth while he was going down on some girl and got it caught in her pubic hair?"

He looked at her. "I told you that?"

"Yeah . . ."

"Well, don't hold it against him. It was sophomore year. I think his technique has probably improved since then."

"Is he a lawyer?"

"Not everyone I know is a lawyer."

"Is he?"

"Yeah—but still."

"Why's he still single?"

Grey looked at her, incredulous. "Didn't you just tell me last weekend that you became enraged when some guy asked that about *you*?"

"Which is exactly why I need to ask it about them."

Grey pulled into the Saks parking lot, leaving the car with the valet. As they walked inside, he asked, "You realize you're actually asking me questions about Mike. As if you're considering dating him."

"I can't answer that until I meet him."

"Normally, you shut me down the minute I mention a setup."

"Well, maybe I'm a little more open these days."

Grey grinned and elbowed her. "Is my wedding inspiring you?"

No, guilt was inspiring her. That and the fact that she was fucked blind last night. Under normal circumstances, she would tell him that, but the fact that Helen had cheated on him during her tryst tainted her story significantly. The guilt overwhelmed the glory.

Once they were at the flask counter, Grey got lost in the details of which leather casing went with which sterling cap. Zadie wandered over to the crystal goblets and checked her messages on her cell phone, half expecting Helen to call with an apology or an excuse or even a threat. She had "no new messages at this time." Helen was probably in the shower, trying to wash the stench of Jimbo and his Chaps off her before the rehearsal. Was she actually going to show up with a smiling innocent face and pretend like nothing had happened? As far as Helen knew, no one suspected anything. The bitch might actually pull it off.

Grey paid for his eight flasks and they left to go pick up his tux. He'd bought it and had it tailored, figuring that Helen would have plenty of Orange County black-tie affairs for him to attend in the coming years. Even though she was moving in with him in Westwood, she couldn't be expected to leave behind her social circle and Junior League events. Grey was more than willing to be her arm candy.

The tailor, an elderly Korean man with a comb-over, made Grey try the tux on one last time to make sure he had the hem right. He looked up at Zadie. "You sister?"

Grey laughed and winked at her. "Yes, she's my sister."

And that was it. There was no way she could ever tell him now.

At Sav-On, Zadie had to look away when they passed the condom aisle. What if Jimbo hadn't worn one? Helen could be infected with God-only-knows-what. Drunken tourist cooties at the very least.

She instead focused on picking out sufficient sunscreen for Grey's Irish-German complexion. As she tossed the bottles into his basket, she warned, "Don't forget your butt crack when you're on the nude beaches. I fell asleep face down and naked on my balcony once, and it looked like I had diaper rash for a week." Having Jack laugh at her while she rubbed aloe vera gel into her crack had only made the situation worse.

When they finally got back to Grey's house, he showed her the suit he was wearing to the rehearsal. "Is this okay?"

She looked at him. "You have never—in the entire time I've known you—asked for my opinion on your clothes."

"I know, but this is important."

Given the fact that Grey dressed far better than Zadie did, she had to chalk it up to his being nervous. Nervous because he was in love and about to marry the girl of his dreams. Who was, as it turned out, a skanky ho.

She looked at the suit. "It's perfect."

He sat down on the edge of his bed. "In twenty-four hours, I'll have a wife. Thank you, by the way."

"For what?" Zadie asked.

"If I'd never met you, I would never have met Helen. My life would be totally different right now."

Yes, Zadie thought. He might be engaged to a nice girl who didn't cheat and he might have a best friend who wasn't such an asshole.

He reached over and squeezed her hand. "I owe you."

Zadie squeezed it back. "No you don't."

thirty-eight

Zadie got home by four and had time to take a one-hour nap before she had to get ready for the rehearsal. Given that she'd gone to bed at four-thirty in the morning and woken up at eleven, the nap was not an indulgence. It was a necessity. In fact, it was crucial to her very existence.

But tired as she was, she could only lie there feeling the weight of her knowledge. If she'd only gotten into the elevator with Trevor and gone home without checking on Helen, she would never have known about Jimbo. She would be peaceful in the belief that Helen was merely a liar and former slut. She could live with that.

When her alarm went off, Zadie had yet to close her eyes. She got up, reshowered to remove the stink of hangover sweat, and put on a black cocktail dress, as per the instructions on the invitation. God forbid she disobey the world's worst bride.

When she got to the Beverly Hills Hotel she left her car with the same valet who had called her a cab at three in the morning. He gave her a friendly nod and a grin, realizing that she probably wasn't feeling tip-top, and took her Camry into the garage to park it as far away from the Bentleys as possible.

The rehearsal was in the garden, where the wedding was to be held. Little white lights were strung everywhere. Perfect Beverly Hills flowers were blooming in abundance. There was surely a swan somewhere nearby.

When Zadie walked out, Gilda squealed and gave her a hug. "How was it?"

At first, Zadie was confused. Consumed with guilt as she was, she'd forgotten that the last time she'd seen Gilda she was on her way up to a hotel room with Trevor.

Zadie smiled and blushed, relieved to be able to tell someone. "It was exactly what I needed." A waiter passed by with a tray, offering them flutes of champagne. Hair of the dog. They took them and sipped greedily.

Jane scurried over and immediately began quizzing her. "Was he as yummy as he looked?" Jane asked.

"He was, indeed, severely yummy," Zadie said. She felt somewhat guilty for describing sweet Trevor in such ridiculously demeaning terms, but since she was half afraid that he was sitting on a surfboard somewhere telling his buddies about her "killer rack," she let it go.

She looked around at the crowd, spotting Betsy over in the corner, chatting up Helen's parents. Denise and her husband were trying to convince Grandma Davis that she didn't need to wear a gardenia in her cleavage.

"Has anyone seen Helen?" Zadie asked.

"She's talking to the minister," Jane said.

If there was anyone in the world who should be talking to a minister right now, it was Helen, so Zadie felt somewhat appeased by this. Perhaps he could exorcise her.

She spotted Grey over by the gazebo. Eloise had pulled him aside for a hushed conversation. Was she telling him about Deep? And the mechanical bull? And Mr. Lovepants? If Grey found out about all the other sordid events of the evening, then perhaps he would dump Helen based on that information alone and wouldn't ever have to know that Helen had cheated on him! Brilliant!

As Zadie got closer to Grey and Eloise, she could hear their conversation.

"Wait until you see what Helen bought for your wedding night," Eloise said. "You're going to die."

Eloise wasn't telling him jackshit.

Zadie walked up to join them. "Hi. What's going on?"

Eloise gave her a meaningful look. "I was just telling Grey about Helen's lingerie trousseau."

"Yep." Zadie nodded. "It's a doozy." She looked at Eloise. "Can you come to the ladies' room with me? I think my bra strap broke and I might need some help."

Eloise was the last of all possible women in the current ten-mile radius that Zadie would ever ask to help with a bra strap situation, but she knew Grey wouldn't question their powwow if she couched it as a girly problem.

"Sure," Eloise said. "Let's go."

Once they were in the ladies' room and sure that no one else was present, Zadie quizzed her. "Did you tell him anything about last night?"

"Nothing. I had a long talk with Helen this morning and she assured me it was all one big drunken blur and that it would never happen again. What happened at the bachelorette party stays at the bachelorette party."

Zadie frowned. This was not the answer she wanted to hear. For once, she thought Eloise's tendency to gossip and overexaggerate would come in handy.

"You realize this is your brother's future happiness we're discussing? You're really going to jeopardize that for some misguided sense of female bonding?"

"I don't see you telling him."

"I was hoping *you* would. You're his sister."

"You're his 'best friend.'"

Goddamn her. Zadie briefly considered telling her about Jimbo's late-night visit to Helen's room. Would she become irate and instantly march over to tell Grey? Or would she somehow find a way to blame it on Zadie? Either way, Zadie still couldn't stand the thought of Grey having to hear those words.

"Besides," Eloise said, "she didn't actually do anything all *that* bad."

Sure. Except for having anal sex with a stranger.

Back in the garden, Zadie was ambushed by her parents. "How was girls' night?" her mom asked.

"It was—great."

"You look beautiful, kiddo." Her dad kissed her on the cheek.

"Thanks, Dad." They stood there staring at each other, the inevitable uncomfortable silence looming over them.

"I bet it felt good to get out of the house," Mavis said. "Maybe you should be looking for some single friends to go out with so you can do it more often." Zadie knew her mother was encouraging this not because she wanted her to forge new friendships, but because she wanted Zadie to take part in weekly organized manhunts.

"Zadie, this is Mike."

Zadie turned around to find Grey and Mike standing behind her. Mike was cute. More than cute. He had cheekbones. Good ones. And brown-gold eyes with thick Italian-looking lashes. For some reason, he looked vaguely familiar. As he held out his hand, Zadie realized he was the broad-shouldered guy in the green shirt from the engagement party. The one she'd been too agitated to check out.

"Grey tells me I get to walk up the aisle with you at the end of the ceremony. I'll try not to trip you."

"I'll try not to fall over anything." Okay, not her best attempt at humor, but it was a stab. She was preoccupied, dammit.

"Zadie teaches English," Grey told him. "Maybe she can finally teach you how to pronounce 'affidavit.'" He looked at Zadie. "He says it 'affadavid' every time."

Mike smiled at her. "Have you ever noticed how annoying Grey is?"

"More than once," Zadie answered, smiling back at him.

"We'll let you kids talk," Mavis said, winking at Zadie as she steered Sam away.

Eloise, realizing that an attractive man was completely ignoring her presence, walked up and made herself known. "Hi, I'm Eloise. Remember? We met at Grey's graduation party?"

Mike squinted, trying to remember, then got a stricken look as the memory of Eloise washed over him. "Right . . . I definitely remember you."

The minister waved everyone over to find their places and line up for the rehearsal.

"Here we go—" Grey said, looking nervous.

Mike looked at Zadie. "I'll see you over there."

As the men walked away, Eloise leaned in close to Zadie. "Don't even bother. He's gay. I tried to have sex with him at Grey's graduation and he wanted nothing to do with me."

And at that exact point, Mike became the perfect man.

thirty-nine

As they lined up to do their practice run down the aisle, Zadie was placed in sixth position. In front of her were Eloise, Jane, Gilda, Marci, and Kim. Betsy was behind her. Denise was matron of honor, so she went last. Thankfully, Snotty and Skinny were not in the wedding party. They'd merely been along on the bachelorette festivities because they were coworkers.

Betsy leaned forward and whispered to Zadie. "I feel like crap. How about you?"

"Crappier," Zadie told her.

"How is it possible that Helen looks beautiful after a night like that?"

"She's a genetic mutant."

"I should thank you," Betsy said. "I know I was opposed to the whole drinking thing at first, but honestly? Last night was a blast."

Zadie gave a halfhearted high five to Betsy over her shoulder, and bent down to adjust the strap on her Payless sling-backs as Pachelbel's Canon in E started.

Eloise started down the aisle, doing the one step, pause, one step, pause. Grey was standing at the altar made of pink roses and eucalyptus leaves. Beaming at all of them. Having no idea that his bride-to-be was walking a little funnier than usual.

. . .

Once they got to the rehearsal dinner on the outside patio of the Polo Lounge, the very same Polo Lounge where Skinny had been indoctrinated into her new profession, Helen finally approached Zadie.

"I know you must think I'm a terrible person for everything that happened last night, but I really appreciate your not mentioning any of it to Grey."

Helen had no idea that Zadie had heard what she'd heard outside the bridal suite at three in the morning. She was merely speaking of the other unsavory details.

"I told you, Helen, it's up to you to tell him." Could she possibly guilt Helen into confessing?

"Maybe someday I will. But now is definitely not the time." She grabbed both of Zadie's hands and looked at her with big, imploring eyes. "You know how much I love Grey. And I swear to you I will never do anything to hurt him. What happened in Cancún isn't important. And what happened last night isn't important. All that's important is that I would die for Grey. I would seriously lie down and die for him. And I need you to know that."

Days of Our Lives should hire Helen immediately, Zadie thought. That was quite a performance. Cheeseball and heartfelt at the same time. She could outact Jack any day.

"I'm going to hold you to that," Zadie told her. "If you hurt him, I might have to kill you. I don't care if we're related."

"And I respect you for that. You're a good friend to him."

Yes, she was such a good friend that she was letting Grey marry a woman who potentially had the semen of another man still lurking in her body. Zadie was the best friend ever.

As everyone sat down to enjoy their salmon or New York strip, Zadie plopped herself down next to Mike, hoping that a little harmless flirtation could take her mind off the fact that she was a wretched, wretched person.

He turned and smiled at her. "Did I do okay with the whole sticking-my-elbow-out-for-you-to-hold-on-to thing? I know that's a tricky maneuver, and I don't have a lot of practice at it."

"You mean you haven't had the pleasure of being in a wedding party before?"

"Only six or seven times, but honestly, it's not enough to get that move down right. It takes some finesse."

"I'd give you a seven point five."

"Excellent. I'll take it."

"So, how was the bachelor party? I hear there were women with low morals involved." She could've been talking about half of the girls at the bachelorette party, herself included, but she left that detail out.

"There were a few ladies who weren't shy about their nudity, this is true."

"Did you get a lap dance?"

Mike blushed. "I cannot lie. I got two. And now you find me repulsive, so I'll just move down and sit with the other degenerates."

"I think I can handle it. You can stay." Zadie smiled at him. He smiled back. His curly brown hair had little ringlets that she wanted to touch. "How was your dinner at Mastro's? Isn't that where you guys went first?"

"You mean the place where the shrimp is as big as your hand? It was obscene. Gastronomical decadence. Far more perverted than anything we did at Crazy Girls. How about you? What did you all get up to at the bachelorette party?"

"Just good, clean, innocent fun. You know us girls."

He looked at her, clearly thinking she didn't look like the good, clean, innocent type. "Somehow, I doubt that."

Zadie wasn't sure if it was her newfound confidence after her post-Trevor experience, or the fact that she was desperate to distract herself from the marital disaster that was about to happen and her own culpability in the matter, but she accepted his implication that she might be a naughty girl and she took it up a notch.

"Maybe you'll have to give *me* a lap dance later to make up for it."

"I've been known to injure people that way, but if you're game, I do a mean grind to 'Purple Rain.'"

Zadie smiled. This was a healthy flirtation with a viable prospect. Something she hadn't done in years. He was age-appropriate, he was gainfully employed, he used proper grammar, and there was no inference at all on his part that she was defective in any way simply due to her availability. And he was Grey-approved. They could double-date. It made it easier for Zadie to forget about the fact that Helen was the devil when she could picture the four of them at the Hollywood Bowl, listening to a jazz concert and sharing a picnic basket, Mike feeding her hummus on little triangles of pita bread.

"I'll take my chances," Zadie said.

The waiter set their entrees down in front of them. They both got salmon. Destiny? Zadie was disgusted with herself for letting the word "destiny" pop into her head two nights in a row. She was definitely not a "destiny" type of girl. Destiny was merely an excuse to misbehave last night. What would Mike think if he knew that she'd had sex with a nineteen-year-old last night? He would surely be horrified.

Zadie blotted the corners of her mouth with her pink cloth napkin. "Can I ask you something, Mike?"

"Sure."

"What's the most disgustingly heinous thing you've ever done?"

"Do you have all night?" he asked.

"Possibly."

"Well . . ." He thought for a minute. "There was the whole eating seventeen hard-boiled eggs in a row when I was pledging, but I'd have to say it was that I had sex with my sister's best friend."

"That's not so bad," Zadie said.

"On their prom night."

"Were you her date?" she asked.

"No, I was their driver. I dropped her date off first, and then I nailed her. She wanted to and all, don't get me wrong—"

"How old were you?"

"Twenty-five."

And at that moment, Zadie knew what destiny truly meant.

forty

When Grey stood up to give a toast, Zadie's whole body tensed, knowing he was toasting a girl who didn't exist.

"Okay, everyone, here's where I get all sappy." The table became quiet, waiting to hear what platitudes of love Grey had conjured for the occasion. "As you all know, I only met Helen six months ago, at Denise's wedding." He nodded toward Denise and Jeff, who were arguing over whether Denise should eat his dessert as well as hers. "Of course, I was immediately struck by her beauty." Helen blushed and smiled. "But, as I got to know her, I was struck by her inner beauty as well. Never had I met someone so pure and so good and so genuinely loving to everyone around her."

If only he knew how loving she'd been to Jimbo, Zadie thought.

"When I asked her to marry me, she teared up, which made her eyes shine even more, and she said yes in a way that I'd never heard sound so beautiful. So I ask you all to raise a glass to the fact that I am so damn lucky."

Helen immediately began sobbing. She stood up and hugged Grey, then kissed him in a way that was both chaste and incredibly romantic.

As the entire table held their glasses high and congratulated Helen and Grey, Zadie was relieved that she hadn't said anything.

Grey was truly in love. She could never be the one to take that away from him.

As the wedding party and all of the relatives trickled out into the lobby, saying their goodbyes until tomorrow, when the blessed event would occur, Zadie got a chill.

"Helen, can I talk to you?"

It was Jimbo. He was sitting in one of the rose-colored velvet chairs under the mammoth chandelier and he got up as soon as he saw Helen walk in.

"Oh, shit," Zadie said.

Mike looked at her. "What's wrong?"

Zadie walked closer, hoping she could somehow diffuse the situation with her proximity.

Helen looked at Jim with a vague sense of confusion, then recognition, then annoyance. "Jim?"

He grabbed her hands. "Before you go through with this wedding tomorrow, I just had to tell you that I felt a real connection with you last night and I could never forgive myself if I didn't take one last shot."

Jimbo had a set of 'nads. That's for sure. Zadie had to give him that. But she wasn't going to. "I think you should leave," she told him.

The other members of the wedding party began to notice what was going on. There were frowns and worried tones.

Gilda frowned. "Isn't that—"

"I think it is," Jane said.

When Eloise spotted him, she turned red with rage. "What the hell are you doing?"

Betsy concurred, marching over and getting right in Jim's face. "Didn't you get the hint last night when we ditched you? Helen is getting married. She has no interest in you."

"I just want to hear that from her."

Grey walked up, stopping a conversation with Helen's mom midstream when he noticed the ruckus. "Who the hell is this guy?" No one replied. He looked at Zadie. "Is someone going to answer me?"

"We met him last night," Zadie said. "At a bar."

"And he shows up at our wedding rehearsal?"

Jimbo looked at Grey. "I mean you no disrespect, but I happened to fall in love with your bride last night and I had to come by and see if we were meant to be."

"You're meant to get your ass kicked, I can assure you of that." Grey was purple. Zadie had never seen him so angry. As his groomsmen—lawyers ever mindful of an assault charge—held Grey back, Jimbo tried to explain.

"It was a moment we shared that I've never felt before. I'm sorry. I just have to know."

Betsy started pushing him toward the door. "Stalker!"

Helen's father agreed, looking around for security. "Can someone get this man out of here? I'm paying a fortune for my daughter to get married in this hotel and she's being harassed by some lunatic."

Jimbo was unapologetic. "I'm just a man in love."

"You're disgusting is what you are," Eloise told him.

Grey looked at Helen. "What the hell was this 'moment'?"

Zadie tensed, preparing for the worst. But Helen merely looked baffled. "I talked to him for maybe twenty minutes at the Sky Bar. I have no idea what he's talking about."

"We had that dance at Deep. Don't tell me you forgot about that," Jimbo said.

Grey was confused. "You went to Deep?"

Helen glared at Jimbo. "So, I danced with you. That gives you the right to try and ruin my wedding?"

Jimbo looked at Helen. "You can deny the night all you want, but I'm in love with you," he said, completely matter-of-fact.

Helen looked at Grey again. "I swear I have no idea what he's talking about. I *just* met him last night. All we did was talk and dance."

"I know," Grey said, as he put his arm around her protectively.

The relatives in the group stood there buzzing. How could something this sordid happen at sweet Helen's rehearsal dinner?

As security finally showed up to remove Jimbo from the premises, he made one last attempt. "If we weren't meant to be, then why did you give me the key to your hotel room?"

The room grew silent. Even the security guards paused. Zadie's stomach knotted up with dread.

"I did no such thing!" Helen said.

"I still have it in my wallet."

"You are a disgusting liar!" Helen said.

"I can prove it," he said, pulling out her room key. He held it up for all to see.

There was a gasp, followed by an incredibly large silence that filled the room. Betsy was the first to think on her feet. "That could be the key to any room in this hotel."

"There's an easy way to find out." He marched over to the registration desk and asked them to swipe it.

The registration clerk looked up at them all, mortified. "Bridal suite."

Zadie's head was ringing with panic. She just wanted to get Grey out of there. She didn't want him to have to hear this.

"He could've stolen it," Denise offered. "He was completely feeling her up on the dance floor." Marci and Kim nodded in agreement.

"His hands were all over her," Marci said.

"He could've taken it out of her pocket, when he was groping her butt," Kim offered.

Helen was now crying. "I can't believe this is happening."

Grey was pale. "Can someone please tell me what the hell is going on?" he asked, looking at Zadie as if she could clear everything up.

Her every instinct told her to make up some charming, witty story as to how this buffoon ended up with Helen's room key, so they could all laugh about it and go on their merry way. But she couldn't do it. This was the moment she should come clean. She knew it. As much as she wanted to protect Grey's feelings, there was no way she could let Helen stand here and lie to his face when the truth was so obvious. She sighed and stepped forward.

"He came by her room after we put her to bed. I heard them having sex from out in the hall around three in the morning."

"What??!" Helen shrieked. "You did not!"

"Believe me, I wish I hadn't."

The rest of the room was too stunned to even gasp. They all looked at Zadie as if she'd just announced that Helen was an al Qaeda operative.

Grey shook his head, confused. "Helen was at my house at three in the morning. She took a cab over from the hotel around two."

Now Zadie was confused. "Then who the hell was in her room screwing Jimbo?"

Eloise raised her hand. "That would be me. I saw him in the hallway and one thing led to another." She shrugged, embarrassed, but not nearly as embarrassed as she should have been. Her parents were in the room, for God's sake. Looking completely mortified.

"So, let me get this straight," Grey said, glaring at Jim. "You showed up to screw my fiancée, but settled for screwing my sister instead?"

"Well, I hate to say it, but yes, that's pretty accurate. I'm a man with a libido and the opportunity presented itself."

"Go to hell, Southern boy, no one settles for me." Leave it to Eloise to make this situation about her.

Jimbo looked back to Helen. "I wish you hadn't had to hear that, Helen. I came to that room for you."

Grey's groomsmen were itching to rip Jim's face off. Bill, the best man, nodded to the security guards that now was the time to take him away. As they dragged him off, Jimbo yelled, "I'm only guilty of love, Helen."

Grey looked at Helen, still confused. "You let him feel you up and then you gave him your key?"

"No!" she sobbed. "I mean, I don't remember *everything* from last night, but I'm sure I didn't—why would I . . ." She trailed off. Then turned to glare at Zadie. "If Zadie hadn't insisted we start drinking, then none of this would've happened."

And there you had it. What Zadie had known would happen all along. It was all her fault. As relieved as she was to hear that Helen *hadn't* let Jimbo violate her, she was enraged that any blame for her potential violation was now squarely upon her shoulders.

"*I* didn't hand him your key, you did—" Zadie said. Perhaps not the most tactful display she could imagine, but the situation had gone far beyond civilized. She knew Mike and her parents were somewhere in the crowd thinking less of her, but that was the least of her concerns at the moment.

Helen's father stepped up, looking around at the rest of the family. "Why don't we all head to the bar and have a much-needed drink while the kids sort this out?"

The old people in the group made a beeline for the bar, leaving just the wedding party in the lobby. Helen again pointed at Zadie, looking up at Grey. "She said you wanted me to loosen up. That you didn't like me the way I was. So I got drunk." She looked at Zadie. "Are you happy now?"

Oh, yes. Zadie was incredibly happy. Bursting with pride. Her best friend was devastated and her cousin was dissolving in a puddle of tears. This was a banner day.

"It's true," Eloise said. "Zadie encouraged her."

"We all encouraged her," Jane said, glaring at Eloise.

Grey closed his eyes, trying to make sense of all this. "You gave some guy your room key two nights before we're getting married?"

Helen just cried in response. "I don't remember."

"How much did you have to drink?"

"Quite a bit," Betsy answered for her.

Grey looked at Helen. "Well, Christ, maybe you screwed a couple guys on the way over to my place and don't remember that either."

Denise put a hand on Grey's arm. "Okay, we all just need to calm down."

"She gave a guy her room key!" Grey shouted. He looked at Zadie before he walked out. "Thanks for making sure Helen had fun."

forty-one

The wedding did not take place. The calla lily bouquets were sent back. The seared ahi on sourdough squares were never passed around. The Taittinger did not flow.

Grey could not quite get over the fact that Helen had been so free and easy with her virtue mere hours before their wedding. And he couldn't quite get over the fact that Zadie was complicit in the evening that caused such a breakdown in trust. He wouldn't return Zadie's calls. Her many, many calls. She dialed his number at least fifty times on the day the wedding was supposed to take place, but there was no answer. She drove by his house, but he wasn't there. She even drove down to Bolsa Chica to look for him on the waves, but there was no sign of him.

She called Helen a few times, but she wouldn't come to the phone.

Zadie felt like shit.

She was a bad friend. She was a bad cousin. She was a bad teacher. In one night, she'd managed to fuck up her entire world.

Tuesday at school, she just went through the motions: listening to the report on Nancy's Saturday night date with Darryl, trading her protein bar for one of Dolores's Rice Krispies Treats, handing out quizzes on Joyce Carol Oates. All was the picture of normal mediocrity, until sixth period, when Trevor walked in and sat down in the first row.

"Hey." He grinned at her.

Zadie immediately tensed at the sight of him and stared at her desk. "Hello, Trevor. How are you?" Faced with the reality of her actions under severe fluorescent lighting, her entire body stung with shame. He was a student. In her class. And he had been inside of her.

"I'm good," he said. She couldn't decide if he was referring to his demeanor or his sexual prowess. She looked up for an instant and noticed that he gave her his best sex-filled look, trying to remind her of the pleasure that could be hers again.

The bell rang again and the rest of the class filed in and sat down. Zadie leaned against the edge of her desk in front of them. "Did everyone have a good Memorial Day weekend?" As her students murmured their answers—ranging from "Hell, yeah" to "It sucked"—she noticed that Trevor winked at her. She ignored it and went on to discuss the social mores inherent in *Pride and Prejudice*. When the end-of-class bell rang and the students shuffled out, eyes glazed over from her less than well-planned lecture, she saw Trevor throw a piece of paper onto her desk. After the last student left, she unfolded it. It was his cell phone number.

Just last week the problem had been that she wanted to fuck Trevor. Now the problem was that she didn't want to fuck Trevor *again*. The fact that she'd lived out her fantasy and then some was shocking, shameful, and immensely gratifying. But there was no way she could condone a repeat performance. A drunken slip on an incredibly difficult night was one thing, but for her to indulge her urges again was unconscionable.

And truthfully, she had no desire to sleep with Trevor again. The fantasy had been fulfilled. It didn't take a shrink to realize she'd fixated on him because he wasn't a viable option. There was no conceivable way she could have a relationship with Trevor.

She looked down at the phone number in her hand and

frowned. Was he saying "Let's go for another tumble," or was he saying "Be my girlfriend"? Trevor didn't think they were dating, did he? That would be bad. Very, very bad.

After her last class, she stopped in the ladies' room. She didn't normally use the student bathrooms, but her last Diet Coke was urgently trying to get out of her. As she was washing her hands, she heard a girl crying in the last stall. She waited a moment, then knocked on the stall door.

"Everything okay?" A stupid question. Obviously everything was far from okay.

She got some sniffles in reply and a quiet "I'm fine."

Zadie frowned. "Amy?"

"What?"

"It's Ms. Roberts. Are you all right?"

Amy pushed open the door to reveal that she was sitting on the toilet, lid down, sobbing into a big wad of toilet paper. "I'm just totally bummed out."

"What happened?"

Amy sighed, wiping her tears away with the sleeve of her soc-cer uniform. "Friday night at Belinda Matthews's party I *finally* made out with Trevor."

Oh, God. Zadie had a feeling she knew where this was going.

"I've been in love with him for, like, *ever,* like I seriously want to marry him, and after Friday, I totally thought we had a shot at being a couple. He said he'd call me this week and everything. And then he tells me at lunch that he met someone else." Amy burst into tears again, blowing her nose into the giant wad.

Zadie paled. The fact that Trevor was breaking poor Amy's heart for *her* was beyond mortifying.

She pulled some fresh toilet paper off the roll and handed Amy a new wad. "Maybe it'll be a short-lived crush and then you two can pick up where you left off."

"Doubtful. He sounded like he was in love with her or some-thing."

"I'm sure he's not," Zadie said. "Just give it some time."

Amy glanced up at her, looking slightly confused as to how Zadie could presume to make assertions about Trevor's capacity for love. "I hope you're right. Because I seriously love him."

Zadie held the stall door open as Amy gathered her bookbag and made her way out, wiping her eyes. "I just hope it wasn't one of those slutty older girls that were at his show on Saturday. They kept trying to get up in front so they could touch him. You should've seen them. They had on these shiny halter tops and stilettos—they looked like hookers."

Snotty and Skinny. It took all the strength Zadie had not to blurt "One of them actually *is* a hooker now." But she refrained, counting her blessings that Amy hadn't spotted *her* at the concert. All she needed was a catfight in the girls' room to make her week complete.

When she got out to her car, she checked her watch. Three-thirty. Still plenty of time to make it to Grey's office. She'd called his assistant during lunch and found out that he'd come to work, but was in a really, really bad mood. Go figure. Zadie thought that if she showed up there, they could have a conversation without him yelling too loud. It was a chicken-shit move and she knew it, but she had to talk to him.

As she pulled out of her parking spot, she heard a slap against her window that made her jump in her seat and slam on the brakes. It was Trevor, on his skateboard, wheeling up alongside of her.

She unrolled the window. "I could've hit you, you know."

"You would never hit me." He grinned.

"I have to go. A friend of mine is very upset."

"Who? Your friend that got ripped off?"

Zadie was confused. One of her friends got ripped off? When?

"That girl with the strap-on. Some guy was going through her purse while you were yelling at her at Deep. I lost him in the crowd before I could do anything. I meant to tell you when I saw you later, but I spaced."

Jimbo. It had to be Jimbo. He *had* stolen the key. That fucker!

"Was he a big guy with a red face?"

"Yeah. With, like, nineties hair."

Now she couldn't get to Grey fast enough.

"I'll see you tomorrow, okay?" She put her car in drive. "And thanks. For telling me that. It fixes a lot of problems." She waved and drove off, leaving him standing there watching her go.

She dialed Helen from the car. "You didn't give him the key. He stole it. Trevor saw him."

"Who's this?"

"Oh, sorry, Aunt Carol. Is Helen there? It's Zadie."

"She doesn't want to talk to you, Zadie."

"She will when you tell her the thing about the key."

"Hold on."

After about thirty seconds, Helen picked up the phone, her voice a hopeful little tremble. "Trevor saw him steal it?"

"He just told me. I'm on my way to tell Grey."

"Oh, my God! Do you think he'll take me back?"

"I don't know. I just wanted you to know that you didn't solicit that idiot hillbilly."

"Call me after you talk to Grey."

"I will."

Zadie hung up and turned right onto Sunset, heading toward Century City. She could kiss Trevor for telling her this news.

But of course she wouldn't.

forty-two

Grey's office was on the twelfth floor of a high-rise. From the window in the lobby, you could see the Hollywood sign against the hill in the distance. On smogfree days, you could see snow-capped mountains to the east. There were perhaps three or four of these days each year.

The model-wannabe receptionist asked her to wait on the brown leather couch while she called Mr. Dillon to see if he was available. After a few seconds, she hung up the phone and told Zadie, "I'm sorry, he's in a meeting right now."

"Can you call him back and tell him that I have a witness who will testify that the room key was stolen from the party in question?"

The receptionist picked up the phone and called Grey again, relaying the message. She hung up and looked up at Zadie. "Mr. Dillon will be with you in a moment."

Grey walked into the lobby a minute later. "Why are you here?"

Zadie gestured to the receptionist. "She just told you."

"Come into my office so no one can see when I throw my coffee at you."

Zadie stood up to follow, betting that he wouldn't *actually* hurl any hot beverages at her once he heard the whole story.

He shut the door behind him once they were inside his cherry wood and brass filled office. "Now, what the hell are you talking about?"

"First of all, where the hell have you been? I called you like a hundred times. I even drove down to Bolsa."

"I've been a little upset, Zadie. That happens when your wedding doesn't. Remember?"

Yes, she remembered. But she spent the days after her wedding didn't happen crying and vomiting at Grey's house. She felt bad that she wasn't providing him with the same service. Of course, he was furious with her, so that changed things somewhat.

"And you're not exactly the person I want to see the most right now," he added. "When I told you to make sure Helen had a good time, I didn't mean get her shit-faced and let her come on to other guys."

"She didn't give him the key. He stole it out of her purse. I have a witness."

"Who? Betsy? I'm not buying it. She tried to tell me she gave the key to that asshole herself so that I'd take Helen back." Wow, Zadie thought. Betsy was a good friend.

"It's not Betsy, it's Trevor."

"Who the hell is Trevor?"

"My student."

Grey frowned, confused. "The one you want to screw?"

Clearly, Zadie didn't have time to go into that story now, so she skipped over the details. "He was there. He saw Jimbo go into her purse and take the key."

"He told you this?"

"Yes, he just told me, just now, after school."

"So, this guy is hitting on her all night, then he goes into her purse and takes her room key?"

"Yes."

"I'm gonna fucking kill him."

"I'll help you."

"What about his hands all over her ass and the whole feeling-her-up thing?"

"That happened, too. But let me remind you that you got five lap dances. At least she wasn't *paying* him to feel her up."

Grey thought about this. "You've got a point." He sat down on the edge of his desk. "I just can't believe any of this happened. It's not the Helen I know. I have no idea who that version of Helen is."

"Well, guess what, your girlfriend isn't perfect after all. But she's still in love with you even though you dumped her the day before your wedding."

"I thought she gave that guy her key! Christ, you thought she'd fucked him! Don't even get me started on that. We spent the whole day together and it never occurred to you to bring that up?"

"Well, it's a good thing I didn't since it wasn't true."

"You didn't know that at the time."

Zadie sighed. "All I could think about that entire day was telling you. But you were so excited and so in love, I didn't want to take that away from you."

"So if I'd thought that Jack screwed some stripper the night before your wedding, you wouldn't have wanted me to tell you?"

"Well, given how everything turned out, it really wouldn't have mattered, would it?"

"Answer the question."

Zadie picked up a paperweight off Grey's desk. It was shaped like a reel of film. "Maybe an anonymous note would've been good."

"So, you would've wanted to know." He said it as if she were on trial and he was gloating to the jury.

"No, I wouldn't have *wanted* to know that. Who would want to know that?"

"You would've let me marry a girl—a girl you don't even like—thinking that she'd slept with another guy the night before?"

"I think we've pretty much established that. Until I saw her lying to your face—or so I thought—I wasn't going to say anything. I didn't want to be the one to break your heart. Maybe that makes me selfish, maybe that makes me a complete shit, maybe that makes you hate me, but that was a risk I was willing to take to not have to see you go through the pain I knew it would cause you."

Grey stared at the floor. Zadie couldn't tell if he was agreeing that she was a complete shit, or if he was appreciating the sentiment behind her complete shitness. He looked up at her. "What else happened that night?"

"You heard the worst of it. We saw some strippers, but they were gay. According to your sister, that doesn't count."

"Great, so Helen saw a bunch of naked men?"

Zadie sighed and gave him a look. "If you're going to sit there and tell me that you're jealous of some guy named Mr. Lovepants, then you've got bigger problems than I thought."

Grey didn't answer. He slumped down on the couch. "It all happened so fast—our whole relationship—when I found out that she wasn't who I thought she was, it just seemed like the whole thing was a lie."

"I can understand that," Zadie said. She'd known he would feel this way. Anyone would feel that way. When she'd found out that Jack was a thoughtless prick instead of an adoring fiancé, it negated every good moment they'd ever had together. "Why don't you just talk to her and see if there's any version of the Helen you know now that you can still live with? I know you're still in love with her. C'mon, you thought it was cute that she got drunk before you found out about the dildos and the redneck."

"The dildos?!" Grey looked stricken.

Zadie frowned, forgetting that he hadn't heard about that part of the evening. "It was an inflatable dildo. It went with the blow-up doll. They were party favors. We bought them at the Hustler store when she was buying lingerie for you."

Grey calmed down a bit. "Have you talked to her?"

"I talked to her before I came over here. She's been in bed crying for two days."

"Really?"

Zadie looked at him, incredulous. "Where did you think she would be?"

"I don't know—out with Mr. We Had a Moment."

Jesus, men were stupid. "Yes, Grey, as soon as you stomped out of the hotel, Helen fell into his arms and they've been partying it up in the bridal suite ever since. And they charged it all to you."

He gave her a "very funny" look, then started hooking together his paper clips. "I should probably call her."

"Yes, you should probably call her."

He looked up from his paper-clip chain. "Why are you doing this? Trying to get us back together? You never wanted us to get married to begin with."

"I never said that."

"Maybe not out loud . . ."

This was true. She'd been pissed off during their entire engagement, and here she was fighting to get them to reunite. "Because I want you to be happy, Grey. And you were happy when you were with Helen." See? Maybe she wasn't such a selfish shit after all. In fact, helping to ensure the happiness of others was far more satisfying than dwelling on her own lack of it. Being a saint was a much better gig than being a martyr. "And for your information there were some moments on Saturday night, when Helen was drunk, where I genuinely liked her." She stood up to go. "I'm leaving now, so you can call her."

"I was in San Diego, by the way. At Mike's. He liked you. He wants to see you again."

Zadie took her hand off the doorknob and turned, intrigued by this bit of news. "Really . . . ?"

"I told him you were a complete bitch and that he shouldn't bother."

"Well, all right then." She opened the door to head out. Grey called after her.

"I'm kidding. I told him I was too mad to talk about you and that he should ask me again when I didn't want to kill you."

"Well, you let me know when that day comes."

When Zadie pulled out of the parking garage, she immediately dialed Helen. "Has he called you yet?"

"He's on the other line."

"You have to promise me one thing. Tell him about Cancún. Not today, but eventually."

Helen sounded stricken. "Why?"

"Helen . . ."

"Okay. I'll tell him."

She clicked back over and Zadie hung up. If they were starting over, Grey needed to have all the facts. Clearly, the Cancún wasn't out of Helen's system.

forty-three

When Zadie walked into her apartment, she felt like celebrating. Love was being restored. Always an excuse for a glass of wine. She opened a bottle of pinot noir and dialed Dorian's phone number.

Dorian answered after three rings. "You're calling during dinner. I'm burning the Spaghetti-O's."

"I had sex and I met a guy that I can date."

"Are these mutually exclusive items?" Dorian asked.

"Yes."

"Hold on, I'm opening some wine. We need to toast this momentous occasion."

"I've already got mine poured," Zadie said.

"Which guy do I want to hear about first?"

"The date potential. His name is Mike and he's a lawyer."

"I like him. Who was the lucky roll in the hay?"

"Trevor."

"And do I get to hear any details about Trevor?"

"He's a model."

"Keep going . . ."

"That's pretty much it. It was just a one-time thing." Zadie sat down on her couch, which was luckily devoid of cat prints now that she'd put up a CLOSE THE FUCKING DOOR sign on her sliding glass door to remind herself.

"How do you know it's just a one-time thing?" Dorian asked.

"Because I'm not sleeping with him again."

"Is this your choice or his?"

"Mine."

"Am I allowed to ask why?"

"No."

"Tiny penis?"

Ha. Hardly. "He's nineteen," Zadie said, figuring that she might as well tell her best friend, since she'd already spilled the beans to Gilda and Jane.

"Oh, my God. Please tell me he was one of your students so I can call Lifetime and tell them they have a new movie."

"You were the one who told me Dan had sex with his teacher!"

"Holy shit, he *is* your student. I love it!"

Zadie was amazed that her moral turpitude was so widely embraced by all of her friends. What did this say about them? Of course, she'd chosen her audience wisely. She was sure her shrink, her mother, and the school board would have quite a different reaction.

"You are sworn to secrecy. If I hear this back from anyone else, you're never getting any gossip ever again."

"Oh, come on. You have to at least let me tell Dan."

"Why would Dan need to know such a thing?"

"Because the most exciting thing he hears from me is what Josh had up his nose this morning. C'mon . . . let me tell him. It'll give us a week's worth of conversation at least," Dorian said.

"You're going to exploit my sex life to make your marriage more interesting?"

"Why do you think I still hang out with you?"

"Fine," Zadie said. "Tell him. God forbid I keep you from an intimate moment of marital bliss where you laugh at what a degenerate I am."

"Was it good?"

"How come you're not asking me anything about Mike?"

There was a knock on Zadie's door. She frowned. Who would knock on her door on a Tuesday night? Could Trevor have found out where she lived? Or was it Grey coming over to report his conversation with Helen?

"Hold on, there's someone at my door." She got up and walked over to look through her peephole. What would she do if it was Trevor? It was just like karma to smack her in the ass for talking about him.

She put her face up to the door and looked out. Every bit of blood in her upper extremities drained out into her feet. "Dorian? I have to call you back." She hung up as autopilot took over her body and she opened the door.

Jack was standing there.

With a rose in his hand.

Smiling at her.

"Hi," he said. Ever the wordsmith.

"Jack." That was all she could muster. What more was she supposed to say? She tried to remember all the scathing things she'd practiced, but none of them came to mind.

"I know this is a little awkward, but I'm hoping we can talk. Can I come in?"

She stared at him for a moment, then stepped back and swung the door open so he could enter. Even though she knew she shouldn't give a crap about anything he had to tell her, she was dying to hear it.

He handed her the rose as he walked in and she set it on the kitchen counter. Deliberately not putting it in water. Fuck his rose.

"New couch. Nice," he said, before he sat down on it and put his feet up on the coffee table. He wasn't wearing leather pants, but he had on a tight Gucci-boy shirt and jeans that cost at least a hundred dollars. He'd been working out too. There wasn't an ounce of fat on him. And his teeth were whiter.

Zadie smacked his feet off her table and sat down on the chair across from him. "Let me guess. You're in a twelve-step program and you've come over to make amends."

Jack frowned. "No . . . what the hell would I be in a twelve-step program for?"

"What the hell would you come over here for?"

"Because I think we have some things to talk about."

"It's taken you seven months to figure that out?" Zadie couldn't believe she was indulging him, but the sad, pathetic part of her was hoping he'd apologize. Not that she'd ever let him see that.

"I admit I did not behave in the best way," Jack said.

"Did your publicist tell you that?"

"Why are you being so sarcastic?"

Jesus. For the second time today, she wondered how men could be so freaking retarded. Maybe she *should* go out with Trevor. He was young. She could mold him. Prevent him from turning out like this. "You're right, Jack. I have no reason at all to be hostile toward you." How's that for sarcasm?

"I've been seeing a therapist, and he's helping me work through some things."

Zadie took a sip of her wine, fortifying herself. "Things like how you didn't bother to show up for our wedding? And things like how I haven't seen you since? Because those are some pretty big things, Jack. I hope you're paying this guy well."

Jack flipped and unflipped the clasp on his watch, trying to avoid eye contact. "I didn't have to come over here tonight, Zadie."

"And I didn't have to let your lame ass in." *Why* was this dickweed sitting on her couch? The couch she bought with her pawned engagement ring.

"I'm sorry. I'm sorry for what I did. Does that make you happy?"

"When you phrase it like that, it makes me ecstatic. What a sincere apology. Did they teach you that in acting class?"

Jack sighed, closing his eyes and leaning his head back on the couch. "I understand that you're angry."

"Do you?"

"I don't blame you. If I were in your position, I'd be angry, too."

He was actually smug enough to validate her anger? Zadie poured herself another glass of wine to keep from hitting him. Her hands were shaking and she spilled a couple drops.

"I should've come over to talk to you after I got back from Vegas," he said.

"You should've shown up at our wedding."

He looked at the floor. "I wasn't ready to get married."

"You picked a great way to tell me."

"I realize that now. But at the time, I didn't know what else to do."

"Maybe a phone call? Before I got to the church and put on the dress? You could've given me a little less distance to fall from."

He started crying. Zadie wasn't sure how to react. She'd never seen him cry in person, but she'd seen him cry on TV. Was he acting now to try and diminish her anger?

"I can't believe I let myself hurt you that way. I loved you."

Zadie sighed and looked out the window. There was cat shit in her cactus pot. "You didn't love me, Jack. If you loved me, you'd never have let me go through the pain of what you did. That's what hurt the most. When I realized that."

She immediately regretted sharing any real feelings with him. He didn't deserve it.

"I did. God, I swear to you, I did. I just couldn't handle it. Everything in my life was changing and I wasn't sure what was real." He stopped crying and wiped his tears away. "But, like I said, I've been to therapy and figured some things out."

Zadie was confused. "Exactly *what* have you figured out?"

"I was genuinely in love with you. I was just scared."

Zadie looked at him. "What am I supposed to do with that, Jack? Applaud your brilliant revelation? Because that really doesn't make me feel any better. I still got left at the altar. You're still the shithead who broke my heart." She was not going to cry, goddammit. She was *not* going to cry.

"I don't want you to feel like you have to do anything. I just want you to consider it."

Zadie's head was ready to explode. "Consider what?"

Jack leaned over and took her hand. "My therapist thinks we should give it another shot."

Zadie stared at him.

Maybe a weaker version of her would have wanted to hear this. Maybe even a version of her as late as last week would have killed to hear these words. Not to act upon them, but simply to relish the irony, the beauty of his retraction in the face of her indifference. But today's version of Zadie had no need for this. Today's version was simply annoyed. She yanked her hand away from him. "I take it back. I hope you're *not* paying this guy well, because clearly he's an idiot."

Her head hurt. She wanted him to leave. She wanted him to leave *now*.

Jack acted confused, as if he couldn't imagine how she wasn't beside herself with happiness at this invitation to renew their brilliant relationship. "Are you seeing someone else?"

It just kept getting more ridiculous.

"Yes, Jack. I'm seeing a shrink who tells me you're the Antichrist. I'm seeing friends who tell me that I should've had you maimed. I'm seeing men on the street that are better than you in every way. I'm seeing plenty of people, and they all make me realize what an ass you are, so get off my couch, get back in your Porsche, and drive over to your therapist and tell him he's wrong. You don't deserve another shot. Unless it's to the head."

"Jesus. You are *really* angry."

"Get off my couch, Jack."

He stood up and walked toward the door. "So, this is it? This is the way we're gonna leave it?"

"This is the way you left it seven months ago. At least I have the decency to say it to your face." She opened the door, gesturing for him to leave. He walked out, turning to look at her once he was outside.

"I really did love you."

"Fuck you."

She shut the door and walked back over to the couch, picking up her glass of wine and dialing Dorian.

"So, where were we?"

forty-four

By Friday, Zadie had been avoiding Trevor as long as she could without incident. The incident happened in the parking lot as she pulled in. He was waiting on the curb.

"What're you doing here? This is where every teacher in school parks." She grabbed her purse and shut the door, looking around to make sure no one had spotted them.

"Why haven't you called me?"

"Why haven't you called Amy?"

He looked at her like she was high. "What're you talking about?"

"Amy really likes you."

"Whatever."

"I just don't think you should blow her off so easily."

He looked at her and shook his head, making little annoyed sighs. "Is this your way of telling me we're not gonna hook up again?" He looked hurt. Zadie immediately felt guilty.

"Trevor, I'm sorry, I just don't think it's a good idea. We had a great night, and I think we should leave it at that."

"But you said you liked it."

"I did. You have no idea how much. And you're going to have a million girls who like—it—as much as I do. But I can't be your girlfriend. You're my student."

"I'm graduating in two weeks. We can hook up then. I won't be your student anymore."

As Zadie was struggling for an answer, Nancy pulled up in her Miata. Zadie gestured for Trevor to leave and he pulled his skateboard out from under his arm and wheeled across the parking lot, looking back at her as if she were the most heartless woman alive.

Nancy got out of her car and looked at Zadie. "What was Trevor Larkin doing in the teachers' parking lot?"

"He had a question about his grade."

"Well, if he needs extra credit, he knows where to find it. . . ." Nancy elbowed her as if it were just the most natural thing in the world to joke about having sex with Trevor. "I'm kidding. Can you imagine? I'd never be able to show my face here again. Lord, I'd never be able to show my face *anywhere* again."

Zadie grimaced. Imagining it only too easily.

Grey showed up on her lunch hour. "Did you know about Cancún?"

She was sitting in the teachers' lounge with Nancy, Dolores, and Mr. Jeffries, the gym teacher, and decided that the conversation might be better suited to the picnic tables on the quad. She rose and excused herself and walked outside with Grey.

"I found out the night of the bachelorette party. Gilda told me in the bathroom at the strip club. That's when I yanked Helen out by the hair and took her back to the hotel."

"Three guys?! In one night?"

"When did she tell you?"

"Last night."

Zadie had been wondering how long it would take. She'd called Grey every day to monitor the progress of the reconciliation. So far, so good. They were talking. She'd spent the night twice. And then there was Cancún.

"So the whole virgin bit, the whole 'I've never had a drink' bit—it's all bullshit. She's a total fake," he said.

"Apparently."

"Who the hell does that?"

"Your girlfriend."

"If she hadn't made such a big deal about being a virgin, I wouldn't even care, but she created a persona that's completely false. Why lie? Why not just omit?"

"Maybe she was trying to convince herself." Zadie could see Trevor across the quad, watching her. He was playing hackeysack with a group of guys, his eyes glued to Zadie.

Grey sat down on a bench and leaned forward, elbows on his knees. Zadie joined him, keeping one eye on Trevor. "Obviously she was ashamed of what happened, so she decided to start over and do a little reinvention."

"I guess," Grey said.

"Did she do anything in this scenario to deliberately hurt you?"

"No."

"And given the fact that you've slept with at least thirty women, are you really that horrified that she had three guys before she met you?"

"It would've been nice if they weren't all on the same night. . . ."

"You did say you wished she would loosen up—"

He looked at her. "Listen to you, it's like you're negotiating a deal."

"I'm just trying to keep things in perspective."

Grey looked up, squinting across the quad. "Why does that kid keep staring at us?"

"Long story."

"Is that your cover boy?"

"Yes. Stop looking at him."

"I think he's got a crush on you. He's eyeing me like he wants to kick my ass."

"Like I said. Long story." She stood up. "Let's go back inside."

Grey smiled. "Oh, my God. You slept with him."

Zadie motioned for him to lower his voice. "I am not going to discuss this at my place of employ." She dragged him up off the bench and started pushing him toward the visitors' lot.

"When did it happen? After Deep?"

"Goodbye, Grey."

"Come on . . ."

"I'll tell you another time."

They got to his car and he beeped his door open. "So, what should I do about Helen?"

"You already know what you're going to do."

"I do?"

"Goodbye, Grey." She walked back toward the school secure in the knowledge that Grey and Helen would remain a couple. As against it as she'd been all along, now she was their biggest champion. For reasons she still wasn't sure of. She only knew that the less perfect Helen was, the more she liked her. And that she much preferred seeing Grey happy to seeing Grey miserable.

Sixth period came and Trevor sat down in the last row, brooding. After class, she called him up to her desk. He walked up, feigning indifference. "Was that your boyfriend?"

"That was my friend Grey. He's marrying my cousin. The one with the strap-on." The fact that Helen would now forever be described as "the one with the strap-on" amused Zadie to no end.

"Oh. Cool." He smiled at her. Thinking he was still in the game.

"I have something for you." She pulled out an envelope and handed it to him. It was Betsy's letter of recommendation to Stanford. She'd called her at her office and had her fax it over, after giving her a quick recap of the latest on the Helen/Grey situation. Betsy wanted to hunt Jimbo down and press charges, but none of them could remember his last name.

Trevor opened it and read it quickly. "Sweet! This is awesome. You rock." He put it in his notebook and looked back up at her, lowering his voice, even though no one else was in the classroom. "Can I see you tonight?"

Zadie looked at him and sighed. Knowing she shouldn't. "There *is* one more thing I've always wanted to do with you."

forty-five

Zadie pulled herself up into a straddling position and shook her hair out of her face. They were in between sets and she needed to rest.

"I always pictured you as a shortboarder."

Trevor was next to her on his 9'0. "Not on these waves."

It was a perfect afternoon in Malibu. At least, perfect for Zadie. Small enough waves so that it wasn't crowded with pros, but big enough for her to catch. The water was warm enough for her to wear her spring wet suit, which only went down to her knees. Trevor opted to brave the ocean in just his board shorts, showing off the torso that probably earned him more money in one photo shoot than Zadie made in six months.

"You're good. Have you ever been in a contest?" she asked.

"Nah. Why get all stressed out about it? I just want it to be fun."

"That's a good philosophy."

"You're not too bad for someone who just learned how. You're pretty flexible, though. I guess that helps." He smiled at her, feeling clever that he'd managed to bring the conversation back to sex.

"Trevor . . ."

"I don't see why we can't do it just one more time. At least."

"Because I feel like a dirty old woman."

"But we've already done it."

"Yes, but I'm sober now."

"We can stop and get a bottle of Cuervo on the way home."

A set was rolling in and she pointed at it. "Here we go."

Trevor let go of the conversation long enough to lie down and paddle. He caught a good one, taking him all the way down to the pier. Zadie caught the next one, but some old man dropped in on her and she had to bail over the back side of the wave, giving her plenty of time to come up with an excuse for Trevor while he paddled back out to the break.

"How about this?" she asked as he sat up on his board next to her. "If I'm still single by the time you graduate from Stanford, I'll be your girlfriend."

"What if I'm over you by then?" he teased.

"Then it's my loss."

"How old will you be?"

"Thirty-five."

He pretended to consider it, then shrugged. "So I just need to kill off all your boyfriends until then?"

Zadie splashed him. "Besides, you'll probably come back from Europe this summer with some supermodel girlfriend."

"Doubtful. Why would I want a girlfriend who lives in Europe?" He was always so logical, Zadie thought. How much easier her life would be if she could share that trait.

She squinted at the beach in front of them, watching as a little kid ran in and out of the water, squealing. "My ex-fiancé came over a few nights ago." Zadie couldn't believe she was telling him this. She hadn't told anyone. Not even Dorian when she called her right afterward. It felt like something she had to process first before she could discuss it. Maybe Trevor was the easiest person to tell because he knew the least about it.

He frowned. "What happened?"

"He wanted to get back together."

"After he dumped you on your wedding day? What a tool."

"My thoughts exactly." Zadie watched as the little kid on the beach flung a handful of wet sand at an unfortunate dog.

"So you told him to go to hell, right?"

"I was probably a little bit meaner than that, but yeah." Another set came through, but they stayed sitting up on their boards, letting the waves pass.

"So are you okay?" he asked.

"Yeah. I am. It was all so ridiculous. Like I was watching him on TV or something."

"Yeah, well, I watched his show once while I was high and he sucked. So it's not like you're missing out on any future Oscar parties or anything, trust me."

That was the first time anyone had ever made her laugh about anything regarding Jack. Okay, that wasn't entirely true. Grey had done an imitation of Jack opening his UPS box of dog doo that had made her pee herself. But Trevor's comments were charming nonetheless.

"You're the only person I've told. About him coming over."

"How come?"

"I don't know." She smiled at him. "Maybe you'll be in charge of all my secrets from now on." She nudged him underwater with her foot and he grinned at her.

"I'm sorry if I've been brusque with you at school, it's just—"

"I know," he said. "It's cool. I don't want you to be unemployed when I come back for you in four years." A piece of seaweed got caught in Trevor's leash. Zadie leaned over to untangle it.

"Uh-oh. I just thought of something," she said. "What if your band becomes famous? I'll look so old next to all your groupies."

"I'll have money to buy you plastic surgery by then."

She reached over to give him a shove as they paddled for the next wave. Riding it in together.

forty-six

When Zadie got to Grey's house, there were already a dozen or so people in the backyard: Bill, his law partner and best man, Betsy and her husband, Denise and Jeff and her now eight-month-pregnant belly, Marci and Kim and their sullen husbands, Jane, three of the groomsmen whose names Zadie had never even learned, and of course, Helen, beaming and glowing at the same time.

Every tree in the yard had been strung with white party lights, and bamboo tiki torches were planted in the lawn, sending their kerosene smoke into the night sky. Grey handed her a glass of wine. "Welcome to the reengagement party." Zadie gave him a kiss, then looked around the yard. Grey noticed. "Don't worry. Mike will be here."

"I know." She smiled.

After the official reconciliation, Mike had called Zadie to congratulate her on her powers of persuasion. They'd talked for three hours. He didn't say a single annoying thing the entire time. He'd called her back four times since then. She'd even been moved to tell her mother about him. Mavis was so excited that she almost dropped the phone.

Grey lowered his voice. "And if you're nice, I won't tell him you prefer hairless pretty boys." Zadie swatted him on the arm.

After reestablishing their Thursday night ritual at Barney's Beanery, Zadie had kept her promise and told Grey all there was to tell about Trevor. Frequency and girth included.

"Don't laugh. If it doesn't work out with Mike, you'll be double-dating with me and Trevor in four years."

"Why wait? Maybe he'll let me be a roadie in his band. I can fill the beer bong."

Zadie tolerated him. "Go ahead. Get it all out of your system now, before Mike shows up."

He spotted his brother and walked over to say hello right as Helen caught sight of Zadie and came rushing over to give her a big hug. "Can you believe it? I told him everything and here we are."

"Of course I believe it," Zadie said. "He loves you."

Helen held up her champagne flute. "Don't worry. Just one glass."

"No striptease tonight?" Zadie asked.

"Maybe a private one." She winked in Grey's direction, then grabbed Zadie's hand.

"I really owe you."

"I know you do," Zadie said. "And I'm still holding you to my earlier threats. Hurt him and I will kill you."

Helen smiled and hugged her again. "If I didn't have a sister, you'd be my maid of honor."

Zadie hugged her back. "Remember all those birthday presents that I never gave you?" She nodded in Grey's direction. "We're even."

"I was always so jealous of you, you know," Helen said. They'd finished hugging and Zadie looked at her, confused. Helen was jealous of *her*? "You've always been so honest. So—who you are— without worrying what anyone thought. I could never do that until now."

Eloise walked up behind them with a new bizarre haircut and an equally hideous new pair of glasses. "Break it up, you two. It's too early to get serious."

Helen gave Eloise a quick kiss on the cheek and rushed off to check the appetizers. Leaving Zadie alone with Eloise.

"Zadie. How are you." She said it in a way that implied no question, so Zadie didn't bother to answer. "I suppose you heard I have a new boyfriend."

No, Zadie hadn't heard. Contrary to Eloise's assumption, people did not discuss her.

"He's a billionaire."

"I'm sure he is," Zadie said.

"Sex like you wouldn't believe."

"I don't doubt it."

"Why are you being so agreeable?" Eloise asked, suspicious.

"Why wouldn't I be?"

Eloise gave her a look and walked away. Zadie marveled at her luck. Jane glided over with her drink and looked Zadie up and down. "You look *fantastic*."

"Thanks," Zadie said. She was wearing a tight knit top and a short black skirt. The first sexy outfit she'd put on in months.

"Need a summer job?" Jane asked.

"I appreciate the offer, but I'll pass," Zadie said.

When Mike walked out onto the patio, he looked around for a moment before spotting her, giving her time to smooth her hair down and stand up straight. When he caught sight of her, he smiled and walked toward her.

"Okay, good, I wasn't too drunk at the rehearsal. You're still hot."

Zadie raised an eyebrow at him.

"I thought I'd lead with my most obnoxious comment," he said, "that way, I've only got room to improve for the rest of the night." He gave her a kiss on the cheek and held out his hand to Jane. "I'm Mike, Grey's roommate from USC."

"Jane, Helen's friend from high school."

Mike looked at both of them. "So what do you think the odds are they'll make it to the altar this time?"

"Significantly higher if she stays home the night before," Jane said. She looked across the lawn and saw Betsy waving her over. "Excuse me, I think Betsy wants to give me a lecture."

"You might be surprised," Zadie said. "I think our night out had some lasting changes for her. Maybe she wants some advice."

"As long as she doesn't want to work for me."

As Jane walked over to Betsy, Mike asked, "Is she a broker or something?"

"In a way," Zadie answered. She turned to smile at him. He was just as good-looking as she'd remembered. Dark, touchable hair. Brown-gold eyes. Dimples. Broad shoulders. Blue button-down and jeans. Appropriate footwear—no visible toes. "How long was the drive up?"

"An hour and forty-five."

"You must drive like an old woman."

"It's one of my best traits."

When they'd talked on the phone, Zadie had discovered that he lived in a loft in the Gaslamp Quarter and walked to work. Which meant that he wouldn't be too burned out from commuting all week to drive to L.A. on the weekends. A definite plus. She'd also discovered that he surfed better than Grey, he'd had long-term relationships with three women, all of whom he was still friendly with, and that he'd never seen a single second of *Days of Our Lives*.

"So you actually have three months off with nothing to do?" he asked.

Graduation had been last week. She'd made sure Amy was sitting next to Trevor.

"Yep. Any suggestions?"

"I hear Crazy Girls is hiring."

"You still owe me that lap dance, by the way," she said.

"I don't know—I hear you're a bad tipper."

"Depends on what you're worth," she teased.

"Got a quarter?"

There was nothing more charming than a man who was confident enough to be self-deprecating. "I've got a whole dollar if you're saucy enough," she said.

"You're on. Just let me get a couple glasses of cabernet in me and we'll retire to the garage. My act includes power tools."

Zadie could not have liked him more at this point. The fact that he had his hand on the small of her back made him even more appealing. She liked a man who wasn't afraid to touch. Right as she was deciding that he was indeed her next boyfriend, Grey stood up on the steps in front of the patio and called for everyone's attention. Helen was beaming by his side.

"We realize some of you may be wondering why we've gathered you here, since the last time you saw us, we were screaming at each other in the lobby of the Beverly Hills Hotel."

"Grey!" Helen swatted him. "You're not supposed to talk about that."

Grey shrugged. "I figure we owe you all an explanation, since you rented tuxes and bought what I've been assured are very tasteful bridesmaid dresses. The situation is—Helen and I are getting married."

The crowd cheered.

"However—"

The crowd booed.

"We're going to take it a little slower this time. As some of you may know, it takes time to get a background check."

Helen swatted him again, as everyone laughed.

"But I'm confident that at the end of this year, we'll actually make it to the ceremony. So if you can keep New Year's Eve open, you'll all have a good party to go to."

Zadie smiled. *Finally* a New Year's Eve worth getting dressed up for.

Mike leaned over to whisper in her ear. "Okay, I know it's short notice, and I know we're both in the wedding so we don't really need dates, but I'm pretty much planning on you being mine, so try not to fuck up before then."

She elbowed him in the ribs and turned back to watch Grey and Helen kiss as everyone raised their glasses.

Love was a beautiful thing.

Acknowledgments

Thanks to Josh Bank, of course, because he is brilliant, and because without him, this book wouldn't exist. Les Morgenstein and Claudia Gabel for their input and good vibes. Jennifer Weis, for buying the book and for all her enthusiasm. Seth Jaret, for his support and encouragement. Mike Bender, Tom O'Neal, and Reggie Hayes, because whenever I attempt to write witty men, I try to channel them. Dana Guilfoyle and Selma B. for providing moments of inspiration from their bachelorette parties. All of the wonderful and wild women I've hung out with over the years who have accompanied me on many, many nights of inspirational debauchery. All of my male friends who gossip on the phone with me for hours longer than the girls. My husband, Walter, for being a good guy who was kind enough to show up at our wedding. My parents, Lanny and Darlene, for my twisted imagination. And of course, huge thanks to the makers of penis confetti.